$12.99

MW01515154

# The Real Gone, Horn Gone Blues

by

*Skoot Larson*

authorHOUSE®

*AuthorHouse™*
*1663 Liberty Drive, Suite 200*
*Bloomington, IN 47403*
*www.authorhouse.com*
*Phone: 1-800-839-8640*

*First published by AuthorHouse 11/6/2007*

*ISBN: 978-1-4343-3637-8 (e)*
*ISBN: 978-1-4343-3635-4 (sc)*
*ISBN: 978-1-4343-3636-1 (hc)*

*Library of Congress Control Number: 2007907396*

*Printed in the United States of America*
*Bloomington, Indiana*

*This book is printed on acid-free paper.*

For the Thursday Night Therapy Group; old friends, some going all the way back to school days, with whom I've almost weekly shared *Vout-O-Reeny* gourmet meals, fine red wines, getting drunk, getting stoned, discussing and debating a wild range of subjects from jazz music to politics and everything in between! You've always been there for me, all you groovy gaters, and I've enjoyed every minute of our *out-there* little hipster brotherhood. Let's keep the good times rollin'!

This story is set in San Pedro, a real California community, and New York City, a place more real than it often seems in legend and stories. Many of the places described herein do exist, however, this is not to be taken as a current or accurate description of either San Pedro or New York including their businesses and landmarks. The author has taken many liberties with people and places for the sake of a good story. Some of the characters in this story; celebrities, close friends of the author and local characters do exist and are real people. Most of the supporting actors in this play, however, exist only in the author's twisted mind. Any similarities between these folks and the ordinary citizens and/or denizens of San Pedro, the Big Apple or other locations described in this tale are strictly coincidental.

# $\mathcal{P}$rologue

Art Pepper was feeling really sick. His stomach kept jumping and lurching as he wandered along Beacon Street in San Pedro. He thought he might feel a little better if he threw up, but even after chugging down a gallon jug of Don Francisco Red Table Wine, nothing wanted to come back up for him. A quick fix was the only answer, the only way he was going to get himself straight and onstage tonight for the gig which would pay him almost enough to cover the heroin he needed right now. It had been almost four days since his last score and fix.

Art paced nervously between the Red Door West jazz club and the Bayside Pawn Shop. Both were on the same block of Beacon, between 5th and 6th Streets. He mumbled a sort of mantra softly to himself as he walked, "Can't play strung out, can't play without a horn. Can't play strung out, can't play without a horn."

A fix would require $50. Art had $4 and change in his pocket after spending the 49-cents for the jug of wine that didn't do shit for him. The only answer was to borrow against his Martin Alto Sax. Someone could loan him another horn for the gig at the Red Door tonight, then tomorrow he could buy his Martin back. Maybe his friend Lester Koenig would help him get the alto back again. That would be easy as all Lester ever asked in return was another recording session for his Contemporary Records label.

Mario, the "Uncle" at Bayside Pawn was no stranger to Art. Mario was an old friend of Art's father, Dick. They used to hang together at The Swan, just a few doors down on Beacon Street, back when Art was just a lad. Art's granddad, Moses, had bought him a clarinet so that he could play in the San Pedro Cleveland Boys Band. Dick and Mario would drag Art and his clarinet along to The Swan where Art would stand on the bar and play the songs he knew while Dick and Mario would cage free drinks from Art's performance.

Art borrowed money for his drug habit at Bayside Pawn more times than he could remember. At first, Mario would just slip him a few dollars "for old times sake," but as the price of a fix went up Art needed more money and larger amounts. Mario started taking Art's saxophone for collateral.

Mario was familiar with the routine; he had dealt with Art often. But he thought to himself that Art had never appeared so desperate. Mario noticed that Art kept glancing anxiously out at the street. At one point, when a police car passed by, Art rolled his body around to half hide behind a shelf stacked with carpenter's tools.

Of course Mario agreed to help out. He actually offered Art $75 for the gold lacquered Martin alto saxophone Art presented. Mario dutifully filled out the card, writing the saxophone's serial number, 472666, from memory and handed him the buff colored pawn ticket along with three twenties, a ten and a five.

Art grabbed the pro-offered bills and ticket, coughed, mumbled a soft, brief "Thanks" and moved quickly out the door. With a couple furtive glances each direction, he hurried across Beacon Street where a huddled figure in trench coat, dark shades and feathered fedora held up a lamppost by the Alexander Hotel. Art placed money in the man's leathery, black hand and waited while "Trenchcoat" reached into the garment's inside breast pocket and produced two pale gray condoms before melting into a nearby alleyway between the old hotel and Tommy's Goodfellows Bar.

Art looked both ways at the curb once more, preparing to cross back to the Red Door. He felt calmer now, just holding the drug in his hand. Escape was close at hand. His euphoria was, however, short lived.

Black Ford sedans approached where he stood from either direction, traveling far too fast for this busy thoroughfare. The westbound Ford crossed over to the wrong side, making for a head-on with its likeness traveling east. Both cars screeched to a halt as bookends to Art's curbside stance and more men in coats and fedoras poured out of them. White men holding out badges. Art turned to the alley, but it was too late to escape and besides, his nausea made running nearly impossible. The men twirled Art deftly to face the Alexander Hotel's brick facade, ran hands over his body and snagged their prize. The two condoms of China White were passed around, tasted and pocketed by the officers who then laced bracelets on Art's wrists and shoved him into the back of the eastbound Ford, hitting Art's head on the door frame as they shoved him in. The time was 4:30 pm on October 24,1960.

# Part I

## On the Waterfront

# Chapter 1

I don't get many visitors at my penthouse address, even fewer coming unannounced, so it was a surprise when my sometime sideman, alto saxophonist Lucian Bezich burst onto my rooftop patio in a state of near-ecstatic glee. "Loose," as he was known around music circles, had a flat, black, plastic square under his arm and the frantic look of someone who'd just been visited by the ghost of Saint Charlie Parker in his eyes. My two feline buddies, Art and Yard, clearly found his ebullient manner distasteful, scurrying for hiding places inside my digs. Normally the boys welcome my guests with loud shouted meows. Yard's voice is an ordinary feline complaint. Art, however, is part Siamese with eyes like a shallow seaside Caribbean lagoon, and vocalizes in his own ethnic cry. Art's excited cries could evoke audio images of a happy human baby's coo.

Loose offered no formal greeting, just dragged a cheap garden chair over to where I was reclined on my chaise and started shoutin'. "Man, you ain't gonna believe, cause, like, I don't believe."

As he spoke, Loose pulled his plastic square into his lap and clam-shelled it half-facing my direction. The upper inside half of the shell burst to life in a dance of colors; a laptop brain-box. Loose let his fingers do the dancin' over four rows of keys as a series of different pictures and logos briefly flashed, one into the next.

"Here, man, check it out!" Loose started vibrating like a kid on a sugar rush. The screen of his brain box showed the familiar red and yellow logo of Net Bid, the Internet auction site where millions of hipsters, flipsters and squares alike found deals on items from the rare to the common.

Loose pointed a shaky finger at the small screen. "That is *IT*, man. Look! It's Art Pepper's old Martin. The sax that established his sound, like, with Kenton and on into the 60s! Its Art Pepper's alto and its up for auction!"

I had heard the rumors and stories myself. Art Pepper's old Martin alto had disappeared when he was busted in 1960 and sent to Quentin. According to legend the horn was either passed on to a friend who has never come forward to admit it, or was stolen from a police evidence locker. The serial number was said to be 472666. There is suppose to be physical evidence to back that up, though I've never seen it, and a Martin alto sax bearing that number has never been found, although jazz fans and collectors alike have searched for some forty-five years.

"This guy says he's got signed, notarized papers to vouch for the axe's authenticity, like, in writing. Claims he acquired the alto from the former owner of an old Beacon Street pawnshop who's had it in his basement all these years! And the guy selling it is right here in Pedro, man! Look, man, look!"

I'm a naturally suspicious cat. Like, anybody can claim to have something. Especially something that is talked about in certain circles until it becomes a fairy-story that cats really *want* to believe. Enough cats have lusted after Pepper's axe. Like, almost as many as have had the hots for Bird's old King Super 20! Are these magic horns with an aura that can create a jazz star from an ordinary stud? Or are they just objects from an assembly line that became the things dreams are made of in the hands of that one genius, a cat that comes along at the right moment with just the right riff and the proper understanding? Loose was lit up like he believed blowin' breath into this horn would make him the next true jazz legend. I didn't know what to say. Loose was a friend and I didn't want to see him hurt or disappointed, but on the other hand, who was I to put a hatpin into his bubble of fame and fortune? I handed Loose a Red Hook ESB from the picnic cooler at my feet and passed him a smile. As we toasted Art Pepper's memory, Loose closed his laptop computer, and I changed the subject to the up-coming "First-Thursday" celebration. Blondy planned to set up a bandstand on 7th Street where we would play the first set to drum up more business for her jazz club, Blondy's Waterfront Dive. The *cat* cats remained in hiding until after Loose had flown the deck.

# Chapter 2

First Thursday came and went. For those of you not familiar with the San Pedro – Los Angeles Harbor scene, First Thursday is a kind of monthly ritual in our artist's community. The first Thursday of each month the community closes off 6th Street from Pacific Avenue to Mesa Street for a sort of wild street fair, and the art galleries in the Old Town neighborhood hold an "open house" with wine, cheese and hors d'oeuvres for all who attend.

When my band had finished our "outdoor" set a large crowd followed us into Blondy's Waterfront Dive, bringing with them an incredible thirst for Blondy's First Thursday Martini Specials. The Lars Lindstrom Sextet had an appreciative audience of jazz heads and Blondy sold more gin than a 1920s Chicago speakeasy.

Blondy's real name is Pearl. She is a life-long jazz fan and, specifically, a fan of my music. She came to San Pedro from Denver some years back to open her club in the basement of the hotel where I have resided with my two furry cat-pals for more years than I care to remember.

Prior to her flip back to California, where she grew up, Blondy was a jazz disc jockey in Denver and published a jazz magazine for the Rocky Mountain music scene. I helped the lady to get established here in L.A., and in return she has provided me with the first semi-permanent gig of my life. Besides paying me very generously for the musicians I bring into her club, Blondy is my "Mother Wendy," a guiding light to protect and keep this "little lost boy" from harm.

And me? I'm a six-foot, over-educated and slightly alcoholic jazz addict. My sandy-colored hair is thinning on top and my green eyes are lookin' tired these days. My Master of Arts degree in music never brought any serious work. For some years after school I spent much of my life bummin' around Europe, where the population has a greater appreciation of jazz; crashing in low-end hotels and youth hostels. I'm athletically thin not because I work out or watch my diet, but mainly because I often get hung up practicing, listening to music or reading and I forget to eat. Again, a good reason to have a Mother Wendy as my boss. Blondy is always asking if I've had a meal recently, and we often end up buggin' out to one of our favorite local haunts for a "decent" breakfast or dinner.

In my work for Blondy, I assemble and lead the house-band at the Dive six nights a week. Monday through Thursday I play trumpet and sing with a trio of piano, bass and drums. On the weekends, or for the First Thursday event each month, I put together a sextet with a couple additional saxophones. My current sextet featured Loose on alto sax and flute along with a killer baritone saxophone and bass flute cat called "Skoot" who has some really strange musical ideas.

Skoot and I are a couple of "gray-beards" . . . over fifty cats that never made the big time but have some good improvisational ideas to share. We're both L.A. cats with San Pedro roots. Although he's a few years younger than me and Skoot, Loose is a Pedro cat too. Loose was born and raised here in a Croatian family who have fished the waters off southern California for one hundred years or more. Loose copped a few seasons at sea, but never really dug coming home the smell of fish and salt water on his olive skin and in his thick, dark hair. He much preferred hanging nights at the Dive, the Hermosa Beach Lighthouse, or the Jazz Bakery in Culver City; places where his heroes ran through the chords and created new music every night

And in this past week, First Thursday through Saturday night, Loose played some remarkable licks, sounding more and more like the ghost of Art Pepper. Just the thought of Pepper's Martin axe being out there for grabs seemed to bring out a new side of my alto-man, spurring him on to greater technique and more intricate harmonic structures. When he showed up for the Dive's Sunday afternoon jam session, he could have been Art Pepper's reincarnation. I had never heard him blow with such facility.

# Chapter 3

On Tuesday, Loose called inviting me to come down to the Dive for a celebration. As of 1:32 p.m., he had been declared high bidder and had won the Net Bid auction for Art Pepper's old Martin alto. He wasn't sure where he would come up with the three thousand he had bid, but the horn was his and he'd do anything to get the bread that would bring it to him.

Daylight faded and Loose showed up once more at the Dive to sit in, but more than that, he wanted to seek the assurance of me and the other band members that he wasn't totally out beyond the last bus stop with his lust for this most desired of "trophy" horns. I wasn't sure what to tell him, but Dave, our piano cat laid out a copasetic rap that got ol' Loose smilin' and noddin'. By the second set, Loose was playin' in such a *vooty* groove that the ghost of Art Pepper could have been hangin' on his shoulder whisperin' the ideas into his lobes. It was a beautiful scene, and when Loose and me went out front on the second break, the night was shining with the luster of his sound. Above the lights of 7th Street stars shimmered like the sequins in a hooker's tank top!

Wednesday morning, Loose was at my door before the crack of noon. His mother had gone to the Bank of San Pedro with him when they opened and withdrew the toll from her savings. She didn't approve, but at the same time she wanted her "wayward" son to cop some happiness.

"If only he could fish with his brothers, or sell real estate like his sister" . . . but jazz was what Lucian loved and she had promised his father, on her husband's deathbed, that she would always be there for their oldest son. Neither of them had understood his fascination with this crazy music but families have to stick together, that was one of the values their forbearers had brought with them from their Adriatic island home.

I tuned my lobes to Loose's rap as we drove out Pacific Avenue. He told me that we would pick up the horn from some stud at 843 West 34th Street, between Pacific and Caroline. Anticipation had laid a major motor mouth on poor Loose. He couldn't stop talking. Turning up the step hill on 34th from Pacific Avenue was a blessing. Nearing the address, Loose asked me to grab the workout bag from behind his seat.

"There's three large in that bag, man. All in fives, tens and twenties. Like, that's what the cat asked for. Almost like some kinda shady deal, like a hold-up or something crazy like that, dig?" Loose chuckled to himself behind his broad happy grin. I don't think he dug to how clued-in he was on this scene.

Loose swung his mother's gold Buick into a driveway near the top of the grade, unfolded his short, stubby body from the ride, and we headed for a turn-of-the-last-century home that stood between modern apartment buildings on the incline. We found the front door half open to an eerie silence within.

"Cat's got to be in here waitin' for us," Loose told me as he pushed through the heavy oak door. I followed as Loose moved from room to room; living room, hallway, glances into two bedrooms and finally the large, old-fashioned kitchen. At each portal he would call out, "Hello? Anybody home?"

No one jumped to his call. It seemed very suspicious to me. If this cat was waiting to receive some major long daddy green, where was he? Had he just stepped out to chat with a neighbor? And if so, hadn't he seen us drive up and park our wheels in his driveway?

I followed Loose to the rear of the kitchen where a sort of dogleg in the back hall revealed a narrow downward staircase. Here was another open door with a bare light bulb hanging halfway down the treads. In the shadows that the light cast, we could just make out the figure of an old man crumpled at the bottom of the basement stairs.

Sax players generally wear a neck strap that supports the weight of the instrument while they play. It's a device that hangs around the neck, with a hook on the end to clip into an eye on the sax's rear tubing. Most sax straps have a sort of sliding pulley thing to adjust the horn's level in relation to the player's chops.

The old man that lay at the bottom of these stairs had a 1960s style neckstrap; a wide leather band around half his neck with a thin chord attached either side that held the hook, and a small plastic device that could be slid up to raise the horn and adjust its level. Unfortunately for this old cat, the pulley had been pulled tight under his chin and the chord knotted to cut off his air supply and cancel his breathing, like, for the entire session.

Loose barged on around the man's lifeless form and into the basement, a puppy off its lead seeking a bone or a hunk of meat. There was no Martin alto sax to be found. There were no clues that could lead to an alto sax. My sax man was just heading past me into the kitchen to start a search of the house when a pair of LAPD uniforms made their debut, stage left, through the opposite portal with drawn guns.

Loose wanted to do confrontational, which got him knocked to the floor with a knee in his back by a young Asian stud in blue. I thought it better to play, like, Submissive City. I backed up against the kitchen sink with my hands over my head and gave a serious mug. The other cop, a young blonde lady, smiled at me without taking her gun from my general direction. I could tell she was fearless and cool. This is the lady that would clue me, so I granted her the space and waited without comment.

Loose, on the other hand, couldn't get his head around the concept of "busted." He wanted to argue, explain, criticize, and make a really *uncool* face of himself. He tried to hold forth on the subject of rip-offs while the cops were more interested in "murder one." I held my peace, sharing knowing smiles with the lady cop, until Loose's batteries ran down.

"Your turn," she beamed at me when Loose had gone still. "Let's hear your take on this call."

I told her about the Net Bid auction, Art Pepper's horn, and the strange request that we show up with some three-grand in small bills. Told it like I was reading the sheet music. She kept grinning, intrigued and interested, while her Asian partner did more sour and serious. They would share the occasional nod. They were obvious skeptics, listening, but not fully buying into the story.

In the end, the Asian cop pulled a set of bracelets from his belt with a pitying shake of his head. He spun Loose around against the cellar door and laced him up. The lady cop cutie did likewise, pulling my wrists behind me as Asian read our rights. The two of them went through Loose's bag of money, tallying up the notes and recording it in their notebooks. "This will be recorded into evidence," the lady in blue told Loose as he moaned about what his mother would say.

As the two cops guided us into the rear of their cruiser, I asked the lady what had brought them out to this address. "Neighborhood watch call," she told me. "Old man across the street saw another car come and go, then you guys pulled up and went right in. He said he was suspicious because the family who lives there is in Zagreb right now on vacation. He thought it might be a drug deal or something."

# Chapter 4

Loose and I sat in the back of the LAPD panda car for somewhere close to an hour, canted forward as our hands were cuffed behind our backs. We watched a navy-blue Caprice pull into the drive, vomiting out its pair of detectives, a man and a woman, who kept glaring over at us while the two young uniforms clued them to the scene. Shortly after the detectives entered the house, the white "crime-scene" van slotted in behind the unmarked blue ride.

The evidence techies carried their gear into the house; tool kits, video cameras and gym bags of who knew what. While they were doing their back-and-forth dance more official vehicles arrived, a beige car with the Los Angeles County seal and "Coroner" on the door, another pair of uniforms in a black-and-white, more plain-clothes cats in large nondescript motors. I recognized Lieutenant Moen, the local Robbery and Homicide Division Commander from another time when I'd been hauled in after a body turned up sitting in my deck chair on the roof of the Channel View Hotel.

Moen never even glanced our direction. By now the interest was focused inside the house. Loose and me were old news until the first two detectives came back outside.

They took Loose out of the ride we were sharing and ducked him into the navy blue short. A trim cop of medium height, probably about four inches shorter than my six feet and just as thin as me, squatted down by the open door of the black and white and pulled a reporter's spiral notepad from the waistband of his dark pants. He had short salt-and-pepper hair with a mustache to match on a friendly enough face, although his voice was all business.

"You men, uh, allege that you found the deceased, one Jakob Rankovich, when you went into the house looking for a saxophone?"

I handed salt-and-pepper our story, at least that to which Loose had hipped me of it, from the Net Bid auction to our discovery of the body on the cellar stairs. The detective scrawled in a scratchy kinda shorthand as I spoke. When I was finished, the cop asked me to tell the whole tale again. Then he asked questions about different parts of my recitation, jumping around all out of sequence from how I had laid it down.

When I had finished for the last time, the man made no comment on my story. "Would you mind running through this again for my partner, Detective Migiani?"

I started to tell him "sure," but he thanked me before I had the word out. I guess his was just a sort of polite rhetorical query. He folded his notebook, shoved it into the waistband at the back of his pants and stood. He shaded his eyes, looking toward the car where Loose was speaking with a trim dark haired lady in brown slacks and white blouse. The female cop, I guessed she must be Detective Migiani, put a hand on Loose's shoulder, and said something more to him as she raised herself from the edge of the car seat and headed our way. She nodded to salt-and-pepper as they passed, then placed herself on the edge of the bench where I sat with my wrists chained. The lady's notebook was sticking out of a plain looking black handbag with a badge and a cell phone clipped to its rim near the leading edge of the shoulder strap.

Detective Migiani folded her gams into the ride's caged rear space, half turned towards me, opened her notepad, and introduced herself.

"At this point," she told me, "we are going to hold you and your friend, Lucian, for further questioning. Your friend's retelling of the events was just a bit disjointed. He seems to be a very excitable fellow.

"Would you mind giving me your version of what happened?" The lady investigator's soft gray eyes locked onto mine. The auburn hair on her head was cut short and radiated strawberry-blonde highlights when the sun hit it. I licked my dry lips and ran through my tale once more, twice more and again in *bits and bobs* according to her directions.

Her bright orbs did cigar-store-Indian as she thanked me for talking with her. She got out of the car and joined her partner on the sidewalk between the two rides. Salt-and-pepper seemed to be holding forth, doin' most of the talking. When their rap session ended, he went over to the other car, took a card out of his shirt pocket and said something to Loose. Whatever he was saying, Loose didn't look happy. Loose dropped his head onto his chest and closed his eyes. I think he might've been cryin'.

I was next. The graying lead detective stood by the panda's door and, after a preamble of "Erik Lars Lyndstrom, I am arresting you on suspicion of the murder of Jakob Rankovich," he read the standard cop-show litany from his pocket card to me once again. When I looked away quickly, I thought I caught his partner, Migiani, winkin' at me.

# Chapter 5

The salt-and-pepper detective transferred Loose back into the black-and-white sedan with me and closed the rear doors. The Asian and the blonde that had met us in the kitchen hours before took their places up front. We made a slow cruise out Pacific to the Harbor Division Station. Mexican housewives and homeless knights-of-the-road gawked in fascination as our tumbrel wheeled past. Everyone was intrigued to view real bad-guys, white guys at that, in a rolling cage. Loose didn't notice. He kept his eyes on the floor giving the occasional loud sniffle as we rode.

The cop car brought us around to the familiar back door, but instead of the interrogation room I'd been taken to when I found the dead terrorist in my garden, the Asian cop opened a different rear portal and took us directly to a large cell, like, *Slam City*! The man took our belts and Loose's shoelaces. I was wearing wooden clogs, so I had none. He put our wallets, keys and geets into plastic bags and brought us a clipboard with papers to sign for our worldly treasures.

Loose started sobbing again when they read off the accounting of the money and the athletic bag that held it. We were offered one phone call each with the hint that an attorney might be a good use of the call.

Loose called his mother. He barely got out a line of explanation when Mrs. Bezich took over. Her voice was loud enough that the jailor and I could understand every word of criticism the mother had for her son's lifestyle.

"I never should have let you talk me into loaning you that money!" she wailed. "Mrs. Riechstien next door said this could come to no good end! And we don't have a lawyer! Why would we ever need a lawyer? We are good, honest, hardworking people."

Her voice droned on. Loose got tired of listening and put the phone back in its cradle. I collared up the blower and dialed up the Dive. Blondy picked up on the second ring. I could picture her in her cramped office going over booze invoices and register tapes. When I had explained the situation, the blonde one laughed and said something about the U.S. Cavalry. "Just keep your cool, baby," she told me. "Mother Wendy'll sort you out once again."

We were led back to the tank, but at least we had lost the bracelets. Loose dive-bombed one of the bunks and buried his face in a soiled gray pillow. I sat back for a long think, but I didn't have to pressure my wig for too long.

Blondy knows a lot of people on the street. I guess its part of running a gin mill. One of her contacts, and I believe part-time boyfriends as well, is Lieutenant Tom Cheatham, a Los Angeles vice cop. The jailor cat had a phone call of his own, which he answered with a series of "yeahs." He cradled the set, and when I looked up, Tom Cheatham was coming through the doors in his starched and pressed blues.

Tom was grinnin' ear to ear. "Well, what have we here? We must be getting' ready for the Police Benevolent Association's charity jazz concert." He chuckled and had the jailor put him into the cell with us. "Blondy's got a lawyer on the way," he said. "A real good one, too. He's a jazz-fan. Handles Blondy's business needs, but he is a good criminal guy as well."

Lieutenant Tom and I chatted, tried to cheer Loose up a bit and waited. In about twenty-five minutes, the jailor's phone rang again. He had a few brief words with someone and he got up to open the door.

I recognized the square in the three-piece drapes from the Dive, but we'd never been introduced. He extended his hand, first to me, then to Loose. "Val Ferguson," he announced. "I'm going to get this mess straightened out for you."

As he said this, he lamped Lieutenant Cheatham up and down with a suspicious eye. Tom Cheatham smiled back at him and shrugged his shoulders. "Hey, I'm just a friend."

They mentally circled each other for a moment and while they did Lieutenant Moen came through the back door to the jail from the parking lot.

Tom caught his eye. "Rich, we've gotta talk." The tall blond Moen kept moving through to the station door, but motioned for Tom to follow. Our attorney, Val, fell in step on Tom's heels and the parade left us in the dust.

Loose was coming around just a little. He blew his nose and gave a hollow laugh at the idea that we could draw an audience of two police lieutenants and a lawyer. I reminded him that if he didn't totally blow his cool and come all unglued, our patron Saint Blondy would swoop up from her basement heaven to rescue us, adding, "Maybe she already has."

And with those words, the trio of law cats returned. Val Ferguson and Tom Cheatham were smiling, Rich Moen looked skeptical, but the consensus was that we could be released "on our own recognizance." Cheatham earned a dirty look from his fellow officer when he jokingly told us, "Don't leave town, guys. We'll be keepin' an eye on you!" Tom took us back into the station where we signed forms and got back our belts and billfolds.

"I'm afraid the bag of money stays here, guys," the property officer told us. "At least until someone tells me it ain't needed as physical evidence in the murder." Loose looked like he'd been punched, but he kept his tongue. Tom Cheatham shrugged and led us out to another unmarked sedan. This time we rode with our hands free. I let Loose ride up front in hopes it might chill him out a tad. Lieutenant Tom drove us back to the crime scene where we rescued Loose's mother's Buick.

# Chapter 6

Back in El Buicko, I decided it was close to *Get Serious City*. I suggested we go back to the Channel View, have a beer and try to figure out what we'd bopped into. Loose was real drug about the three-large he borrowed from his mother to buy the horn. He was focused into flailing himself and sobbin' some major "Cotton Field" Blues. I told him he better stop the cryin' jag, lay down that mental eleven-foot sack and give some powerful whiggage to what he was going to do about it!

We found an un-metered parking place just up Centre from Blondy's. Loose vaulted from his ride and set a brisk pace toward the Dive. "Uh-uh," I told him grabbing his elbow. "We don't want this business *too* public just yet. Hit the stairs and we'll sort this in the lonesome of my crib. I've got plenty of beer and I'm gonna bribe you with it to get some answers."

When we were settled in my living room with a couple cold Red Hooks, Loose said, "At least I've still got the cash. I mean *if* and *when* we get it back from the cops."

"That's thinkin' too far ahead for right now, Loose. First we got to figure a few things out about the 'why' and 'wherefore' of this. Was this just a robbery? Why was the man strangled with a sax strap, but there wasn't any horn there?  Hell, man, there wasn't even a horn *case!*  Was this even the *Clyde* who was selling the horn?"

Poor Lucian started weeping again.  After a minute, he dried his eyes on his sleeve, gave a raucous sniffle and said, "Man, I don't know.  I can't understand any of this.  It seemed like it was so simple.  Someone has the horn, they put it up for auction and I buy it.  I went over there and I should have just been able to give the cat the brass and take my new axe home.  How could I know, like, the sky would darken and all this *bad jive* would rain down upon us!?!"

Loose's eyes started leaking again.  I gave him more time to pull himself up.

"Aw *reet*, ol' buddy.  First, tell me about the Net Bid auction, I mean I've copped some LPs and CDs from there; sometimes they give you real hip descriptions, or photos.  Tell me about this horn auction."

Loose rubbed his eyes then dragged his hands back to pull at the short hairs above his ears.  "Man, I *showed* it to you, you saw it!  I had it here on my brother's laptop."

"I didn't see much," I replied.  "You were so excited you were jumpin' all over and bouncin' that computer around on your knees.

"So humor me.  Lay it on me again.  Was there a photo of the actual horn?  How did they paint the word picture?  What were they promising?"

Loose's face brightened.  "Man, Lars, there were seven or eight photos, Photos from all angles.  There was a close-up of the serial number, 472666, right below the brass loop for the strap.  And he showed a couple close-ups of a scratch on the bell and a little dent in the bow, near the 'C' tone hole."

"Okay," I told him.  "So that should establish that he *had* the horn, unless he copped an envelope full of photos somewhere . . . "

"Oh, man, don't *DO* that to me," Loose wailed, stepping on my line.  He waved his hands in the air, spillin' beer foam down on his shirt.

"Well, you never *saw* the actual horn," I reminded him. "Cat can do some *bad* deeds in Photoshop or something crazy like that.

"But he said the horn was here in Pedro? And he claimed to have some kind of certificate to back up his claims?"

"Yeah, sure, all that jive." Loose was doin' the 'bobble-head' thing at me. "It was just, like, you know, like any other auction. I know I was pretty puffed up over this thing, but I did have my eyes wide, man, I really did!"

"*Reet*, so it *looked* like the real deal. That's a cool start. Now is there any way to check the guy out with Net Bid? Can they tell you if it's the dead cat we found or someone else?"

Loose did a deep think, absent-mindedly rubbing the cool brown bottle along the side of his face. "Like, I checked the dude's Net Bid feed-back, but he hadn't sold too many things on the auction before so it was just a few lines. All positive, though. I guess I can try to e-mail Net Bid and ask for the dude's credentials or whatever."

"If push comes to shove, I'll bet the cops can get the info if the Net Bid cats won't give it up to *you*, so you're kinda covered . . . maybe." The look I gave my friend was more harsh than I had intended.

"Thanks heaps, man!" Loose shot me fierce eyes as he reached for another brew. I grabbed another myself and we sipped in silence for a while.

After his second beer, Loose lit his face with an almost happy grin. "I'm so drug that, like I'm chillin' now, cause I know it can't get any worse. Lets go and blow a few licks."

My friend led the way into my spare room and sat at my old black Wurlitzer spinet. Yard and Art were still on the lam, tucked under my duvet or cowering in some cupboard. Loose fumbled a few real "out" chords, resolved them into some funky-feeling blues with weird voicings and told me to grab my horn. I followed his thoughts as we composed a heavy new line. Loose told me he was taggin' it "The Horn Gone Blues." I found some music paper in a desk drawer and noted the melody as Loose worked out the changes. When I had it down, Loose asked if I could run through it on the keys while he went down to the Buick and retrieved his old Selmer.

Loose's Mark VI made it swing as I accompanied him, then we traded places and I blew a little flugel over it.

We decided to work on it more tomorrow. By Friday we'd have parts written for everyone and we'd be ready to try it out at Blondy's when Skoot joined us for the sextet thing. As Loose's footfalls faded down the stairwell, two brown and white fuzz-faces peered around my kitchen doorway. Art's half-Siamese blue eyes seemed to be asking, "Has that overly-excitable dude split for good? We'd like to scarf something fishy now."

# Chapter 7

On Loose's departure, I fed the boys and decided I'd better sit down, have another drink and dig this score in its entirety. A hassle this gianormous needed more than a "beer" solution, so I retrieved the Linnie brand aquavit from the freezer and poured a generous shot into a water glass. I started out to my rooftop patio, thought about it a minute, and decided to bring the Aquavit with me. The bottle and I sat on my favorite lounger and watched a cruise ship setting sail for Mexico. Partiers on the liner's top deck waved my direction so I raised my juice jug in salute.

Loose believed this saxophone existed, and that it was the magic horn Art Pepper had sounded in one of his most creative periods. But then Loose really *wanted* to believe in this horn, so how far did his opinion count? Murder and deception had no place in his fantasy.

Back in the real world, deception abounded and this golden axe Loose wanted so bad seemed to be carryin' a curse. Its bad luck aura had already cost Loose three large and the man we'd found had paid with his life. And who had the horn now?

Was the person who had it going to have some bad luck as well? If only I knew where fantasy left off and reality began!

This made me laugh, as those thoughts didn't just apply to Art Pepper's lost horn. I've had trouble most of my life, as teachers, friends and relatives had always been quick to point out, from an innate problem with fantasy and reality.

Somewhere in my musings on what was happening with Loose and the horn, and how I might be able to help him as a friend, I must have gone on the nod. I awoke to a low sun in the sky and a chilly breeze across my elevated garden. No time to eat anything, just enough time for a quick shower and swing into some class vines for work.

I walked in to find a fair number of patrons in the Dive. Blondy was having a drink with some visitors from Denver in a booth near the jukebox. She introduced me to a cat named donnie l. betts, name spelled all in lower case letters, who was just finishing up a video documentary on singer Oscar Brown Jr., gave me a one-armed hug and turned back to her company. The trio was already warming up on the bandstand.

We tuned up, kicked off and swung a couple standards for the crowd. The folks were getting into our sound and the applause was a soothing balm to my troubled soul. The unpleasant memories of the day slipped away with the solid groove.

At least until halfway through the first set when Loose walked in with his light brown leather gig-bag under his arm. When we took our first break, around 9:45, Loose came up to tell me that he'd been thinkin' about "The Horn Gone Blues" and wanted to try it out with the rhythm cats right away.

"Maybe if it sounds like a good-enough riff, I can put some lyrics to the tune," he announced. "Then I can lay this down, distressing and depressing story on the world."

Dave, the piano man, turned a curious face our way. "Like, depressing story?" He went into a little Harry-the-Hipster ragtime riff on the keyboard and sang "Hey man, what's your story," at us, then turned on his bench and gave an inquisitive stare while doing a "Groucho" thing with his eyebrows.

We took it out to the alley where me and Loose teamed up to relate the day's haps. Loose provided the background information about the horn and the auction. I did my best to keep his story truthful and on track; weeding out the heavy exaggerations.

Dave listened along with the others in the band. Everyone agreed that it was a rough riff and wished Loose luck in finding his horn, or at least getting his gold back. They also liked the tune as Loose and I hummed it for them. Loose had written it out and showed them the sheet music, fumbling with some possible lyrics. We could dig where "Horn Gone" might rhyme with "in pawn," but no one could think of a rhyme for "auction" or "Net Bid."

We were, however, all anxious to get back on the stand and give the melody a run through. "Maybe, like, if we record it and get some airplay on NPR stations, someone will call us with an answer to the mystery," Dave said. John, our drummer, pointed out that by the time we booked a studio, pressed the discs and got it to market, the sax could be in Ghana or Tibet. "I like the tune," he told us. "And I'm all for recording it, but I don't think a song is gonna find a missing sax *or* a missing murderer. Lars'll hav'ta do that for you. He's the detective cat around here."

# Chapter 8

The next morning, Blondy woke me with a phone call just after 10 a.m. She told me that I was being "summoned" to an informal interview with her friend, Lieutenant Cheatham and another detective. She promised to have some breakfast for me if I could get down there within the hour.

I showered, dressed informally, checked the cat-kiddies' water dish and headed down to the Dive in a black tee-shirt sporting Dizzy Gillespie blowing a pink bubble-gum bubble, olive colored Swedish Army fatigue pants and my old wooden clogs. I found Lieutenant Tom, Blondy and the petite young lady-cop with the dark auburn hair seated in the back booth. White plastic take-away cartons of eggs, potatoes and toast littered the table. Blondy had set out some mismatched plates for us along with plastic forks, and real spoons for divvying up the grub. As we were loading our platters, Loose shuffled in doin' a hangdog number with downcast eyes and hands behind his back. I got up and fetched a chair for him, and Loose took his place on the end of the table, sitting half out into the aisle. Besides our little "breakfast party" the Dive's only other occupants were Sid, the bartender and a couple retired day-drinker Longshore dudes.

Tom re-introduced us to his female partner, Detective Salli Migiani, the one-and-the-same chick that had sounded us yesterday about the murder thing. He described her as one of his top investigators, adding that Detective Migiani had been assigned to investigate the murder of Jakob Rankovich, the man Loose and I had found strangled in the house on 34th Street.

Detective Migiani had a few interesting facts to lay on us. First, the address where we met Jakob Rankovich was not his home. The owners of the house, Dan and Marja Szizich, were on an extended visit with family members in Croatia. They were close friends of Rankovich's daughter, Katrin, who had been given the key to the house on 34th Street and was suppose to be "feeding the cat and watering plants."

"So what was Rankovich doing there," I asked?

Detective Migiani answered that the daughter had no idea. She had mentioned to her father that she was "house-sitting" for her friends, but didn't believe her father had paid her much attention. Katrin knew nothing about a saxophone.

"My father wasn't very interested in music," she had told the police. "Especially not in jazz." She had expressed doubts that Jakob Rankovich had ever listened to jazz or would have known who Art Pepper was.

Loose and I didn't know what to think about this information. Loose had, however, brought along "printouts" of the Net Bid pages advertising the auction. He also had the page stating that he was the high bidder and had won the auction in his shirt pocket, as well as printed copies of his emails from the seller telling him he must "send cash in a plain envelope, preferably small bills. Nothing larger than a $50." The email address was on the free "Hotmail" site. The police stated that they already had the Hotmail address and had looked into it.

I let these police officers know that I had thought these instructions about cash in an envelope were a bit strange, and I had said as much to Loose. Loose told the cops just what he had said to me: "Hey, lots'a these Net Bidder cats are a touch eccentric. They're always doin' quirky numbers like not trusting checks or banks or things. At first this dude didn't even want to meet me in person. Like, I had to do the chat thing for quite some time to convince him it was cool and, like, this way he'd get his bread faster, dig?"

Lieutenant Tom gave Loose a weird once-over, but didn't say anything. Blondy put her hand on Tom's arm, gave him a pat, and turned her eyes to the lady detective.

Salli Migiani explained that the email address Loose had for the auction seller was a new account that had been opened a few weeks before the saxophone was put up for bid. The information given to open the account proved a dead end. Both the Net Bid account and the email were registered to one Bobby Smith at a non-existent San Pedro address on a street that had years ago slid down the bluff in an area now known as "Sunken City." The credit card number Net Bid had *was* for a Robert Smith, but turned out to be a Visa card that had been reported stolen back in New York a few weeks before the auction began. Net Bid had verified the card when the seller first signed up, but then just kept the number "on file," so they were unaware that it had become listed as a bad card.

As to Art Pepper's old Martin saxophone, no one had a clue. No instrument with that serial number had been reported stolen. A team of detectives had called on all the pawn shops in San Pedro and surrounding communities, as far away as Torrance, Long Beach and the other L.A. coastal towns but found no-one that could recall ever seeing such a horn or having it in their possession. The consensus of the local "uncles" was that if such a horn existed and was what it was purported to be, it was probably hidden away in someone's private collection and wouldn't surface until the collector died and family went through his estate. Even then, the owner's heirs might not know what they had and could well put it out at a garage sale or cast it off to some charity thrift store.

None of this proved a lift to Loose's demeanor. His pale face sunk lower as we listened. His voice issued the intermittent

"Oh *no*," or "*Doomsville*, daddy." When Salli Migiani asked if she could keep the computer printouts Loose had brought, Lucian told her that they were copies he had brought for her.

At the meeting's end, Lieutenant Tom assured Loose that he believed we were innocents who just showed up at the wrong moment, and it looked like Loose'd eventually get his three-grand back. Detective Migiani seemed pleasant enough towards us as she shook our hands, but offered no such assurances as to her beliefs about our case.

# Chapter 9

It is never easy figuring out just where to begin. I knew I had to do some research on my own as Loose wasn't in any condition to help himself. I remembered that the San Pedro Historical Society was open to the public on Wednesday afternoons, so I figured that was as good a place as any to begin. It was also about three blocks away in the old City Hall building, convenient to my pad and Blondy's.

The elderly gentleman at the desk wasn't sure where to start either, but he gave it some thought and decided that we might start with photographs of Beacon Street in the 1950s. Beacon Street had been known as "The Toughest Ten Blocks in the World" back then. There were, at one time, 264 saloons within that ten-block stretch and at least a dozen pawnshops. Three of the pawnshops had relocated to Pacific Avenue and were still open and active. The others were a puff of smoke in the Pedro legend.

I wrote down as much *gen* as I could find about all the pawn brokers that were pictured or mentioned in historic records. Some photographs had owner names and phone numbers listed in the records; some had only their faces looking out the window of time from a distant scene. The phone numbers in the records were dated, most starting with the "Terminal" prefix, which became "83" when telephone area codes were introduced in the 1960s.

I took my notes back to the Channel View where I tried to organize everything I'd found. I started dialing numbers. The first three were obviously "new" subscribers, so wrong numbers. The next was a disconnect. On my fifth dial-up I got lucky.

A man named Mario Bernini had owned Bayside Pawn. His son, Gian-Carlo, remembered that his father had been a big Art Pepper fan and often spoke about Art and his father, Richard Pepper. Gian-Carlo said he thought they still had an old Martin alto saxophone in their possession that could be the Art Pepper horn. He promised me he would take a look in their storage facility and would meet with me tomorrow afternoon at 3:30 to share whatever he found out.

My appointment made for the following bright, I took five, swung with an ale, swooped to the porch and parked it in my recliner for a little unwind before my regular gig at Blondy's. I wasn't sure where all this was coming from or where it might be going, but at least I was doing something to move it forward. Bailing out Loose wasn't really my responsibility, but I did feel an obligation to help the kid if I could. We jazz cats have to stick together, through thick and thin as well as through smart and "too obsessed to think clearly."

# Chapter 10

Gian-Carlo was cool. He was probably a few years older than me, a lifelong Pedro cat who had worked all his adult years as a high school history teacher and had a great knowledge of the town's chronology. He remembered his father talking about the many evenings he had gone out drinking with Dick Pepper. They usually brought little Art along because Art could play the clarinet, and when young Art stood on the bar and played for the folks, either the crowd would buy Dick and Mario drinks or the bartender at the White Swan would give them free beers. Because they both had to be at work early in the morning, Dick and Mario would take the 11:05 Red Car up Crescent Avenue to their homes. Mario had lived on the bluff by 19th Street and Crescent, overlooking the main channel. Dick and Art had a place farther out toward Point Fermin, on the edge of the huge Fort McArthur military complex. The Pacific Electric streetcars had stopped going out to Point Fermin in 1937 when much of the coastal bluff area had collapsed into the sea, so the time had to have been early to mid 30s. The area that slid down the bluff, known as "Sunken City" had taken the streetcar tracks with it putting an end to trolley service at the southern edge of town. This was also where the Net Bid cat had placed his false address.

Gian-Carlo also remembered when Art came back from the war. Gian-Carlo had been a child, but he recalled his father saying that the Peppers had moved into Watts before the war. Art, however, came back to Pedro when he got out of the Army. He had rented a little house up on 19th Street overlooking the port and the town. He and his wife, Diane, lived there with a small white poodle named Bijou. They often came to visit Mario at the Bayside Pawn Shop. Whether his visits were purely social or for money to buy drugs Gian-Carlo had no idea. He recalled that one time Art had brought Chet Baker in to meet Mario, knowing Mario was a fan. At that time Gian-Carlo had been a teenager. He had listened politely to his father's stories, but he had been too wrapped up in his own social life at San Pedro High School and hadn't paid much attention.

The Bayside Pawn records were still somewhere in Gian-Carlo's cellar and could easily be checked, but for the moment there was no need as Gian-Carlo knew that Art Pepper had borrowed money on his horn many times over the years. He remembered Mario often bragging that he owned the horn Art Pepper played when he became a jazz super-star. He had often told friends that having that horn was worth more to him than any money he had ever given Art, and that he was proud to have helped Art keep playing his music through his rough drug-addicted times. Mario had always said that, while he didn't approve of heroin use, if it had contributed to the greatness of Art Pepper's *bella, bella* sound, God would surely forgive it.

A quick inspection of the family storage container at a Wilmington facility had not produced the Martin alto, but Gian-Carlo was sure it was there somewhere. He promised to make a more thorough search over the weekend, when he had more time. He would call me as soon as he had some more information. I left his South Shores home, where the family had moved to in the 60s, and caught the local DASH bus back to the Channel View to get ready for the night's gig at Blondy's.

# Chapter 11

Detective Salli Migiani was at the front desk of the hotel when I arrived. She turned, eyed me up and down, gave a seductive wink and told me, "You are just the man I'm looking for. Is there somewhere private we can talk?" I invited her upstairs, offered her the rooftop lounger and a Red Hook Ale. I pulled up a plastic garden chair for myself and took a long swallow from my own bottle. My fickle feline kids were out here to greet *this* new visitor. They must have sensed something good about the lady detective, as they circled her ankles and nudged her hands seeking attention and recognition. Salli Migiani stroked each of their heads and cooed soft noises at both Yard and Art. She commented on what large eyes Yard had, and how blue were Art's. When both cats were purring contentedly, the lady cop got down to business.

"We've been interviewing a few friends and neighbors of our deceased friend Rankovich," she told me for openers. "... found a drinking buddy of ol' Jakob's who 'tipped back a few' with our man just before his murder. He was very likely the last one to see Rankovich alive, except for his murderer. I'm not sure how reliable a witness we have in someone who starts off drinkin' before nine in the morning, but he's what we've got.

"The buddy's name is Adrian Samich, he claims he was driving Jakob home from a bar where they had met earlier in the morning for a breakfast coffee with brandy. Breakfast apparently stretched into a few Budweiser's for dessert. Samich had a doctor's appointment at 11:30, so they left the bar but were planning on going back that afternoon for a few more beers.

"They were driving up 34th Street when Jakob saw the door open on the house where he remembered his daughter was house sitting. He was thinking his daughter had to be there watering house plants, so he asked Adrian to drop him off. He wanted his daughter to take him shopping and said he'd call Adrian later so they could go back to the Alhambra Bar for a couple more beers. Adrian says he drove off without looking back."

The lady Detective fell silent, took an absent minded pull on her Red Hook and stared off toward the channel, where a large ship jam packed with green China Shipping containers drifted seaward. When the silence became uncomfortable, I decided I should fill it. I asked, "So what do we know about the saxophone neck strap? Any idea where it came from? Or how it got around the ol' stud's neck?"

Salli Migiani turned her eyes to mine. I couldn't help but notice that those orbs were a deep and fetching shade of blue-gray set off by the pale highlights in her wine-red hair. "That's the mystery," she told me. "Lieutenant Cheatham says you're good with mysteries. While technically, you are still one of our prime suspects, Tom says he knows you're okay and we can trust you."

Her eyes searched my eyes. "And I want to trust you. My gut feeling is to agree with the Lieutenant." She hesitated a few seconds, then continued.

"I don't know much about music, but my father is a jazz fan. He told me all about Art Pepper. And he had some good things to say about you as well. He says he's almost a regular at Blondy's."

She reached down beside the chair and dug in her handbag, bringing forth a compact disc I had made some years before. Not one of my best efforts, its notoriety rested in that it was probably my rarest and most obscure. I had recorded the session in a friend's garage in an effort to get some gigs. I had mainly given it out to promoters and club owners. I had sold off the leftovers at live performances to pay for the production costs.

"Can you autograph this for my dad? Just something like 'good luck to Joe Migiani?'"

I started laughing at her solemn expression, then excused myself as I saw how serious her face remained. "Sure," I told her, "I can sign this, but I've got a better, more recent CD of my current band I could sign for your dad. I'll be happy to give that one to you."

"That's nice," she replied, "but dad says this is the one he wants autographed. He told me that this is the one his other collector friends are most jealous of, cause they can't find this record anywhere. One of his friends has apparently had a search going on Net Bid for over a year. He's willing to pay $100 or more if someone has a copy to sell."

I offered to give her more copies of the old CD for her father's buddies as I still had a few somewhere in my closet. She gave an emphatic, "Don't you dare! They're envious because they can't find it and dad is very pleased to be the only one to have it. He'll have even more prestige when he has not just the only copy, but a personalized one at that!"

I laughed again, took a swig of beer and headed to the house to find a pen and another newer CD to give the detective as well. I started to pull a copy of my latest release, cut with the guys from Blondy's, then gave it more thought and went to my closet where I had some other old recordings in a box on the top shelf. I dug out a disc I'd made in Oslo a few years back, accompanied by some very vouty Norwegians and Swedes with whom I'd performed at the Molde Jazz Festival.

When I returned, Art was flattened out in Salli's lap, head against her groin and tail flipping around her knees. Yard covered the toes of her low-heeled shoes, looking up wistfully at her face.

I signed both the pro-offered CD of her father's and the Scandinavian disc. "Not as obscure as your dads, but another one his friends aren't likely to have in their collections."

Her grin had some real candlepower to it when I handed over the CDs. She shook her auburn locks and said I was wonderful. With the discs in her purse, she returned to business. "What are your thoughts on this murder," she asked me? "Was Rankovich the man trying to fence the horn? Was he someone's errand boy? Or did he just stumble by at the wrong moment?"

I told her my vote went toward the last option, but that was just my feeling, not a logical decision. "Rankovich seems a bit old to be some hood's helper," I told her. "It also doesn't fit in my head that a retired longie day drinker would be clever enough to make an appointment at which he was to receive big bucks, then gamble on a friend driving by and dropping him off on time for his meeting after they'd been drinking. And what about the saxophone? Did he stash the horn earlier?

"No," I told her, "It just don't jive in my thinking. Someone else is out there in the shadows and I wouldn't have a clue as to who, or even what shadows to bet on."

I noticed that Salli had finished her beer. I offered another, but she stood and told me she had to get back to work. "Can I walk you back down to the street?" I asked, adding, "Those three floors between here and there are a pretty rough neighborhood."

Now it was her turn to laugh. "I'm a big girl," she reassured. "Besides, I'm a detective, a trained killer, and I'm armed with a large Glock automatic." By now we were headed for the stairwell, doin' the slow stroll across my rooftop. Yard and Art had gone back inside. At my front door, she turned and gave me a hug that turned into a kiss and grew to *full swing* with, like, a heat of solid passion behind it.

I was momentarily off guard. My single-o fly-chick, Astrid, lives eight thousand miles away in Norway, but I still felt some minor guilt. What was I doing? First I was a suspect, then I was a consultant, now where was I headed?

Salli must have sensed something of my unease. She broke off the kiss and took a step back. Her beautiful eyes clouded, then cleared and finished up smiling. "Yeah," she told me, "I think maybe you'd better escort me through the badlands and back to my car."

# Chapter 12

Salli and I bid a businesslike farewell. She slid into a slick-back panda and drove away down 7<sup>th</sup> Street. I made an upward slink carrying a load of useless guilt to my crib.

I had strong feelings for Astrid, my *earth-angel* dream redhead who drove a streetcar in Oslo. We both enjoyed each other's company when we were together and I even felt as though she could be the major love interest in my life. Yet Salli the cop had stirred something deep inside me as well. Salli was here and Astrid was one third of the way around the globe. When I was a young cat, I wouldn't have given it a second thought, but now it was buggin' me in the high numbers.

At the top of my four flights, I took the aquavit bottle from the freezer and found my small blown-glass tumbler. I put a couple 'George Shearing with Strings' discs on the changer and sat cross-legged on the floor, my back propped against the sofa, to look out at the skyline of downtown Long Beach across the harbor. I poured a shot, tossed it back and pondered. The cats book-ended me, one on each side vying for my attention.

Why was I feelin' drug? I mean, a most attractive lady had just paid me quite a compliment, but she hadn't actually dragged me off to bed or anything. There might not even be anything shakin' there. The kiss might never be mentioned again; life and the murder investigation would carry on as usual. I'll drink to that, I thought . . . and I did!

On the other hand, the prospect of her becoming just another cop figure bothered as well. I had enjoyed that kiss. Heck, man, I had grooved on the full interview thing and had eyes for our next meeting, hoping things might escalate. And my cat kids obviously dug her. They had given a *unanimous* vote of approval, something most visitors to my lair *never* received. I poured another shot and decided my choices were the girl, the guilt, or both. I tried to make a decision, taking a drink straight from the bottle to fire up my gray cells.

I must have nodded off again. I woke from a dream in which Astrid and Salli were both tugging my outstretched arms in opposite directions. They were on either side of a fast flowing river. I was precariously balanced on the sharp peak of a slippery moss-covered stone. Whichever lady might win the tug-of-war, I would most likely be lost to the strong current parting around my narrow foothold, a watery grave taking me from both ladies.

My crossed legs had gone to sleep giving me trouble when I tried to unfold them and stand. My Viking shot glass lay on its side. My supply of aquavit appeared to have evaporated while I was out. Adding to my troubles, the daylight was fading which meant I was due to open the show at Blondy's at any moment.

# Chapter 13

I took the stand at Blondy's under the weight of double guilt and a strong aquavit buzz. The band had already launched into the first set without me. The blonde one had nasty in her eyes when I walked in, those green orbs telling me I had picked the wrong night to screw up. She would probably give me another lecture about my drinking at break time.

Drinking was a sore subject right at the moment. Lady thought that I should consider joining Alcoholic's Anonymous. I told her she knew me well enough to realize my rebellious nature wouldn't work in that kinda scene. She had recently mentioned it again and I had made light of it, telling her I would go to an AA meeting if I could find one in Beverly Hills.

"You meet a better class of drunk there than you would here in Pedro," I'd joked, but she didn't find any humor in the subject.

I was saved by the entrance of Jay Abramson, an old school friend from San Pedro High. When Mickey's little gloved hand crept up to break time I made a beeline for Jay's table. Jay was a clerk on the docks. Back in 1964, however, he'd been a promising trombone player. His parents had been jazz fans in their native Sweden and Jay had some solid old LP's of Kai Winding and Åke Persson his parents had brought from Ystad, a town in Skåne. Jay still had his axe somewhere in a dusty closet. Every few years he'd bring it out, practice for a few weeks and come by the Dive to sit in on a Sunday jam.

Remembering that Rankovich and Samich had both been retired from the docks, I hoped maybe he could give me some understanding of how things work with the longshoremen of our harbor. Every other cat in Pedro was somehow connected to the harbor: longshore, warehouse men, fishing folk or sailors. And every third chick that *did* work either worked the docks or owned a hair and nail salon.

We started talking old times. Jay always wanted to talk about music with me, but tonight, I steered him towards his own career. I showed a friendly interest in what he did for a living and Jay took the ball down the field to his own goal.

As a clerk, he checked manifests, kept records of the goods coming in-and-out of the harbor and knew which crews were off-loading goods, operating cranes or other tasks. Just like in the old days, the largest part of the workforce handled cargo. Technology, however, computers, cranes and forklift trucks, made the job much easier than it had once been. The rank and file guys didn't mind, as they were paid for many more hours than they actually worked. A large group of them collected their hourly wage while soaking up the juices in one of Pedro's or Wilmington's many gin-mills, waiting for the call, waiting on trucks or trains or just waiting through a required rest period.

Although dockworkers were not supposed to come to work juiced or high, everyone looked out for each other. Supervisors often looked the other way. Any drug testing was broadcast long before it was scheduled. The International Brotherhood of Longshore and Warehousemen boasted an amazing "jungle telegraph" on the docks. They not only kept their members informed on situations with work, but also proved a superb source of local San Pedro gossip.

We were just getting into the subject of pilferage and theft when Blondy started casting nervous glances toward the stage. Time to get back to work.

"Fascinating stuff," I told Jay. "I'd like to hear more sometime." I hadn't mentioned any of Loose's problems, but if it looked like there might be a tie in, I had set the stage to get more information.

"Bring your 'bone down Sunday, man," I told Jay. "We miss your riffs here. Just like in old times, bro, we always sound good together."

By the second break, Jay had gotten in the wind. It was time for me to face the lady's rough mood. Smile and nod, I was thinkin'. Watch my smart mouth and I could get by without too much grief.

# Chapter 14

Gian-Carlo woke me up with a phone call the next morning sending my feline sleep-mates scurrying. The time, 10:30, was earlier than I normally open my conscious mind for business, but I hadn't slept well and was already half awake anyway. I must have sounded sleepy as Gian-Carlo apologized for calling so early. When I assured him that I already had eyes and ears wide open, he got down to the crème-filled-center of the communication.

Gian-Carlo had a teen-age son, Greg, who lived in Orange County with his mother, somewhere in the Garden Grove area. But Gian-Carlo's boy had been hanging out here in Pedro lately. He had entered his name in a lottery the Maritime people were sponsoring an order to fill some 3,000 longshore jobs. Greg wanted to work on the docks with some of his old school buddies from the harbor area, kids he knew from Dana Junior High before his parents, like, split the legal partnership thing.

Gian-Carlo had been having his son around often for meals. He was happy for the opportunity to spend time with his only child. They talked about San Pedro, about the new development going on, the Promenade that the City of Los Angeles was building along the channel, and about work on the docks.

Greg had mentioned one friend who sounded like trouble. This particular mate of his, Jeremy, always had some shady side deal going. Greg suspected that Jeremy was stealing from the containers that were unloaded during his shift and selling the goods he stole at flea markets in other parts of Southern California.

Jeremy had recently been asking a lot of questions about the pawnbroker business in general and about granddad's pawnshop specifically. He had been joking with some of the other guys at the union hall that he planned to open a shop so he'd have a more convenient address for unloading *"his percentage"* of the cargo he was handling everyday.

Under pressure from Gian-Carlo, Greg admitted that he has bragged about the family storage where some of the old pawned items were stored. He had been bragging about how they intended to sell all this shit off when his granddad died, but never got around to it. He had also told friends he has access to a key. They might have "borrowed" the key once or twice, just to go marvel at all the junk Greg kept bragging about the family having there. What was the harm in that? After all, they *were* his friends, and you've got to trust your friends.

Only now, after Gian-Carlo told him about the missing saxophone, Greg was getting nervous, feeling guilty and suspecting he might have been betrayed by Jeremy or some other buddycat from the docks. Gian-Carlo thought that maybe I should pay a call on Jeremy, unannounced, to check him out and pick his brain a little. Even if this Jeremy was just makin' like Mr. Bigshot by talkin' trash, he must have picked up the idea somewhere, and probably could point me in the right direction.

# Chapter 15

Jeremy di Stefani lived in an aging duplex up the steep hill on 22nd Street. It was a heavy climb from where I got off the DASH bus on Gaffey Street. I had called Salli Migiani before I headed up to check this stud out so if I should get into trouble, someone would know where I had been and could maybe help me out. As I explained to Salli what Gian-Carlo had told me, I could sense the "cop" side head of her kicking in.

"You go on up there and talk to him if you want, Lars," she told me. "While you're doing that, I'm going to put his vitals into the computer and see how he looks from here. If I don't like what I see, I may be joining you there before you have time to finish your interview."

Jeremy greeted me at his front door, a grinning fair-haired, brown-eyed kid, around 5'9 and 180 pounds. He looked like he'd been lifting weights for some years. His neck, arms and chest bulged obscenely in a too-small navy tee shirt. He invited me in without questioning why I was there and offered me a banana from an open wooden crate in the corner of his living room.

"You the guy lookin' for the, uh, sample plasma TV," he asked?

"Tell me about the TV," I fired back non-commitally.

"I've only got a couple of these big-screen plasmas. Samsungs. They, uh, fell off a truck, but nothin' got hurt, *if you know what I mean.*" He winked lasciviously. "We're guaranteed to be in perfect working order. Of course the guarantee comes through me, cause you don't want to send in the registration card on this baby. Anything wrong, I'll replace it with another one. Hey, but at the price I'm offering, I don't think anyone's gonna complain."

I stared him down and kept silent. After an uncomfortable sweep of the second hand Jeremy offered, "I'm sorry, were you the guy for the lap-tops? I got a dozen Dells, right from the factory, you might say. Just happened to fall off the boat."

"Actually," I told Jeremy, "I came here to ask you if you had helped yourself to anything from the Bernini's family storage, the goods from the old Bayside Pawn Shop." I definitely had him off guard. His first reaction was surprise, but anger quickly came in behind it.

"Who the fuck are you? If you're here lookin' for trouble, you might just be findin' more than you can handle! If you're tryin' to shake me down, I got some heavy protection that could mess up your life in a hurry. So what is it?"

He started towards me, cracking his knuckles and puffing himself up to appear threatening. My take was that the cat was bluffing. I hoped I was right. I stared him down and held my ground.

I was saved from findin' out if I was crazy or not by another knock on the front door. Jeremy sidestepped that direction, keeping an eye on me as he shuffled a parallel path toward the portal. He was reaching out to grab the knob when a loud and deep voice sounded out "police, open up."

Jeremy's face radiated hatred my way, his eyes telling me that it wasn't over until it was over and he still might have the last word. As he turned toward his callers, he spread a cold smile across his face. In a friendly voice, he greeted the detectives who waited outside asking, "Is something wrong?"

The first detective through the door was tall and so black his skin almost appeared purple. I looked for Salli behind him, but saw only an older cat with snow-white hair and a large beer gut. The tall detective zeroed right in on the crate of fruit.

"You must really like bananas, man. You some kinda monkey?"

Jeremy was flummoxed. He hemmed-and-hawed a bit, but couldn't seem to get a coherent sentence out.

The tall cop was cool. "Hey, man, no offense. We're just wantin' to see your bill of sale for these goods."

Jeremy's face was a bank of heavy clouds. "Bill of sale?"

"Yeah, man, like the receipt, y'know? You buy these at Von's or one o'them little Mexican grocers?"

The white haired partner had disappeared into the hallway of Jeremy's pad. Suddenly, his voice rang out from somewhere in the rear of the flat. "Might want to show us a receipt for these lap-top computers as well. And is this a plasma TV in the carton you've got in your spare bedroom?"

Jeremy shrunk into himself, looking like a hurt child. "Come-on, guys, dock workers have always helped themselves to a few things from the cargo, it's a tradition man."

That earned him a solemn, deadpan stare. The older detective had come back into the room with a white Dell carton in his hand. Jeremy's confused look traveled back and forth between the two gendarmes.

"Did someone complain? I mean if someone wants this stuff back, they can have it. Or did someone rat me out? Hey, man, what is all this?

"First this cat," a nod in my direction, "comes here to shake me down for some bread, then you guys show up. I wanna know what the fuck's goin' on!"

The tall detective started reciting some Miranda at our boy. The old cat was pullin' on my coat. "You're Lars, right?" I nodded. "Salli says to say 'Hi' and 'thanks'. We're under a different lieutenant, but we're grateful for the tip. You might give Detective Migiani a call when you get home. Just between you and me, I think the lady is kinda stuck on you. "

# Chapter 16

Detective Salli saved me the nickel. Walking back down the 22nd Street hill, I caught a short burst of siren behind me. A dark blue unmarked squad car pulled up to the curb where 22nd met Meyler Street and the passenger door opened in my path.

When I got in Salli asked, "You like to walk all the time or what. I never see you drivin'."

I told her I didn't own a car, she replied, "Yeah, I know. I hope you don't mind, but I took the liberty of checking your record. No registered auto and no current license." Salli was chewing gum. She blew a small pink bubble and popped it without getting any on her face.

"Tough break about those 802s you got; the DUIs. But that was a few years ago. You could get your ticket back now and buy a car if you wanted."

"Yeah," I told her, "but then I'd have more expenses; monthly payments, repairs, insurance." I didn't care to discuss the fact that I still enjoyed the sauce too much and didn't trust myself with a motor at my disposal. "Anyway, the other cats take me

The Real Gone, Horn Gone Blues

to any gigs we got away from the Dive, Blondy's place, and I ain't got the need to go far from the Channel View, anyway."

"A real homebody." She turned her head and smiled at me. "Not like that's a bad thing. My ex was *never* home. Conflicting schedules. That's when I was still working patrol, so my shifts were pretty screwy." Her cop ride was just pulling up to the stop sign across from Blondy's and my hotel. Salli parked us in the loading zone out front of the Whale and Ale Pub.

"Anyway, I wanted to thank you for the tip. Skinny around the station was that the union and the Maritime Association were investigating some recent major thefts of cargo. It isn't in our squad's area, but it never hurts to have a few cards you can trade with the other teams. We all need to call in favors at some time or another.

"You gonna be around later? I'll stop by and let you know what we learn from your buddy Jeremy. I think he's gonna start singin' some interesting lyrics when he sees the seriousness of his woeful ways."

"Sure," I told her. "You want to meet down at the dive for a drink?"

Salli thought about it, blew another gum bubble, popped it, then answered. "Naw, I'd better come up to your place, if that's okay?" She sent a conspiratorial face my way. "This is confidential stuff, y'know? We don't want some other longshore type overhearing and breeching our security."

# Chapter 17

I did the homeward hike to my aerie and headed for the freezer. As I opened the 'fridge door, I remembered that the aquavit had died. I opened an ale, making a mental note to myself to bum a ride out to Alpine Village, eight miles up the freeway in Torrance, to restock the Norsky Juice. Local liquor stores didn't offer any decent aquavit, not even Trader Joe's.

At my piano I fiddled with some changes, wrote out some ideas for a ballad that was running around in my head, but it couldn't hold my concentration. That little "guardian" voice in my head kept buggin' me about, like, what have I got myself into now. I really did want to get Loose out of danger and even help him find his "golden horn" if I could. I didn't want to get mixed up in some major hassle on the waterfront. My heart was confused between Astrid, for whom I had strong feelings, and Salli Migiani, who was stirring something pretty heavy inside me as well. I carried my bottle out to the patio to give all this more heavy thought.

Art and Yard squeezed into the recliner on either side of my form. The cat kids were happy just being close to me. I watched some ships coming and going on the channel. I listened to a couple arguing down in the street, hurling insults back and forth. Mainly I tried to figure out how a stolen saxophone, an instrument that had value mainly among jazz memorabilia collectors, could be tied into pilferage from overseas ships. It cooked my brain, simmering it in bitter ale, until I closed my eyes for a brief rest.

The phone brought me back to the present, ringing in the distance beyond my open glass slider and sending the cats out for cover. I was sure it would stop its chirping by the time I got to the receiver, I counted a dozen rings before I got my hand around it, but there was Salli's voice in the earpiece to greet me.

"Am I interrupting anything?" In my mind I could see a sarcastic grin painting her question.

"I was outside. Sorry I took so long, I don't hear the phone goin' off from out there."

"Especially after a few beers," she replied. "And I hope you saved a few more for me. Or, should I stop and get a bottle of wine to share while I tell you what I've learned from the Special Cases squad?"

"I've got plenty of Red Hook in the fridge, but if you'd prefer heavier sauce a nice red would work."

I caught her laugh as she hung up. I went in to run some cold water over my face and straighten up the kitchen a little. The detective was rapping on my door before I got started. She walked in, set a pricey looking bottle on the counter, and gave me a hug accompanied by a peck on the mug. Once again, my feline friends were makin' figure eights around the lady's shapely ankles, lettin' her know she was welcome, maybe even more welcome than old meal-ticket me.

"Community policing," she told me as she reached down to scratch little furry heads. "We try to maintain a friendly rapport with the public we're watching over."

I returned her kiss and got some tongue for my efforts. When we broke for air, Salli sent her eyes wandering to take in my cookery digs. "So where does a lady find a corkscrew in this mess," she laughed. "And I trust you *do* have proper wine glasses?"

"Hey, I'm a musician, girl. We just break the jug off at the neck and drink straight from the bottle! I mean when we can't find wine in a cardboard box." I fished in my junk drawer for the high-end contraption someone had given me as a gift that levered out the cork with ease, after which I opened the cupboard that held my classy collection of English beer mugs, French wine glasses and thimble-sized Norwegian shot glasses.

I received another kiss for my efforts along with an, "I'm impressed, you've got quite an assortment to choose from." She picked out a pair of stem glasses that were almost brandy snifters and proceeded to overfill them. She offered me a healthy drop or two of the juice and took a sampling sip from her own.

Salli hooked her purse over her shoulder, gathered up her glass in one hand and the bottle in the other. "Lead me to your sofa and I'll call this meeting to order."

# Chapter 18

In my living room, the cats rallied round for the best seats, playing quotes to the lady cop's position and vying for her attention. She gave them obligatory strokes, but focused her attention on me, all business.

Salli told me that Jeremy had been, like, a real uncool face. He had entered the cop shop full of bluster, sticking to his story that workers on the waterfront had always helped themselves to the occasional item from ship's cargo. Taking things from the ships was an accepted and time-honored tradition. The shippers, he had told them, expected it and always packed a little extra because they knew items could go missing or get broken at sea. He had scoffed when read his rights, repeatedly askin' who had it in for him. He hinted at a sizable bribe if they'd let him go and tell him "whose ass he needed to kick to settle the beef" that someone was puttin' on him.

When a bigwig from the Maritime Association and one of the top union officers were brought into the interview room along with a pair of FBI men, Jeremy started to realize that his thievery was a serious matter. The feebs told the detectives that they intended to make an example of Jeremy. They would hold him up before the other longshoremen to let everyone see that shippers were tired of losing money and goods, paying continually increasing premiums for insurance and putting up with workers who had no respect for their employers.

By the time the officials and the feds were through, Jeremy had agreed to turn states evidence. He hadn't understood any of the part about racketeering, or asking for protection money. Jeremy had only been involved with breaking into the containers and boosting the goods, but he would tell the police and the Maritime Association all he knew about those stolen goods, how they were removed from the containers and how they were transferred to the black market for sale. He would give them someone higher up the food chain for their example: someone who might have information about the insurance scheme as well.

In the end, Jeremy "cut a deal" for leniency and a promise that he would be relocated into a witness protection program. The union man offered to provide an attorney to help him get fair treatment as long as Jeremy was willing to tell all that he knew, holding nothing back. In the meantime, the union would put up his bail. Jeremy would be suspended from his duties on the docks while awaiting his hearing and further meetings with government agents and Maritime people. He would be talking with one of the union attorneys in the meantime, putting together some names, dates and places for the federal cops. This was, indeed, a heavy charge: one that could put him in prison for many years if his information didn't prove useful in stopping the theft.

Salli had snuggled up close to me while she told her tale, squeezing Yard out of his prime position between us. At the stories end, she took another drink of her wine, and rested her head on my chest. "Have you eaten yet," she asked? "Now that we've covered the secret stuff, I could risk bein' seen with you someplace like 22$^{nd}$ Street Landing or The Green Onion."

Suggesting two of my favorite restaurants made it a difficult offer to refuse. "Green Onion is closer," I said.

"There is that," she countered. "But then lots of cops go there to eat and drink. Besides, the landing is nicer atmosphere with a cool view of the yacht harbor."

"You gonna make me ride in the cage of a cop car to get there?"

That earned a loud laugh. "I hadn't thought of that," she confessed with a mischievous grin. "But you're too late with the suggestion. I have my own personal vehicle downstairs."

# Chapter 19

Just across 7<sup>th</sup> street at the curb by the Lazy Dog Studio
Art Gallery, the lights flashed on the light gray BMW urban
assault lorry when Salli pushed her key chain clicker button.
She turned to me, her eyes seeking approval of her ride. I tried
to send an impressed face her way, though I'm not much of a
fan of these pseudo-military things everyone's driving these
days.

"I bought this for myself as a reward when I made Detective
II last year," she cooed. "So much more comfortable then all
those huge black and white Crown Vics and Caprices."

Salli pulled down her seat belt to its fastener and watched
to see that I was doing the same. When my belt had clicked
home, she turned the key and propelled us past The Sheraton,
City Hall and the Red Car tracks, turning toward Ports O'Call
village along the main channel.

At 22<sup>nd</sup> Street Landing, the day charters were just doin'
their homeward thing, but it was still a little early for the
dinner crowd, so we copped a parking place right near the
entrance. Salli and I hit the flight of stairs to the bar and main
dining area where we had our choice of seats. Salli picked a

table overlooking the dinner cruise boat that was preparing to leave from its moorings. We ordered a couple house reds and some fried calamari for starters, halibut dinners to follow. A mini-loaf of bread and small plates before us, we chilled out to enjoy the view.

They were filming a movie off Cabrillo Beach. Blue and white striped marques were spread across the parking area by the fishing pier. A small knot of people in bikinis and surfer-jams stood around near the colorful tents. Gypsy caravans with signs that proclaimed "Star Wagon" crowded the car park across the bay from us.

Salli Migiani didn't seem to notice. She was completely focused on me. "Did you always want to be a musician?" she asked twirling the stem of her wineglass between her thumb and two fingers. "Never a fireman or a cowboy?"

"Well," I admitted, "in my earliest years, I idolized Roy Rogers, Wild Bill Hickock and some other cowboys on TV. But I also watched Captain somebody, a guy who used to show up at McCowan's Market with his flying saucer on a flatbed truck and throw out handfuls of bubble-gum. And I was fascinated with Engineer Bill and all his model trains. I was probably more into the trains than anything else, until I got my first horn and joined the band at school.

"My first axe was a mellophone, kind of an alto trumpet that looked more like a French horn. Then I heard Dizzy Gillespie on a jukebox at Disneyland. I burned down that record, over and over, until I was out of nickels. When I got home, I went to the local record man searching for more Dizzy Gillespie, where I also discovered Chet Baker, Art Farmer and Joe Gordon. I started saving to buy a trumpet. Never thought seriously of bein' anything else since then."

Salli's moony look was most un-cop-like, but I kinda dug it. The waiter brought our fish. When he was gone, I met her stare, asking, "And you?"

"You know us Catholic Italian girls, I was just gonna be a housewife and have lots of kids. For a while in junior high, I thought about bein' a nurse, but when it came right down to it, I felt squeamish cutting up frogs in Biology, so bye-bye nursing goals.

"Then at Harbor College I had a boyfriend who was a solid cop wanna-be. Police work was all he talked about. He had a part-time job as a security guard and went around dressed in black boots and a uniform type shirt. He talked about it so much, he got me interested."

"So is he in the LAPD now too?"

Salli laughed her musical laugh. "No. Jack discovered marijuana. He u-turned into a sort of late blooming hippy and dropped out of sight. I ran into him some years later. He was in town for an uncle's funeral. Wow, had he *changed*!" She laughed again, shaking her head at the memory. "Bald on top but hair to his waist. Some sort of string vest with shredded jeans.

"He still had the black boots, I'm sure it was the same pair, but I don't think he had shined them since the day he discovered dope. He was a sad sorry sight!"

I laughed with her. "Ah, young love and missed opportunities."

"Oh, right," she countered. "Anyway, I had started talking with a recruiter, thinking it was also a great opportunity to do my thing for womens' rights. The officer who counseled me advised that I should finish my four year degree first, not only to help me advance a law enforcement career faster but also because they needed police officers with more than just street smarts."

"A smart man," I commented, just to show I was listening.

"Yeah, he is. You know him, of course." She took another sip of wine and continued. "He's advanced himself well. It was Tom Cheatham, my Lieutenant and Blondy's sort-of boyfriend."

Such a small town, San Pedro. My plate was nearly cleared, Salli's was barely touched, but the mention of Blondy reminded that work called. "Maybe I better talk for a while and let you eat," I told her. "I'm on in about 45 minutes."

The lady reached across the table and took my hand in both of hers. "That's okay," she said. "I wasn't all that hungry. But I wanted the opportunity to spend some non-work time with you." Her pretty head made a tiny nod toward the waiter who rushed over with the check. I offered, but Salli told me, "No, I invited you. You can take me to dinner next time?"

I caught the upturned question in her voice and assured her that we'd dine again soon. "Can you pencil me in for Sunday night?" I asked. "I'm off on Sundays. We could maybe drive up the coast and check out one of those fish places in Santa Barbara for dinner."

"Okay," she replied with mischief in her eyes. "But only if you'll take me for a quick walk along the yacht harbor now before I bring you back to the club."

# Chapter 20

I fell into the dive with five minutes to spare but Blondy wasn't in. Ruth, the bartender told me Blondy had received a phone call around 7:00 and had left in kind of a hurry.

The other cats in my sextet were warming up their horns on the Dive's small stage before a healthy Friday night crowd. My dinner with Salli had inspired me. I felt like a world-beater, ready to play my *voutiest* licks. We launched into "Little Melanie," a tune alto saxophonist Jackie McLean had composed in the early 1950s and named for his infant daughter. Loose and Skoot caught my heat and we began a rapid-fire series of four-bar exchanges after the main solos. The pace was set. We laid it straight for two solid sets.

On our second break, Blondy walked in. Her shoulders were set tight as though carrying the weight of the world and her face was troubled. She headed straight into her private office.

I followed the lady, hoping to find out what was troubling her and lay some comfort on her if I could. Bringing Lady out of a funk is never easy. When angered, she becomes defensive, striking out at friend and foe alike. I feline-footed the eggshells and breached her private threshold.

"Bobby Campbell," she offered in a flat, matter-of-fact tone. Campbell was our landlord, owner of the building that housed both my crib and the Dive. He had been a longshoreman all his life, was a work-a-holic that often put in 60 or 70 hours a week on the docks and ran the Channel View in his "spare time." In his absence, one of his grown children would "manage" Bobby's holdings, though with little care or enthusiasm. Bobby had been more than happy to lease the bar space to Blondy, as his own family had mis-managed the establishment when they had helped to run it. He also had a drug-addict daughter who had almost cost him his liquor license by dealing heroin and cocaine out of Fran's Spot, as the Dive had been called in its former incarnation. The daughter had gone on to that great "Fran's Spot" in the sky on the back of a drunk boyfriend's Harley a few years back. Blondy came along to save the place at just the right moment. She took over the ticket with Alcoholic Beverage Control promising to start a fresh and run a clean operation.

"Bobby's taking heat on the docks," she told me. "He claims he isn't stealing anything himself, but some of his friends around the waterfront are feeling the fire of the ongoing investigation into pilferage. He seems to think that, as Tom Cheatham is my *boy*friend, I can somehow get Tom to halt the proceedings.

"He said that some of the younger trouble makers have let it be known that the Channel View was considered to be a fire trap and could very likely burn down in the near future. They are offering Bobby protection Quid-Pro-Quo for sheltering their little illegal waterfront enterprise to see that the cops don't bring down their happy little scene. Bobby feels that if I can't get Tom to at least screw things up and slow the feds, the fire is going to start right here in my club."

Bobby Campbell had already been brought up on "slum lord" charges a few times by tenants in the building beneath my digs, so a fire would definitely burn more than just his building. The aging longshoreman/slum lord would probably end his days in the slam for mass murder through negligence, or at least heavy manslaughter charges.

"Better call Tom," I told her.

"Already have," came her response. "He's on his way over as we speak. Probably stopping on the way to pick up his little *helper* who's got the hots for you."

That brought me up short on the double take. The lady and I have always been good buddies, never an "item," and she was always encouraging me to meet more potential girl friends; embarrassing me in super market check out lines when she saw someone she thought I'd like and tried to get them talking to her "favorite uncle *Lasse*." Lasse being a Norwegian nickname for Lars, and what my mother had always called me. At the same time, Blondy often seemed jealous of any female who paid too much attention to me. Go figure!

"Come join us when they get here," the lady ordered. "The rest of the band can finish up the last set."

I went out to let my fellow cats know the plan and we kicked off a nameless blues while I watched the door for Blondy's conferees.

# Chapter 21

Salli Migiani arrived before we'd finished the first chorus. She took a seat up front and gave me a "thumbs up" right away and a big hand when I'd taken my solo. When the tune finished she was clapping so hard I thought she was going to injure both her hands.

Lieutenant Tom made his entrance as the applause was dying down, spotted Salli, dipped his head a slight nod in her direction, and headed for Blondy's office. I knew there was barely room for two chairs and a desk in there, so I waited with Salli by the closed door. Blondy and Tom came out after a few minutes and called our meeting to order in the back booth where the lady often did business.

Tom and Blondy recapped what she had told me earlier, the lieutenant looking concerned as he drummed nervous fingers along the tabletop.

"I think this Campbell roach is going to get pulled in as a material witness," he said. "I think we may even do it tonight. You have his address, right?"

The blonde one pulled a sticky-note from her purse, wrote something as she told Tom, "He's out by Point Fermin on

Caroline Street, if he's home. Bobby puts in a lot of hours at work."

Tom turned to Salli. "You mind a little overtime? This might prove a long night."

The lady sleuth gave him a full grin. "We serve and protect," she replied. "Count me in."

They asked my opinion of my landlord and how I got along with ol' Bobby. I told them that I had no problems with the guy personally. "He gave me a great home with rent of less than half what anyone else I know is payin', so I don't mind that he's very slow to fix things or make improvements. Usually, I just do my own maintenance if I can and hand him my receipts. Bobby just takes it off the rent."

"The problem Lars has had," Blondy cut in with a heated tone, "is the guy can be a creep and a peeper. I was crashin' up there on Lars' sofa one night after a party at the Dive. I'm walking around the room in my night drapes and there's Bobby sneakin' looks in the side window at me.

"He also goes up to Lars' place if he sees too many lights on late at night. Claims that, since Lars doesn't have a meter, he's paying Lars' light bill with the rest of the hotel and so he has the right to turn off Lars' lights! Campbell disconnected the security lights on the roof some time ago. If he hadn't done that Lars probably wouldn't have had that dead Arab dumped in his chair last year. Or the stabbed policeman out on the roof either."

We let Blondy wind down before Tom continued. "Campbell is a creep and a pervert. I hear that. He's also a big time taxpayer as he owns a number of these old downtown buildings, most of them not maintained up to standard.

"And as a long time union man with lots of seniority, I would guess he knows everything that goes on down on the waterfront. If he isn't reporting criminal activities of which he is aware, he is an accessory to the crime. Because the unions have to deal with the Maritime Association, they can only go so far to protect members who are outright thieves stealing from their bread-and-butter client."

Blondy reached over and took Tom's hand. "Just protect my business and my employees. Please, Tom. Bring Campbell in and sweat the truth out of him, but find out who the real threat is before they destroy what I've built here."

Tom put an arm around the Lady's shoulders and gave a squeeze. "Don't worry, kid," he told her. "I'll handle it. You just relax and stay beautiful for me." Then to Salli he said, "Let's roll," as he pulled his cell phone from his belt to call for backup.

# Chapter 22

I was able to get back on stage for two more songs before last-call. Loose was curious, asking me what was goin' down as he swabbed out his alto and packed it away. I wasn't sure just how much I could tell him, so I just said, "The cops think they got a lead on your horn, but nothing definite so don't get your hopes set too high."

Loose pressed for details. I admitted that a team was going to check out the lead sometime before dawn, a midnight raid, but that I didn't know any details. My sax man was disappointed, but glad just the same that things appeared to be moving along.

After the cats had packed up and gone, I stopped by Blondy's office. I found her just sitting and staring off into space. When she noticed me standing by the door, she got up and came over to give me a long, tight hug.

"I don't know how we get into these things," she moaned. She broke the hug but kept her hands on my upper arms, holding me in front of her.

"You look tired," she told me. "Go up and get some sleep so you'll be fresh tomorrow for a big Saturday night. And no alcohol! No nightcap, no shots of your Norway joy juice, no beer for breakfast.

"Good night," she said shoving me out of her doorway.

I walked around to the front of the Channel View on Centre Street. The hotel was closed for the night but the front desk buzzed me in. Mike, the night porter, asked how I was doin'. I told him "Aw reet" and returned the pleasantry. Mike said he couldn't complain. "Not that anyone's listenin' but you," he added.

I climbed my four flights, brushed my teeth, shed my vines, and joined the fur-ball fellows on my bed. I started petting them, one hand for each, on either side of me, and I quickly dropped into Dreamsville. The telephone woke me up. It was still dark out. Who would ring me at this time of day?

I fumbled for the offending instrument, which sent Art and Yard scurrying, mumbled a rude "Yeah," and was greeted by Salli Migiani's dulcet tones.

"I thought you might want to know how it went," she told me.

"You could've waited to tell me in the morning," I replied, trying not to sound cross with her.

"Well," she drawled, "I'm down in the lobby here anyway. Is it too late for you to ask me up?" She paused as I pondered, but before I could formulate an answer, I heard her say, "Alright, babe, I'm on my way."

She must have taken the stairs two at a time. She was knocking before I had time to pull on shorts and a singlet. I opened the door: she gave me a hug straight away. "Did I wake you up," she purred? "I'm sorry, we'd better get you back to bed. You lay back down and I'll tell you what happened."

Salli took my hand and led me back to my bedroom. When we'd entered my chambers, she began to undress herself. "You could help a girl out here, y'know," she laughed. I fumbled with her bra catch as she stepped out of her jeans. She pushed me back onto my bed, burrowed her way under my duvet and patted a spot next to her.

Art was quick to take her invitation, jumping right up as Yard looked on from my bureau top. I lifted Art to the other side of the bed and climbed in beside the undressed detective. She rolled her body my way and threw arms around me.

"Bobby Campbell was just getting home from a late shift when we pulled up. He ran into the house and got right on the phone, but then let us in. He came without a complaint or a struggle.

"The union lawyer, however, beat us to the stationhouse, so we didn't get much out of Mr. Campbell. He does know that we know about the threats and we are taking them seriously. He was warned that if he can't tell us otherwise, we will have to assume the threats came from him.

"He was quite loud and adamant that he was just passing on gossip he'd heard and wasn't threatening anyone. His lawyer agreed with us, that he would be safer in our custody than on his own, so we're holding him. If he cooperates, we can offer him protection. If he won't talk to us he's on his own.

"Now, about the other action tonight." With that, she moved her body onto me, began running hands over me and placed her lips firmly on mine.

Art and Yard slunk off, likely feeling jealous and slighted.

# Chapter 23

I have only a vague memory of Salli getting up and leaving. There was a rosy glow of dawn coming in the window and she asked if she could make some coffee. I told her to help herself to anything in the fridge.

"There isn't much in your fridge beside coffee and beer," she giggled as she kissed me goodbye. "Call me."

I turned over and slept until almost 3:00. Salli had kept me up late and been very demanding, but had brought me some serious joy. Just as thinking of Astrid driving her tram through the streets of Oslo brought me some righteous guilt. I decided to put it all behind me and enjoy the here-and-now, starting with a hearty breakfast.

Salli had been right about my larder, seven bottles of Red Hook Ale, an empty egg carton, the heel end from a loaf of rye, and a bag of Skåne Roast Swedish coffee in the freezer with the ice cubes. It was too late for the Omelette and Waffle Shop so I walked down to Harbor Boulevard and a spot called The Grinder.

The Grinder was one of those chain style coffee shops that serve breakfast 24-hours. I indulged myself in a cheese omelet, mounds of potatoes, a couple English muffins and three cups of coffee.

The food was satisfying to my tum, but there was too much weighing down my gray matter. Criminals on the dock were intruding into my life by threatening Blondy and my home. Loose was still counting on me to help him find the missing saxophone, as well as to help get his mom's money back if it came to that. Did I love that fantastic Norwegian goddess I had been calling and writing to in Oslo for months with hints that she should move here to the U.S.? And, how seriously? And, all around the edges and corners of my brain, Detective Salli Migiani's musical laugh taunted me with that "instant gratification" promise of love and pleasure.

All I ever wanted was to just play my music so that it might touch some intelligent and caring hearts. Was that too much to ask? Or was my musical goal only to be found at the center of this "life maze" of other knots and puzzles. Could Art Pepper's real gone horn be a sort of Zen koan promising enlightenment to he who plays it, or even to the cat that finds it, or knows what he's found?

I slurped up the last of my coffee, left an overly large tip on the counter and walked out. I could hear the Red Car trolley whistle approaching, so on impulse; I sprinted across the boulevard to the 6th Street Platform, deciding to take a ride to Cabrillo Beach and back.

I recognized the lady conductor who sold me my ticket as I boarded the train. Her nametag said "Erin." She had been working on this same trolley last fall when a terrorist who had been following me had knocked her down in his hurry to escape from her streetcar and the scene. She had also been working on the car that later struck and killed a rogue FBI man who ran in front of her train without looking while in pursuit of another player in the terrorism plot.

In spite of all this, Erin was smiling and cheerful in her uniform black vest and slacks, with her long dark hair spilling from beneath her conductor hat. She obviously loved her job and the people she met everyday aboard her historic rail car.

In some respects, she was fortunate to be a bubbly, positive kind of kitten so these past events didn't stay with her too very long. We exchanged some pleasantries and I took a seat in the forward open-air section while she went back to chat with a mom and two kids obviously under the grip of youthful "train fever." She placed paper train hats on both the youngsters and gave them coloring books that told about the days when Pacific Electric Red Cars like these connected the towns of the Los Angeles area.

I watched the channel and Ports O'Call Village roll by out my window. The gentle rocking of the streetcar was relaxing. The cool breeze from the ocean refreshed my soul and helped me to build some confidence that I could handle all these different events that were filling my life. I made the decision that I could enjoy a relationship with Salli, if that was what this was becoming, without diminishing my love for Astrid.

If, someday, Astrid *did* want to move to America, I might have to make a choice. But that would only be if Salli's and my infatuation continued to grow and blossomed into a love thing. In the meantime, I reasoned that I was sort of blessed and I should just enjoy these gifts from the Gods that I received.

That settled, I closed my eyes and pondered how serious Bobby Campbell's threat might be, or who might be behind it. And, how did it connect with the saxophone Loose was seeking? No good answers.

I stayed on the car when we arrived at Cabrillo Beach, looking out at a dozen or so windsurfers who zigzagged near the point. In five minutes, we were eastbound again, back toward the downtown and my little world. I was feeling wired and inspired, charged up with newfound energy, so at 6th Street, I got off the trolley, went back to my crib, and tried out some new ideas on my flugelhorn. By show time, I was ready to tear-up Loose's Horn Gone Blues with some alternate chord changes that raise the bar on *"killer-diller"* to an unprecedented height.

# Chapter 24

Salli came into the club just before nine, sat at the bar with a longneck beer and watched until break time. We were into some old Shorty Rogers baroque-sounding chamber jazz and I could tell that she dug it.

When I came off the stand, she locked her arm into my elbow and led me out to 7th Street.

"Your friend Campbell isn't much help," she told me after giving me a hug and a peck. "Last night he seemed shaken enough to give us something. Today, after meeting with the union attorney, he's saying that he only heard some gossip on the job and was just warning Blondy in case there might be something to it. He' swearing by that story now. Plus, someone made 500-thousand bail for him. The union says it wasn't any of their people."

We shared a more intense hug and a serious kiss. Salli looked into my soul windows and continued. "I'm gonna have a long night. We're keeping a tail on old Campbell to see who he's talking to. Campbell's pulling another double shift on Terminal Island right now. Me and Carl Berger lucked out with the next watch, so I'm gonna be cruising the docks and the streets as Campbell's shadow into the wee hours."

I got another very soulful kiss, followed by a long caring look. "I'd rather be hangin' with you, Lars! But duty calls, I guess" I told her Yard and Art were going to miss her if she didn't make it upstairs, but I'd console them and they could console me.

"You are so kooky and cute," she said, patting my bottom and trying to drag me into the alley. Out of the streetlamp's glare, the pecking heated up until I wasn't sure if my lip would hold for another set of high-note licks.

I walked Salli up 7th Street to her ride, which was parked in front of the old San Pedro News Pilot building. When our local daily newspaper had been purchased by a big publishing chain some five years ago, the building had been transformed into a series of high-ceilinged artist's lofts. We stopped briefly to look at a new acrylic canvas in the front window, a dizzy splash of reds, blues and greens with hints of forms and oriental characters blending through the wash of colors. We shared another one-for-the-road kiss, I handed the lady into her urban assault lorry and she sped off into the black.

Back in the dive, my lip held up fine. The exercise might even have done it some good. My high notes were coming often and with ease, and I used a couple choruses of those screamers when we closed the night with our latest arrangement of Loose's "Horn Gone Blues."

Local songbird Rosanne Drago had stopped in on the way home from her gig at the Ports O'Call Restaurant. Loose had gone down off the stage to talk to her while I was doing a solo ballad of "Moonlight in Vermont." While I savored my applause, Loose lead Rosanne up. He had laid the lyrics to his composition on her and talked her into trying them out. Rosanne really did Loose credit. She moaned and emoted so you might believe it was her who had lost the brass treasure, then she brightened the mood some four choruses of her own hot, sophisticated scat. Our "Horn Gone Blues" ended up filling

the last set and running into overtime. We were all smilin'
wide as Rosanne hit the final chorus:

*"Art Pepper was a jazz man, he played a mellow golden*
*horn,*
*Art Pepper was a jazz man, he played a mellow golden*
*horn,"*

Soto voce, she spoke, "Yeah, it was a Martin!" then went
back to singin',

*"But when he needed money, he put that axe in pawn.*

*"Art lived here in San Pedro, with his poodle dog and wife,*
*Art lived here in San Pedro, with his poodle dog and wife,*
*He had a righteous black-tar monkey,on his back to cause him*
*strife*

*"He went down the uncle, to get some drug-fix cash,*
*But the man was waitin' right outside, to bust him with his stash*

*"Oh, oh, Art Pepper, how we miss your vooty sound,*
*Hey my soulful Mr. Pepper, how we miss your vooty sound,*
*Someone has copped your golden horn, and now it can't be*
*found*

*"Well I saw your horn on Net Bid, I laid my money down,*
*And now I come to find out, that some stud has burned me*
*down*

*"Oh hey Art Pepper, I tried to save your real gone axe,*
*I so loved your sound that I tried to save your axe,*
*Now the man's likin' me for murder, and your horn has hit*
*the tracks"*

When the song had ended, the energy level was too high in
the room. Ruth and Blondy had trouble clearing the customers
that were suddenly wideawake and wanting more. Rosanne,
Loose, David, Skoot and I sat in Blondy's back booth and talked
shop; like who was coming to town, personnel changes in local

bands, and like that, until the Blond one threw us out into the street. It was just after three when I opened my door to my two hungry waiting wee-beasties.

There was one call on my answering machine. Salli had phoned from the stakeout on her cell around two to tell me there was **nathen shakin'**. Bobby Campbell had gone into his office and not come out. As his shift had ended, Salli's partner, Carl, had snuck up to the trailer in the container yard and peeked in a window. Campbell appeared to be asleep in his chair with a copy of Hustler magazine open in his lap.

# Chapter 25

The beat up old Chevy Blazer without headlights cruised into the container yard, eased up behind a three-tiered stack of the cargo boxes and parked. From his driver's seat, the truck's lone occupant had an excellent view of the mobile temporary office building where the clerks put in their hours and where, now, Bobby Campbell was the lone longie on night duty.

The man also could keep tabs on the two plain-clothes police officers that thought they were so cleverly disguised with their dark blue Crown Vic sitting in the shadow of the first stack of shipping boxes. He sat and watched for an hour or so. Dressed all in black, the Blazer's driver then opened his car door, after checking that the interior light had been set not to respond to this action. He cat-walked forward, chuckling to himself at how clueless these cops seemed, passing their boredom in conversation as they held one eye on the longshore clerk's office.

As the man tiptoed by the rear of the large police Ford, he risked a brief glance at the occupants and mentally recorded their features. The young, dark-haired lady was talking to someone on a cell phone. The heavy-set man with the salt-and-pepper hair had his eyes closed and rested his neck against the car's head restraint. Neither stirred as he passed into the shadows to their right and circumnavigated the pile of containers to come out behind the office trailer.

The shadow found the office's back window, the one that wasn't visible from where the two police officers sat. He placed a pair of black suction cups on the glass, applied light pressure and lifted the pane from its aluminum frame. He set the window down at his feet and climbed easily into the room, where he dropped to the floor and crawled to Bobby Campbell's side, keeping his head below window level.

The man knew Campbell's habits. Bobby would usually grab an hour or so of sleep on these late watches if there were no cranes at work on his berth. And he was **not** a light sleeper. The shadow drew a large syringe from his coat pocket, aimed it at the sleeping form's back and pushed the needle between two ribs, where he plunged home a concoction designed to stop the heart while leaving few traces of its presence in the bloodstream.

Campbell awoke as his body convulsed in one quick jerk, the magazine he'd been looking at sliding from its face down position against his chest into his lap as his heart stopped beating. He appeared to be peacefully sawing logs when the shadow man replaced the glass and glided off into the night.

# Chapter 26

Sunday morning I was awoken by a relentless pounding on my penthouse door. The cats went scurrying. The clock read 9:17 and my body still said "tired." I pulled on an old pair of shorts and shuffled out to the passageway.

It was Salli, minus the usual appearance of sweetness and light. "May I come in," she asked, wringing her hands?

I stepped aside and swept my right arm in a welcoming motion. The lady detective brushed past me and took a seat in my living room, thought about it for a minute with her head cocked at a funny angle, and patted the cushion beside her.

"I'm sorry, Lars, it isn't your fault. Come give us a hug."

When I had parked it next to her she wrapped anxious arms around me and squeezed me hard enough to break ribs.

"Bobby Campbell is dead," she breathed into my chest. "The Lieutenant doesn't think it was natural, which means somebody got to him while Carl and I were sitting there at Berth 231 watching the trailer."

"Wait a minute," I interrupted. "Bobby died in his office? What did he die from?"

"Heart attack," she moaned. "At least that's what it was supposed to look like. But toxicology found some traces in his blood, some chemical I can't pronounce. Then the docs found a needle prick in his back, just behind his heart.

"But Carl and I were there. We were watching and we didn't see anyone around the berth area. No one came or went. We didn't hear anything, so now we're being accused of not being vigilant . . . not paying attention. This is so *weird*!"

I really didn't know what to say, what questions to ask. There had to be an explanation. Had Bobby been about to rollover on one of his co-workers? And, if so, how did they know, and how did they get to him so *fast*. It was beginning to look like there was much more at stake here than a few crates of stolen bananas and a missing saxophone.

"You didn't see anyone coming-or-going, could someone have dosed him before you got there, like a slow acting drug?"

"The medical examiner says his death was almost instantaneous. The stuff they shot him up with went right to his heart. Carl and I had both seen Campbell walk by the window, pacing, just after we arrived, but then we didn't see anything for an hour or more." Salli was talking fast. She pulled back and let her peepers search mine, curious as to whether or not I believed her.

"Carl went up to the trailer around 1:30 and stole a glance in. Campbell seemed to be asleep in his chair. Carl said he had a porno magazine open in his lap, looked like he had just dosed off."

The lady returned her head to my chest, breathed the rest into my tee shirt. "Around 2:20, a white SUV from the port arrived to see why Bobby wasn't answering the phone. Apparently they're used to him taking a little nap and feel its no harm done. He's suppose to check-in every two hours, but on night shifts, if he doesn't call, his buddy in the main office calls him and gets the report.

"These guys all break the rules and they all cover for each other. But Bobby always wakes up when the phone rings. It's like a little running joke around the docks."

"But last night he didn't wake up." I was stating the obvious, more to reassure myself than for Salli's benefit. "Didn't wake up cause he was doin' the *big sleep* number."

"Yeah," she answered. "So Carl and I have to be standing tall before the lieutenant at three to explain ourselves officially. They might even take us off this case. Now I'll be a Detective II until I *die*. Something like this will keep surfacing every time I go for promotion and I'll never have any real future here." Salli was weeping softly.

I stood and took Salli's hand, led her back to my bedroom and pulled her down onto my mattress. We wrapped arms around each other and snuggled. It wasn't about passion, strictly Comfort-Zone-City. After a while, Salli nodded off and my spinning head joined her.

# Chapter 27

Salli stirred around noon, which brought me around as well. Fortunately, I'd made it to the market the day before in my wanderings. I fried up some eggs and local calamari for us with strong Skåne Roast coffee and rye toast covered in lingonberry jam. The lady detective was in considerably higher spirits when she left for her meeting.

I had assured her that Lieutenant Tom was a fair man. "I know," she said with downcast eyes. "And I know he has always been in my corner, very supportive."

"Right," I pressed on. "Everything will work out fine. Just keep a positive attitude! You know, like, keep your chin up and it'll prevent the beer from dripping on your shirt." Salli giggled as I walked her to the door. We traversed the narrow steps side-by-side, arms around each other like moony high school kids.

At six, she was back at my door. Salli was smiling, much less nervous. "You were right, of course," she told me after a healthy kiss. "Tom Cheatham believes in me. He told me that in the hall before we went into the official de-briefing.

"He said that the fact that someone would go to so much trouble to kill Campbell right under our noses means we are on to something. Obviously, our surveillance was under their surveillance as well. Tom said even he wouldn't have thought this was serious enough that someone would be watching us.

"In our meeting, the forensics guys had some things to add," she told me. "They found two black marks on the trailer window facing the water. They believe our murderer used suction cups to grab the pane of glass and lift it out of the frame. Then he was careful enough to put it back when he had finished."

I nodded my head to show I was paying attention. "Experienced burglar," I asked?

"Don't know, maybe. Anyway, the wind off the channel is always blowing dust and dirt along that section of dock," Salli continued. "A layer of muck tends to pile up around the office's temporary foundation, which in this case had been disturbed by the bottom of the window frame being set in it and someone's size 10 ½ boot. That's what got the forensics guys looking at the window. At first they were looking for jimmy marks around the frame. That's when an alert officer noticed the black cup marks."

"And the boot?" I asked.

"Not much help," Salli continued. "The tread is fairly new, no cuts or marks on the sole. A very common brand, the union guys say it's the most popular among the workers there. And Union War Surplus Store on 6th Street confirms that. It's their biggest seller. They probably move an average of twenty pairs of those boots a week, a good percentage of them size 10 ½.

"And they only found one clear set of boot prints. Probably from our man hitting the ground hard coming out of the window. He was probably walking on his toes to and from there. The brass has decided, thanks again to the lieutenant, that our murderer could have come by boat, tied up beside one of the cargo ships and climbed a rope up the dock. He could well have arrived and departed without ever passing our field of vision as we sat in the car."

"So basically, you're off the hook, and still on the case," I stated.

"Right, baby," Salli barked, lightly punching my shoulder. "More interested in what's goin' on than ever, and I will solve this one no matter what it takes!"

I gave my cop cutie a big hug and told her that if she would drive us to the Taco Bell on Gaffey Street, I'd treat her to a big dinner. We were both laughing as we descended to her waiting chariot. That's when her cell phone rang.

I could see her face fall as she listened, though her replies were a stream of yes and no's. Mostly yeses, punctuated by a couple "oh shits."

I got a hug and kiss up against Salli's car door. As she slipped into her ride, she told me, "More trouble, Lars. Possibly another murder. Another of our witnesses."

My lady cop rolled down the window and kissed me again before she u-turned and sped off down 7$^{th}$ toward the channel.

# Chapter 28

Jeremy diStefani had been to see his girlfriend, Billie, a clerk on the docks where he worked. Billie lived in Harbor City, across from the big regional park and the hospital. She had warned him that it could be dangerous to say too much about the docks and the people working there, longshoremen have a reputation for sticking together and for being pretty rough with anyone who isn't a team player. But he told her "it's just a bit of pilfering we're talking about, no big thing." He isn't worried. Billie is nervous just the same as she walks him to his new silver Honda Civic GTI and kisses him goodbye.

Jeremy heads back to 'Pedro. He's supposed to meet James Mitchum, the union's lawyer at the San Pedro Fish Market in the Ports O'Call Village. They will discuss their options over a paper plate of red snapper and a beer or two.

As Jeremy's Honda approaches the San Pedro Girl's Softball Field on a lonely, unpopulated section of North Gaffey Street, a beat-up black Chevy Blazer rockets out from the parking lot of the Los Angeles Police Pistol Range with tires screaming and rubber burning over the pavement. The old truck cuts Jeremy off by such a narrow margin that he almost loses control, braking hard and momentarily crossing into oncoming lanes. Fortunately, there is no opposing traffic. Instinctively, Jeremy speeds up to pursue the asshole and give the miscreant a piece of his mind.

There are no other cars on the road; just the aging Chevrolet and Jeremy's silver Honda. Jeremy redlines the Honda's sophisticated V-Tec engine, closing the distance quickly. Both cars are approaching a slight curve on Gaffey that will bring them back into a less rural stretch with businesses on the right hand side. As Jeremy gets within a car length of his prey, something sails out through the Blazer's sunroof.

Now he's gonna throw his trash out of the car to mess up my paintwork, Jeremy thinks, a coke or a beer can. But the object hits the tarmac right in front of the Honda, bounces once and starts to roll toward the double yellow line. Has to be heavier than an empty can, he thinks. Jeremy swerves slightly, putting the object between his wheels, so as not to ruin a tire crushing it, whatever it is.

As he's thinking about what the object might be, the world around Jeremy and his Honda turn into a hellish ball of flames. The "Oh shit" he started to shout was lost in the wave of heat that vaporized Jeremy's mind and body. A thousand tiny bits of metal tore the flesh from his bones. The ball of fire from the Honda's gas tank ignited trees on either side of Gaffey Street.

The Chevy Blazer turned right up Capitol Drive, disappearing at a high rate of speed through the residential neighborhood behind the Home Depot complex.

# Chapter 29

"The explosion shook Home Depot like an 8-point earthquake," Lieutenant Tom told us. "Some folks in the garden center there, just about fifty feet from the road and crowded with weekend shoppers, thought it was either the end of the world or terrorists blowing up the Tosco oil refinery across the boulevard."

It was a little past seven on Sunday evening. The "free-jazz" jam was in full swing. Some guy from Manhattan Beach had hauled in a set of rust-spotted vibes that looked like they'd gone down with the Titanic and been brought back for a second incarnation. The dark featured young tenor player that had come in with him seemed to know the chord changes, but much of what he played was seriously out of tune. He sounded like he was trying to play Indian music. Either that or he wanted to revive the Don Ellis quarter-tone thing. He kept hittin' close, but he couldn't seem to nail the notes right on the head.

"So what happened?" Blondy asked.

"Well, it looks like someone rolled a hand grenade under diStefani's car. Forensics says it wasn't *in* the car, it was definitely on the road underneath him, so our killer had to be by the side of Gaffey Street waiting in some kinda ambush."

Salli remained quiet, sitting close by my side in the corner of the back booth. Both her arms were around my right arm. She would give an occasional squeeze, but she didn't seem to have much to add to the speculation. I looked at her face, thought I could read something there which she was too timid to say.

"Could someone in another short have tossed it," I asked? Salli tightened her grip on me and nodded against my shoulder. I had read her right.

"Someone in a car maybe comin' the other way, or overtakin' Jeremy on the road? Like, I can't see someone just standin' there waiting for him. More like somebody tailin' him. Makes sense cause then they'd get away faster too."

Lieutenant Tom ran a tired hand over his face and nodded agreement. "Yeah, that makes good sense, Lars. My infantry time in Viet Nam still has me programmed to think 'grenade' and a soldier 'lobbing it' from somewhere nearby. But a guy could easily toss it out of a moving car and plan it just right to roll under another vehicle. Hell, it wouldn't even have to go right under it! Our man must have got lucky with a direct hit so close to the gas tank, but if he had just come close, he still would most likely have taken out his target just as easily."

Salli eased up on her grip and joined the conversation. "I think you guys have hit on it. Throwing an explosive out of a moving car right in front of our vic, I mean if it didn't blow him up, like, even if it went off just in front of him, he'd almost surely lose control and crash with an excellent chance of dying or being badly injured in the process."

"I believe our suspect wanted Jeremy dead; silenced forever," Tom emphasized. "Obviously someone doesn't like co-workers talking about what's going on out there on the docks."

"Which means it's got to be a big business," Blondy added. "Big bucks, lots of them, and a growth industry to protect. Enough of an enterprise to make murder a viable option to protect it."

"Murder is *never* a viable option," Tom aimed her way.

"You never heard of the Mafia," Blondy countered? "And you're a policeman?"

"Organized crime is . . ." the lieutenant began, but Blondy cut him off.

"This isn't Romper Room Play School out here you know. There are billions of dollars comin' into this port every week. Just a percent of a percent can equal enough wealth to turn quite a few heads. Look at it, Tom. What makes organized crime? Someone here in Pedro is stealing big time, and they are well organized!"

The Lieutenant started to protest, but the blonde one stepped on his words again. "Don't interrupt me," she stated loudly. "You've got some major crime here and it's well organized. Organized enough that they can take out witnesses right under your noses, and so far they're getting away with it. Hell, we got enough Sicilians in this town, it could even *be* the mafia!"

While Blondy was holding forth, Salli's surveillance partner, Carl arrived and pulled a chair up to the end of the table. He tipped his head to Salli, Blondy and I, then focused his attention on Tom Cheatham.

"No witnesses that we can find," he stated to enter the conversation. "Jeremy's attorney had an appointment to meet him this afternoon at the Fish Market in Port's O'Call. As close as we can call it, that's where he was headed."

"Good work, Carl," Tom told him. He introduced Blondy and I, and then asked, "What was he doing on that part of Gaffey? Doesn't he live up on 22$^{nd}$ somewhere? Totally opposite direction?"

Officer Carl flipped a page or two in his notebook and continued. "A couple guys we talked to, one bein' the attorney, thought he had been visiting his girlfriend. That would make sense." He consulted the page again as he spoke.

"Wilma Frankov, Billie, lives in Harbor City. But she claims she hasn't spoken with Jeremy in a couple days, since before his arrest. Salli, I think you should come with me and take the lead on this interview. I'm fairly sure Jeremy phoned her to cry the blues when we pulled him in. That would just make logical sense, when you get in trouble you call someone that cares about you. So why would she deny that they talked?"

"Who talked to her?" the lieutenant wanted to know.

"One of the uniforms," Carl opened his notebook to another page. "Sergeant Tanaka." Carl looked up and continued. "Tanaka is a good man at reading people." Carl gave his notes a further scan. "He said she acted broken up, but he could feel anxiety more than grief. Fred is sure she's not being up front with us."

"Maybe our killer has threatened this Billie woman as well," offered Salli.

Tom Cheatham moved his head in agreement. "Okay," he said, "to recap, it looks like our suspect tossed a grenade under Jeremy's car, possibly from another vehicle to shut him up. This same person, or persons, is probably making it known around the port that longshoremen should be watching what they say, especially leaning on anyone we might already be watching, like the late Jeremy's girlfriend.

"Jeremy and Bobby Campbell both had something to tell us about what's going on regarding losses at the port, and both of them have died under suspicious circumstances, murder suspected. We have no witnesses to either murder, and no one wants to come forward to help us." The lieutenant turned his attention to my corner, looking directly at my lady sleuth.

"Salli, how about you and Carl go over to see this Billie Frankov right away. Do what you have to do, but find out something. If she's not telling us the truth, try and catch her in a lie so we get some leverage, and hopefully we can get some answers." His eyes turned to meet mine.

"Lars, I know you're still trying to help Loose find this mysterious old saxophone, but this is becoming a dangerous business. Please watch what you say and to who you say it. If the sax is tied in with the problems at the port, or even if your snooping around steps on someone's toes at the port, it could put you at risk for some real hurt. I don't want to have to explain your being the next innocent victim. I'd ask you to just stay out of all this, but I know you probably wouldn't listen. Just be real careful. And tell your buddy Lucian to do the same."

Tom stood, signaling the end of our meeting. I slid out of the booth to let Salli pass and she stood for a tense moment unsure if we should make a display of our affection in front of her fellow officers. Both Tom and Carl seemed to sense her awkwardness. Carl mumbled that he had to check his cell phone messages, turning to walk outside, and Tom followed Blondy into her office.

Salli threaded an arm around my middle, gave a squeeze and led me down the steps to the Dive's backroom, where it was just the two of us beside the vacant pool table. "Sunday's come and gone," she commented. "Can I get a rain check on Santa Barbara for another Sunday?" I assured her that we'd have lots of good Sunday's when things calmed down a bit. We shared a quick kiss, told each other to watch out and be careful. I then walked her outside to join Carl in the waiting Crown Vic.

# Chapter 30

I hung for a while with Blondy at the dive listening to the young cats blow, nursing a Sam Adam's Draught, and wondering what I'd gotten myself into for the umpteenth time.

When the young guys took five, the Lady turned to me and said, "That guy's vibraphone looks like hell, but he sounds pretty damn good!" I agreed. The blonde one thought for a long pause then told me. "If you ever lose one of your sax players, maybe you should find someone that can keep up with you on mallets. I could dig your brass with that ringing sound behind it."

We yakked on 'til around half ten, when I told Blondy that I was shot down and flamin', in need of some serious Zs. I left her alone in her favorite booth, walked around to the hotel's main entrance and pushed my feet up the flights to my crib.

Suddenly, I was wide-awake again. I had a feeling that Salli would probably either call or come up to tell me how her interview went and what else she and Carl might have uncovered. I carried a Red Hook out to my rooftop lounger and parked myself where I could watch the ships on the water and the cranes that were servicing them.

Yard and Art seemed restless as well. They came out to be near me, but played tag around the big clay pots of Birds of Paradise plants. Every now and then they would pounce on one another with growls, loud meows and drawn-back ears. They would roll around, the fur on their tails getting electro-statically thick as they postured for supremacy of the roost.

I watched the boys, dozed a bit, woke up and checked the downtown city lights. At 2:00 am I was about to give up and pack it in when my phone rang.

Salli was on the line, but she didn't sound good. My lady detective seemed paranoid that people were watching her. She didn't say who it might be, but she wanted me to come down and bring her up the back stairs, from the dark alley behind the Dive. What could I say? I told her I'd be right there, not to worry.

When I opened the fire door at the foot of the rear stairs, I didn't see anything. Within seconds, my girl emerged from the shadows, scurried into the foyer and rushed to my arms, kicking the door closed behind her.

"Quick, Lars, up the stairs," she breathed. I took her hand and complied. Once we'd closed my door and fallen together on my bed she said, "Lars, this is all too weird. That Billie women denied that she had anything going with Jeremy. She said they were co-workers and nothing more.

"Everyone we've talked to on the docks said they've been an item for a long time! She told me he was a foolish young boy and was probably trying to cover for his own indiscretions by selling us some conspiracy theory. That she knew there was nothing illegal going on at the harbor. And Jeremy was just a casual friend.

"When Carl was walking to the car, she pulled me aside and told me I could be hurt badly if I tried to push further investigation of the longshoreman. She was crushing my hand and her eyes were so fierce. I motioned Carl back and asked her to repeat what she had said. She denied that she'd said anything. Told Carl I must have been hallucinating and I was unstable. She said they should pull me off duty until they could determine if I was sane or not."

I held Salli close and cooed soothing words, but I couldn't calm her.

"Back in the unit, Carl told me he knew she was bullshitting and we needed to keep an eye on her, but she really pissed me off! I'm so sure she was Jeremy's lover, but she can so coldly deny him. I mean, what is going on here?"

I held her close, didn't say anything. In a few minutes she started to shake and to cry. I kept her in my arms, kissed her neck, her shoulders, and finally we shared a full on passionate buss.

Salli and I made love with a heat and passion that earlier would have been difficult to imagine. When we had both been satisfied, she lay back on my chest and found some peace.

"I'm sorry Lars," she told me. "I shouldn't be bringing you my problems. I think I love you and I don't want to burden your life. You have such a simple and beautiful existence and I'm spreading shit all over it."

"Hey," I told her. "What are friends for? Loose brought me into this. It might be getting' heavy, but if Loose hadn't dumped this on me, I wouldn't have gotten to know you. And I'm just diggin' the heck outta knowin' you, babe. So don't apologize to me. Now that I know you, I got some warm feelin's for you, too. I wanna be here for you, I mean you an' me are suddenly closer than me an' Loose have ever been!" I could feel her smile against my chest. Her tears faded as she squirmed against me, moving closer with arms entwined about my body. She was quickly breathing that slow rhythm that told me sleep had brought her peace. I lay for some time longer pondering just how deep I was getting into troubles that really didn't concern me. I mean, Salli was well paid to take these risks while I just wanted to play my music and keep a good alcohol buzz going when I wasn't creating.

It wasn't like I needed love. Astrid was there and she loved me. But Astrid was half-way around the world in Oslo, and

Salli was right here, snuggled against my side. And, while Salli was the big, bad lady cop, she had eyes for me, and she also needed me in her world right now. Sleep overtook my brain somewhere amongst these thoughts.

# Chapter 31

The telephone rang to wake us at some ungodly hour. By the time I'd climbed out of a fleeting dream, Salli was sitting on the edge of my bed with the handset to her ear. She gave my caller a few questions, punctuated by, "I see," and then passed me the receiver as she gave me a questioning look.

Loose's voice was hurling excited babble my way. There was no space to even greet him. He was going on about e-mails, the Martin saxophone, meeting someone, and more; his words and sentences collided like a train wreck, running together as his thoughts jumped the rails.

"Wait, stop, hold the weddin'," I begged him. "Take this piece of music from letter A and run it slow so's I can catch a little more of what you're sayin'."

My lady detective kept inquisitive eyes on me as Loose finally started to organize his thoughts for me through the wire. Loose had apparently not slept well. At four in the morning, he had decided to hop on his computer, as it was too early to practice his saxophone. He had a couple e-mails on his Hot Mail account, an address he rarely used, but stayed in touch with.

He hadn't recognized the name of the sender on the note in question, and had almost decided to delete the communication as spam, but for some reason, Loose had opened this message. My friend described chills flooding his body as he noted reference to the recent Net Bid auction and the Art Pepper saxophone.

The e-mail's sender said that the horn was waiting for Loose in San Pedro's old Warehouse One, a huge concrete and steel behemoth that has stood on the main channel for nearly a century. This historic structure was seldom used anymore. There had been talk of demolishing it, turning it into a tourist hotel, using it as a maintenance facility for the Waterfront Red Car trolleys and other schemes. For the time being, it was just a sort of catchall location for cargo that overflowed the more modern facilities.

According to Loose's e-mail, some cargo on odd pallets had been stacked in the old warehouse recently, and the Martin sax was among these items. The sender stated simply that he knew the horn should rightfully belong to Lucian, and this person wanted to see that he would get it.

To aid Loose in getting his horn, the sender told him that one of the doors facing the dockside railroad tracks had been left unlocked for him. All he had to do was go in and pick up his saxophone, but he should move quickly "before it fell into someone else's hands.

"So we gotta head over there right now, Lars." His voice was rising in excitement once more. "Like, under cover of darkness is best, don't you think? I'll come and pick you up. Can you be ready in ten minutes?"

I had been holding the phone just a little out from my ear so Salli could pick up on what Loose was putting down. She nodded, I should tell him yes.

"Yeah, ten minutes," I told Loose. "I'll meet you on Centre, in front of the hotel."

As soon as I hung it up, Salli had her mobile out. She woke up Tom Cheatham, then Carl Berger, explaining that Loose had been summoned to the old warehouse supposedly to retrieve his sax.

With the cavalry alerted, my lady pushed me back down on the bed, gave me a strong embrace and told me, "You better be careful you big dumb animal. I'm gonna be behind you guys, backin' you up, but that won't stop bullets in a crossfire.

"You better hold Loose in check, don't just let him charge ahead and get you both hurt or killed, okay?"

# Chapter 32

The door from the loading dock to Warehouse One was ajar, just as Lucian's informer had said it would be. Our footfalls echoed endlessly through the concrete-walled open space. Train tracks ran down the aisles between stacks of pallets rising skyward. Loose held a crude floor plan printed from his computer. We crossed a first aisle, a second, then, at the third, Loose's eyes lit up and he took off running between precarious stacks of cardboard cartons. I ran behind him, spying the brown suitcase looking object at the end of the row, near the back wall. We stumbled between cargos piled precariously on either side. Nearing his target, Loose appeared to trip on something, a wire or chord stretched between piles of goods. He started to fall, but recovered and stumbled forward. As he flew toward the target case, I saw the stacks of goods begin to totter, falling in a trajectory that would easily crush my friend as he clutched after the promised saxophone.

I threw myself forward, delivered a flying tackle behind my sax man's thighs that carried him forward into the cement wall taking the brown leather coated Martin sax case with him. A mountain of heavy boxes thundered down with a roar and a clatter to seal the passage behind us sending a cloud of dust that filled the enclosed space.

Loose turned his eyes to mine, blinked a couple times, and then rolled back into his head. Concussion? Or just frustration.

We laid there for a minute or two, coughing and choking on the settling dust as we tried to catch our breath, before we heard Salli calling my name on the other side of the landslide. As I shouted back that we were okay, Loose raised his head, got to his hands and knees and started for the brown case at the edge of the pile of rubble.

"My sax," he cried. "My Art Pepper horn!"

I popped up and tackled Loose once more, unsure as to what might be waiting in that ominous case. And on closer perusal, it was a Martin alto saxophone case, brown faux leather in two-tone with the trademark 1-inch by 2-inch brass label stating "Martin, Elkhart, Indiana." Loose fought me and finally managed to undo the snaps, only to discover that the case was empty. No saxophone. He groaned loudly, rolled back and started rocking his body, his arms laced about his knees.

As Loose was reveling in his weirdness, I detected the sound of a forklift starting up beyond the pallet landslide. The goods that imprisoned us began to shift. Among the torn and shredded pasteboard the aisle was filled with bricks and chunks of broken concrete breezeblocks. When a space had been cleared through the rubble to free us I saw Salli and Tom, weapons drawn, flanking a very large and very dark giant enthroned on an oversized cargo shifter.

The giant dismounted his machine and came to me with his hand extended. He had to be nearly seven-feet tall, his frame proportionally large, with skin like polished walnut paneling. When I took the pro-offered hand, his dark, serious face cracked into a broad smile.

"Michael Mallory," he rumbled in a basso that shook the remaining stacks of cargo. "Good thing I stopped by. Someone reported suspicious goin's on here, and I like to keep an eye on my, ah, kingdom, as it is."

I filled Michael in on Loose's Net Bid auction, Art's axe and such as my police guardians holstered their weapons and started taking notes on our little disaster. It turned out that Michael was a jazz fan. He remembered Art Pepper, though he told me that he personally thought Sonny Criss could have played Art under the table any day. We were reminiscing on the old Central Avenue scene and the Dunbar Hotel when Lieutenant Tom stalked back into view.

The lieutenant held up a piece of ¾ -inch dowel trailing what could have been piano wire or a very long guitar string. "Looks like all those blocks and bricks were balanced on these dowels. The way the sticks were wired together across the passage, somebody knew it wouldn't take much to dump everything. You're just damn lucky you got out of the way, my friend." His face did the concerned thing as he focused on Loose, still rocking on his heels and moaning.

"Salli found a crate of European machine pistols back by the bay doors," he continued. "These are not on any manifest the port can come up with, so I think we've stumbled onto another major, ah, situation here."

"We have no weapon's scheduled into the Port of Los Angeles," Michael replied, his face a serious stone mask. "Every item of cargo crosses my desk and I have never seen *any* manifest for automatic weapons. California hasn't allowed such imports in over six years!"

Tom Cheatham informed him that U.S. Customs agents had been summoned. Other Federal agents would probably soon be on scene as well. Pilferage was one thing, and a vital concern at that, but large shipments of illegal arms elevated this case to a new, advanced level.

Coast Guard and Custom men were soon swarming the scene. Other union officials came in close behind them, talking about public relations and avoiding any negative spin in the media. The port was too big an asset for the City of Los Angeles to let it be dragged through the mud!

Between cameos with various politicos, Michael drew me aside. "You and me need to talk. And without these face-savin' clowns around us. Where can I reach you?"

I told him to stop by Blondy's Waterfront Dive any night of the week. I'd be playin' there, and when the band took a break, we could find someplace to talk where no one could eavesdrop or overhear. Michael promised to be there the next night, without fail. He told me that straightening out this situation was crucial to the future of the waterfront and the San Pedro community, which relies heavily on the economic engine that overseas shipping, *legitimate* shipping, provides. I believed him and gave my word that I would help.

# Chapter 33

True to his word, Michael Mallory was at The Dive the next night just after 8:30. At intermission, I joined him in Blondy's back booth. Ruth, the duty bartender brought me a pint of Sam Adams and asked if Michael would like another. The union man said he was fine for the moment looking up at her dismissively. When she had resumed her place behind the bar, Michael addressed me.

"You know by now that pilferage has become a major problem in this port. It's getting so serious that the shipping companies are paying twice as much for legitimate insurance. If that isn't bad enough, we suspect that someone working on the docks, most likely one of our union members, is selling protection to the shippers. The shipping lines have been warned that if they don't pay the weekly 'bite' they will lose more goods, and possibly have warehouse fires, containers 'accidentally' dropped from cranes and more." He stared at me in silence to let his words sink in.

"I have worked hard for many years to attain a position of some power and stature in the Brotherhood of Longshore and

Warehousemen, but in many ways I am still an outsider, which can be both good and bad."

Michael clued me as to how he had fought his way up from a "casual" worker to a clerk and, finally, an elected member of the union's board. "I was determined when I started that I was going keep this job. Working here paid too well for me to just get scared off and let it go. I took a heap of disrespect for the money I made. When they called me 'nigger' and 'spear-chucker,' I just smiled and held my temper in check.

"I don't know if you are aware of it, Lars, but as late as the 1950s there was a major Ku Klux Klan presence here in San Pedro. The docks were white man's territory when I started out. Federal marshals were walkin' James Meredith around Ol' Miss at that time, and in many U.S. cities black children still attended their own sub-standard schools.

"My co-workers took every opportunity to make it clear I wasn't welcome here, but I stood up to them. I made a few hard-won friends among the old guys and did the best job I could. I tried to be honest and fair. I did more than my share of the work on my shift, while some of the other young men goofed off, took extra smoke breaks, or just stood around staring me down.

"I didn't grab lots of overtime, I left that for the others. I put in all the hours I was assigned and impressed the leadership with my work ethic and my efforts in the face of harassment and adversity. It was slow in coming, but I eventually won some grudging respect from my fellows. When civil rights starting changing things, the union decided it would look good to elect me to the board. Someone up in the main office saw to it that I won the election. Promotions started coming. My efforts were finally being recognized."

I heard the trio starting up without me and checked my watch. The break had gone on too long, but Blondy was on a barstool smiling, so I guess she thought I should continue talking to my new friend. The Blond One noticed me looking and gave a slight nod to tell me I was okay.

Michael caught my eyeball exchange with the Lady wrinkling his ebony brow in a question. "Go ahead, man," I told him. "Boss lady knows this is important, so we're *voot-a- root.*"

"I am a religious man," Michael continued. "I've always trusted in my God and felt that if I did the right things and treated people properly, my God would look out for me. I assumed that an important part of my job was to see that my work was done honestly and properly. I've kept my bargain with my God and I've done well for myself. I've put three children through college, one all the way through medical school. Just as I owe my God, I owe a special loyalty to the Port of Los Angeles and my union for helping me to realize my dreams. I don't like to see others taking advantage of our situation here, stealing from the port and disrespecting the people that give them all a comfortable livelihood."

The big man reached across the tabletop to place his large hand over mine. "I sense that you are a good man, Lars. I can see that the police have a certain amount of respect for you; they seem to trust you. They tell me you're helping one of your musicians to find that missing Art Pepper saxophone."

Michael locked eyes with me, lightly patting my hand as it rested on the Formica. "There may or may not be a connection here," he told me. "But while you're looking for that instrument, if you could keep your ears open for me . . ."

"Hey, no problemo, pops," I replied. "Anything I can do, man, I'll try it."

"Well, Lars, there is something, but I hesitate to ask."

"Hey, pops, it don't cost anything to ask, like, if I can do somethin', I will."

Michael withdrew his hand and reached into the breast pocket of his expensively tailored dark blue jacket drawing out some folded pages of paper. "I've already talked with FBI and customs. The federal boys say you've gone out of your way to help them at least once before."

Now I could feel the short hairs on my neck rising. What did I just get myself into? I thought back to the last time I "helped" the FBI, when they'd sent me halfway around the world as bait to draw out a terrorist.

"They told me that you were able to aid them before because you were playing jazz somewhere and it proved a perfect cover."

My jaw dropped. "They think Art's Martin is in Europe or something?"

"New York, actually," Michael corrected. "Not the saxophone, but similar problems with this sort of organized crime on the docks. I wanted to go myself, to speak with my opposite number back in Manhattan, but I was told the connection would surely draw the wrong kind of attention.

"The agent suggested that you carry some papers to the union officers in New York for me, have a little talk with them and bring their answers back to me. You won't look at all suspicious, cause you'll be playing for a few nights at a club on the upper west side."

"I will?" It came out as almost a squeak. "I ain't got no New York bookings, baby, none that I know about."

The big man set the papers down in front of me; a printed airline itinerary and another paper that looked like a schedule.

"It's cool," he assured. "My brother in Harlem has a buddy who owns a part interest in this place, called 'Dig!' and he has an open spot week after next. They're willing to pay for all five of your men and you to blow there.

"Did I tell you my brother is a fan? Anyway, he'll pay for the gig and some rooms at a local boarding house. The union will spring for the air fare."

I didn't know what to say. Somebody had my number. They knew I love to travel and make music, so they had set me up without asking. Of course it would be a good gig; a chance to show off my band, and Loose's new tune, to a different audience.

Michael stood and reached down to give me some skin, taking my hand in both of his and spilling sincerity all over me. I stood as he was leaving, zombied up to the stand and picked up my horn.  I called an old Dick Twardzik tune, "The Girl From Greenland" to lose my thoughts in the unique changes of the line.

# Chapter 34

Tuesday morning when I woke up I read through the papers Michael had given me. The New York gig sounded like a good one. According to the photocopied newspaper clippings, **Dig!** was a smallish venue, seating about 65 with another 15 or 20 places to stand at the bar. Some giants from the past had appeared there and **Dig!**'s reputation was building fast.

Besides, it had been a few years since I'd appeared anywhere on the east coast. If I was concerned about career moves for the band, it was definitely time to be heard somewhere outside LA.

The second page gave details on our reserved crash space. We were booked into a boarding house on the Upper West side that specialized in rooms for jazz musicians. The owner was a Swedish lady, Barbro, who really dug the music and catered to cats from all over the world that came into New York for their gigs. We would be sharing three rooms with breakfast included.

Folded into the package were six round-trip tickets on Jet Blue Airlines from Long Beach Airport to New York. These "electronic tickets" would serve as our boarding cards, so we didn't have to do much more than show up for the flight. Someone had been fairly confident that I would jump for this deal.

I phoned my sidemen, one at a time, with the news. Skoot, Loose and Dave were excited about the trip. Skoot told me he hadn't been to New York since he was, like, 9-years old! Trav, my bassman, said he really would like to go, but as his wife worked a straight job, he was the daytime child-care person. He promised to find a sub that would make the trip, which probably wouldn't be too difficult considering that it was a very *vooty* New York thing. Our drummer, John, said he could make the scene, no problem, but that his wife would be unhappy that she was not invited along. And, no, there was no way he could cough the long daddy green to bring her on his own budget.

Now I figured the tough sell would be Blondy. In the past, when I took myself out-of-town for the odd gig, my sidemen filled in the gaps for me at Divesville. This time, I would be taking the pack with me, and it was real short notice for Blondy to get a show together. I procrastinated my fall down the stairs to lay the news on her. Around half-past-two, when I finally made the scene, I found Blondy in her office humming along with some old Trane and Dolphy kicks on KKJZ Jazz Radio. As I hesitated by her door, the Blonde One turned a few thousand candlepower of smile on me.

"The lucky musical gumshoe goes out to hit the big-time! Is New York ready for you?"

I tried to, like, catch my falling jaw before it banged onto her desktop.

"Tom told me all about it," she grinned. "I think it's great. You need to get better known. When you're a true 'Jazz Legend' you'll draw even bigger crowds for me."

"Wha, what about . . . who's gonna fill in, like play here while we're gone?"

The Lady shot a wink my way. "I've got some performers lined up. There's lots of cats that would like to be playing here, you know. I'm thinking of having a couple weeks featuring girl singers, or female players. I've got calls in to Ann Patterson, Nedra Wheeler, Sherry Luchette and Diane Hubka. And I'm confident that Rosanna Drago will give me a few days. It should be a fun break for our regulars.

"But don't worry, I'll hold your spot here no matter how successful the ladies are for Blondy's. Go tell Syd to lay a taste on you, bring your drink in here and tell Mother Blondy all about what's going on."

I copped a double gin-and-tonic, then I filled in the background gaps and laid my conversation with Michael Mallory on the Blonde One. She listened, asked a few good questions along the way and, when I had concluded what I knew, she asked if Mike Mallory was married or not. "From the way you describe him, he sounds like my kinda man," she laughed. "But don't tell Tom I said that."

I raised my empty glass to her, but Blondy shook her head. "No more free drinks for you right now," she told me. "Go get some solid dinner so you'll be in good and sober form to play for me in a few hours. I'm glad to give you time off to do what you need to do as well as to be a big star on the East Coast, but I want some exceptional performances from you right here before you go." I decided I would just go back upstairs and have a beer and a frozen pizza.

# Chapter 35

I walked around the corner, into the Channel View and started up the stairs when I heard light running feet behind me.

"Hang on there, cowboy. Don't move so fast!"

Salli was at the bottom of the stairwell in a dark blue sweater, black jeans and her badge pinned to a dark, narrow belt. Her auburn hair was drawn back into a tight bun.

"I need to take you upstairs for questioning," she told me, all serious face and business. I half turned and waited on the first landing.

Salli caught up to me, threaded an arm around my waist and pulled me forward toward the next flight. "Questioning," I queried?

The lady detective gave my wrist a twist that backed me into the wall, grabbed both my hands and pressed them tightly against the plaster over my head. She crowded me into the side of the stairwell, beamed a grin at me in my captive position and said, "Do you really love me or are you just getting off on my position of power?" Salli then burst into laughter, raised on her toes and parked her laughing lips on mine, lacing her arms around me.

The lady detective broke away with an audible sigh after a minute or two and we resumed our climb hand in hand. Inside the penthouse, she took a seat on my couch, patted the place next to her and rested against my side when I sat.

"Good news of sorts," she told me. "Still no saxophone, but the Customs guys said that Loose can keep the empty case, so he'll have someplace to keep the horn when you do find it."

"That's something, I guess." I thought about it. "Not much really, unless we do locate Art's axe, but something. Get you a beer?"

"No thanks, I'm on duty for a few more hours." Salli did a minor pout. "Can I get a midnight rain check?" I told her my door was always open for her, but as soon as I said it, I thought about Astrid. What would happen someday if Astrid came to visit and Salli showed at my door. More guilt, like major size.

The lady beside me asserted herself and pulled my face down for another kiss. "To hold you through the rest of the evening," she told me, "while I'm out chasing bad guys and looking for your friend's alto."

We got up and I said I'd walk her back down to her cop ride. As we treaded the steps back down, I told her about the gig in New York and the favor I was to do there for Michael Mallory. We were just coming to that same first landing. Once again she maneuvered me against the wall, almost in the same spot.

"No Lars, I don't want you to go." Her look was pleading with a hint of *upset* tinting the edges.

"Hey, Sal, this is a done deal, kid. And you know I'm always careful. This is something I can handle."

She shook her head slowly. "Sorry, Lars, I just have a bad feeling about this. A premonition of disaster." I could see tears forming in the outer corners of her eyes. "I just . . . its like . . . " Then the waterworks went to full flow. "Lars, I've got this feeling that if you go to New York, I'll never see you again."

She hugged me tighter, a rib-cracking kinda thing. I could feel her tears against my chest as we stood there, oblivious to time's passage. Her shouting cell phone broke the spell. Salli turned away from me to answer it, sniffled loudly then said "hello" to her caller, followed by a series of two "yeahs," three "rights," and an "okay." She turned back to me, pleading eyes into mine once more.

"You gotta do what you gotta do, Lars, but please think about it. If you can get out of going, for me . . ."

I told her I would think about it. And, that was the truth. I'd probably think about it endlessly, but I was committed to going. I *had* to go because I gave my word to Michael, but also because I had already got the band excited about it, and because it was a solid positive career thing. The artist ego thing in me needed this boost right now, and someplace deep inside me, I looked forward to the adrenaline rush of checking things for Michael as well.

# Chapter 36

Back on the top landing, I could hear my phone through my industrial steel front door. I rushed in expecting more tearful protests from down below or maybe Loose to say he had the horn case.

"I just got off the late shift." It was Astrid, calling from Oslo where the time had to be around one in the morning. "For some reason, I've had you on my mind all night so I was hoping you'd be in if I called."

My guilt thing pulled the reigns in tight. "Astrid, *elske*, it is so good to hear your voice. I was thinking about you, too." Guilty thoughts, my mind added silently. I told her about my gig in New York.

"Great," she exclaimed! "I have some time off coming and I'd love to fly to New York for some shopping. I can come to the club and cheer you on! I haven't heard the full group since the last time I was in San Pedro!"

"Yeah," I laughed, "at least four months ago. But it will be so nice to be with you again.

"I'm supposed to be sharing a room with Loose in a boarding house on the upper west side. Loose probably won't mind having a room to himself, though. Do you have someplace you want to stay, or shall I book us a suite?"

Astrid laughed her musical laugh. "No rooms left at the inn where I can bunk in with the boys?" I told her I honestly didn't know. The paperwork was still sitting out on my night table. I checked to see if I had a number for Barbro. I did.

"Wait a minute, babe, I've got her number here. I'll call and see. If the boarding house can't accommodate us, where is your second choice?"

"First, tell me a little about this boarding house," she asked. "Knowing the places musicians hang out, I might have another first choice." She was still chortling.

"It's kind of a hostel for jazz cats. A Swedish chick named Barbro runs the place. Its suppose to be really vouty, kinda quaint and with lots of historical vibes, and, ah, like that."

Her voice turned serious for a nano-second. "Staying with a Swedish *frøken*, no, no. You'd better get me a room there close by, where I can protect you." Then the tittering resumed. "It sounds charming. And I'm sure she'll find a spare room for us. If she doesn't, just get us a nice room somewhere close by. I want to hang out with your band. I can be your, how do you say? Your groupie." Another giggle.

I gave Astrid exact times and dates, our flight number and the phone number for Barbro's place. We exchanged *I love you's* and rang off. I rested back on my bed to do another analysis of my life and what was I doing. Yard and Art did their bookend thing against my sides and I went on the nod for a few minutes.

Yard woke me up when he heard a bird outside the window or something. Good thing! It was time to grab a bite to eat and get myself to the club.

# Chapter 37

The prospect of a New York gig had everyone fired up! Loose and Skoot showed for the Tuesday night quartet gig "just to get in step," they said. Man, did we cook and burn! We played a bit of Monk, some Benny Golson, a few of my own tunes and, just before the second break, we tore through Loose's Horn Gone Blues, the man woefully vocalizin' his own lyrics, and Dave tweakin' his keyboard into a Hammond B-3 sound. It doesn't happen often, but we got a standing ovation from the room, including the Dive's regular drinking crowd. It was beautiful, and we all suddenly felt like world-beaters.

When I went up to my nest after the last show I was sailin' around the fourth moon of Saturn, or some similar place in the *Voutesphere*. My high lasted until I found Salli crashed out on my deck with a tear-stained face and sweater. She said she'd come right from work to wait for me, still insisting that if I went to New York, we'd never see each other again.

I wished that I could bring her with me, but at the same time I was really anxious to spend some time with Astrid, to make up for my perceived infidelities. I picked Salli up, carried her inside and set her on my bed. Before I knew what was happening, she had slid out of her jeans and was tugging at mine. She ravaged me like a mad woman. When I thought I had died or passed out for the count, she dragged me back and made me satisfy her again. The rosy light of dawn was sneaking in my windows when she finally laid still and allowed me a few hours sleep. Her passion had been so wild and obsessed that the cats had both run off to hide, questioning the sanity of humans as cats are often want to do.

When I awoke again, the lady was gone. I had fallen out so soundly I hadn't heard her prepare coffee, get dressed or leave. There was just a note, watermarked, by more tears I guessed, to tell me that whatever should happen, she would always remember me and love me: that I was the most real and powerful love of her life, and she would miss me horribly should I go to New York and never return to her.

Salli's strong words almost had me doubting my own sanity in going, but in my soul I knew she was wrong. I would be safe. Maybe she sensed that I would be spending my time with another, my Astrid, and that was her panic. Maybe, somewhere down deep, she knew that Astrid was the one who would end up with my heart. Whatever the source of her panic, I knew she was over-reacting and that I would return unscathed and fine from my East Coast gig. Setting her worries aside, I phoned Barbro in New York.

It turned out that there had been a cancellation, and her one other room was available for our entire stay. I was so happy to hear it, to know Astrid and I would have a room together, that I immediately called John and let him know that his wife was invited if he could pay her airfare. I would make sure they had a room to share, on me. John started to grovel and cringe at my verbal feet. His wife would be so happy! They had always wanted to go to New York together, had talked about a second honeymoon there. I was his savior, and like that.

I put the blush-and-aw-shucks in my voice, telling him he was, like, super valuable to me and the band, superb timekeeper that he was, and I just wanted to make sure he was happy with what we were doing. John assured me that I was the best leader-cat he had ever drummed for, and that he would work even harder to make sure we sounded superb throughout our Big Apple time.

# Chapter 38

As I broke the connection on my phone, the instrument began ringing. I lifted my finger off the hang-up button to hear the excited voice of Blondy repeating my name.

"Yes," I replied, "it's none other."

"Well get your 'none other' down here," she snickered. "Lieutenant Tom is with me and he'd like to have a chat with you."

I ankled it in double time through the Channel View maze and into the dive. There were only a handful of day drinkers spread down the bar. Ruth was arguing about some team in a recent sporting event with a couple retired dockworkers. She moved her head to indicate the blonde one's favorite booth to me as she stared down her protagonist. There was a mug of Samuel Adam's draft waiting for me on the tabletop.

"Figured you'd be looking for breakfast," Blondy told me, motioning to the beer as I sat. "Have a quick snort and listen to what Tom has to say.

"By the way, you don't happen to have one of Tom's detectives stashed up there in your crib, do you?"

I looked at Tom. "Salli phoned in sick today," he told me. "The caller ID said that the call came from your number. I was just curious."

I told them she had been there this morning, but she wasn't there now. Blondy gave me a knowing so-you-got-lucky smirk, but my word was enough for Tom.

"I could use the extra manpower today, but she has the time coming, so we'll work around it." Tom glanced at his notebook, flipped some pages, then set it down and addressed me again.

"Last night two containers full of big screen, high definition plasma televisions disappeared. Televisions with a street value of 4-grand or more each. The duty crane crew said that they must have set them on the wrong truck, and they're sure the containers will turn up eventually. The union rep says not to hassle this crew; that the insurance will cover it and mistakes can happen. At the same time, the shipper was told that he would be losing this shipment because he hadn't paid the protection money yet.

"This same crew has a history of losing loads. They always blame the truck drivers saying we just can't trust a bunch of illegal foreign-born truckers." Tom glanced at his notepad again. "Actually, they called them something nastier and not, uh, politically correct. I get the feeling that there's a large helping of prejudice between this mostly Croatian crane crew and the Latinos they are compelled to work with. I think they'd like to see us bust the truckers even though it wouldn't change anything for the crew."

I was getting a bit lost here. I was knocking my lobes at Tom and he was painting me a picture, but the brush strokes he was layin' down were all wrong, so I asked him, "Has this got something to do with the horn Loose bought that we can't find?"

He sent a grave look my way. "It might be connected, but that's not why I'm talking to you. You were approached by a union representative, Michael Mallory, about doing some investigating for him."

"Not really investigating," I told Tom. "He asked if I could talk to someone in New York for him, that's all." Tom did an eye contact thing with Blondy. They both had long faces. Lady gave him a nod, then he turned back to me. "I'm sorry, Lars. Michael Mallory refuses to cooperate with the police. He told us he doesn't want any publicity, and bringing the police in is inviting the press out to roast the union and the Port of Los Angeles. He told us that you were making 'discrete inquiries' for him and that he couldn't say any more. So, are you sure you're just talking to someone for him? I don't want to have to charge you with obstruction of justice."

Panic was startin' to set in, with a double helping of paranoia. I checked the blonde one's face for a hint of a grin, but found only gloom and doom. "Is Mallory the guy tryin' to rip off the port," I asked? "Is someone usin' me or something?"

Tom finally flashed a hint of smile. "Nothing like that, or at least I don't believe so. He's just doing his job, *as he sees it.* Or maybe he hasn't told you all he expects of you yet?

"We need to know exactly what he is doing, however. We need to know just what he's told you and exactly what he's expecting you to do for him. This is a double-homicide now, beside the fact that we're already into serious federal crime where the thefts on the docks is concerned. You don't need to tell Mallory that you're talking to us, but you *do* need to keep us up to speed. We'll work with you, and we'll try not to give you away before we have to.

"Since you already have a, uh, a relationship with Officer Migiani, there's no reason for anyone to suspect you're helping us. You're just spending time with your girlfriend, nothing more. I'll keep in touch through Miss Van Weirden here, to keep you up on my end, otherwise, Salli Migiani will be working with you directly on a day to day basis."

"You know that Mike Mallory is sending the band to New York, don't you?" I looked from Tom to Blondy and back. Lady smiled at me. Tom said, "Yeah, Pearl told me. We thought about sending Salli along with you, but then we figured that might seem like too much, after all, you guys haven't been hanging together for all that long yet."

"Ah, well, ah." I was stumbling. "Yeah, like, I don't need the distraction. I mean, ah, this is a career thing, ah, I need to concentrate on my gig there."

Blondy was giggling. Tom remained serious. "Pearl told me about your girlfriend in Oslo. She hinted that this Norwegian lady might be joining you in New York. That's not a problem. I'm not here to bust you with Salli . . . as long as your relationship doesn't interfere with her work for LAPD." Blondy's hand rested on Tom's and patted it. The lieutenant put an arm around her shoulder and gave her a small squeeze. Tom gave Lady a quick kiss and slid out of the booth. As he walked away, she asked if I wanted another brew. I looked down to see that my Sam Adams had been drained. I didn't even remember drinking any of it.

# Chapter 39

A duce of blacks passed with *nathen* special *shakin'*. Our gig moved along fine at the Dive. Loose kept his wig tight, no freakin' out over his missing horn. And Salli Migiani remained scarce. No appearance, no calls, no nothin'.

Then Thursday late, Friday morning, actually, I came home to find her pacing the edge of my rooftop. The air was charged with her hyper-ness. She looked like a spaced cat that had been shooting speed for a week or so. When she heard my footsteps, she ran to me and threw herself against my chest. She wound her arms around my neck and squeezed, but her body couldn't stop squirming.

"I did it, Lars," she breathed into my shirt. "I made a move that will either put my career on the fast-track or bust me down to nothin'."

"Huh? Sal, what are your talkin' about?"

Salli pulled her arms tighter around my neck and threaded her legs around my middle. "Carry me inside and I'll tell you all about it. I can't wait to tell you about it!" She tilted her head back to look up at me. Her eyes were burning with a fierce glow. I complied, bringing her into the bedroom where we fell back onto the bed together. Salli rolled us over, pushed me down against the mattress and raised up on her arms to look down on me.

"I put a task force together on my own and I busted the crane crew that lost the televisions. I didn't ask Tom Cheatham, so he wouldn't have to answer for me if I was stepping on someone's toes. I just organized a team of detectives and uniforms, requisitioned a paddy wagon and we *boogied!* It was *soooo cool!* Those bastards didn't even know what hit'm.

"We were waitin' when they came off shift. My guys rounded'm up, put'm in the van and brought'm back to Harbor Division. I had five teams of detectives to sweat'm, one for each of those monkeys. I threatened'm with grand theft, murder one and racketeering, and sweat is just what they did!"

I was blown away, like, couldn't believe and all that. This girl was solid. Maybe too solid for her own good! "So did anyone roll over," I asked her?

"Not exactly." She registered a small pout. "They had a battery of lawyers there within' twelve minutes of the first phone call. Two of the grunt workers swore it was the Mexican truck drivers that have been stealing everything. They said the Port shouldn't trust the stinkin' wetbacks with anything of value. The crew chief wouldn't say dick, and the crane operator actually threatened me!

"But the fun part is we found a plasma TV still in the box in one of the vans belonging to one of the low-life's that was all anti-Hispanic. Like, red handed! He claims he doesn't know how it could have gotten there. He swears that one of the Mexicans must have put it there to discredit him. For him, I got a judge to ask 2-million bail. The others got bond posted real fast by the union.

"The Brotherhood of Longshoremen seems to want to distance themselves from my one sticky-fingered scruff, though. We'll hold onto this one until he sings. He's my 'in' to clear the case before the feds even get their interest together."

I was startin' to feel seasick from Salli bouncing around above me. I felt like we were on a waterbed, though I knew it was just my old and thin IKEA foam pad.

"You say someone threatened you?" I was incredulous. "Like, one of these guys threatened your life?"

"Yeah," she smiled, "the crane operator. Right in the interview room, so we've got it on tape. That gives us a good excuse to keep a close eye on him."

"Sal, baby, are you sure you know what you're doin'?" She was still bouncing, squirming and grinning; eyes as bright as lighthouse beacons.

"I don't have a heavy plan," she said, "if that's what you mean. I'm improvising detective jazz riffs: just like you guys do on your horns. And its cool fun, man, I'm havin' a ball!

"Oh, and guess who was the lead clerk on the shift out there? Our old girlfriend Billie. I just wish I'd had an excuse to drag her in as well, a material witness or something. Maybe I'll still do that!" Then her face fell a tiny bit; I could sense tears forming around the corners of her eyes. "So you can't leave me and go to New York now, Lars, you've gotta stick around and see how I'm gonna handle this."

With that, all the hyper life vacated Salli's young body. She crashed down into my arms and started ballin' again. We shared some torrid passion, but her tears never completely quit her. When we had stopped moving against each other, she cried herself to sleep in my arms, while I lay awake analyzing what I was doing with my life.

# Chapter 40

I had slept so little and so lightly that Salli's sneakin' out of the bed drapes got me up as well. I went into the kitchen and made coffee for her. It was somethin' like seven in the early hours, ungodly time to be awake. The lady detective was tryin' hard to put on a happy face, but the water kept bubblin' around the corners of her peeps.

Salli was avoiding eye contact as we nibbled on toast and sipped coffee. She gave me a sorta lightweight kiss goodbye and told me she had a really heavy schedule ahead of her this morning, but she would check with me later. My cop hat quickly turned and stumbled down the stairs without lookin' back.

I put myself back under my duvet. In spite of the espresso, I fell back into dreamland for most of the remainin' morning hours, but when I awoke, I didn't feel rested or refreshed. I brewed up another coffee and carried it out onto the roof.

Coming through my sliding door, I spied Michael Mallory standing at the south railing, lookin' down on 7th Street. "Figured you'd be coming around pretty soon," he offered in greeting. "We need to talk some more. Your police lady friend is stirring things up out there on the docks, and it's making things difficult for the good guys as well as for the bad."

Mallory turned to face me, leaning his large frame back against the steel pipe railing. "We, I mean the union and the feds, have been keeping an eye on this thing for awhile, gathering information and evidence. Now your friend has these rats scurrying to cover their tracks. She's locked up one of the small, less smart players, but sent a loud warning to the big fish, the smarter guys pulling strings behind the scenes.

"Before this saxophone con job burned your friend, we had a good working relationship with the Port Police. They were assisting us when needed, but staying out of the way most of the time. The Port Police Commander told us that he put the word out to Lieutenant Tom Cheatham after Bobby Campbell turned up dead, and Cheatham promised cooperation. Then suddenly there's a busload of LAPD detectives down there attracting attention. Attention from the guys we're watching and, inevitably, from the media as well. If we don't get control of this, it flushes six months of hard work by us." The big man was nervously massaging his knuckles as he spoke, one hand, then the other.

"It isn't going to prevent us from catching whoever is organizing this theft, but it will make it much more difficult to do it without putting both the Port of Los Angeles and the unions into a bad light. A major scandal here draws too much attention to all of us; makes it more difficult for the unions to do their job and protect their members, 95-percent of whom are honest and responsible workers."

Mike gave a casual glance around my aerie and continued. "Many people in this port town and all across Los Angeles already have the perception that longshoremen are overpaid and given far too much in the way of benefits for the job they're doing. If the common man, the hard-working other citizens of this area start believing that our members are stealing large amounts of cargo on top of being so well paid, we will have great difficulty maintaining our level of benefits and pay. Just maintaining, not even figuring cost-of-living increases." He turned to survey the harbor again. With his back to me, he added, "And as you can see, there is new development going on here in San Pedro. Property values are going up, so housing is becoming more expensive. The cost of living here is going up exponentially. Do you understand what I'm saying?"

I joined Mike at the railing, where he was gazing down at a large pit across Centre Street with a sign on the fence in front of it announcing that pricey condos were on the way. In the silence, I wondered how long I'd have cheap digs here at the Channel View, and how long Blondy's could remain as a neighborhood jazz bar if someone with big bucks decided they wanted the space and the liquor license.

"I know what you mean," I told Mike after some minutes of silence. "I also know that Detective Migiani was acting on her own initiative. She didn't consult Tom Cheatham on her raid idea. Thought she could earn some kudos by takin' on the bad guys as a complete surprise. I didn't even know anything about it until she showed up here late last night."

"Maybe you could talk to her." Mike's dark eyes bore into mine from a head above me. "I mean talk to her and make her understand our position. What we are trying to do and why we are using the feds. If she could back off a little . . ."

I told Michael Mallory I would make her aware. He offered one word, "Thanks," and then turned on his heel with a military precision and marched through the fire door and down to the street.

# Chapter 41

The Friday night crowd was large and loud. Requests were shouted by fans as well as by the tourists from the Sheraton, two blocks away, who had discovered Blondy's Waterfront Dive and come back for more. There was, apparently, a large group or two booked to leave on a Saturday cruise aboard the Island Princess to Hawaii. They had flown into Pedro a few days early to begin the party before the boat was to sail. They knew a thing or two about jazz, and were very enthusiastic about our playing. We fed off their admiration, took very short breaks, and played our hearts out for them.

By last call we were all dripping with sweat and exhausted. Skoot and Loose had stolen the last set with a chase-o-rooney thing ala Wardell Gray and Dexter Gordon, only bari against alto rather than tenor on tenor. They had both played so many choruses back and forth that I'd lost track. The audience was on their feet through much of the saxophone battle, cheering, screaming, and calling for more drinks.

Blondy was one very happy lady. The only sound she enjoyed more than a good jazz solo was the electronic beep of her cash registers as the alcohol flowed.

Too tired for even a short nightcap, I stumbled straight up the flights to my crib with intensions of a solid black of Zs. My meeting with Michael Mallory, Salli's raid, everything from the day was way back in my consciousness and as blurred as the multi-colored wax on a pizzeria drip candle. I even unplugged my telephone from the wall jack. I figured that if Salli was going to come, she could just walk up without phoning and crawl in beside me. And if she rang up, got no answer, and decided to crash at her own pad, that was fine too. I just needed to get some deep slumber to tighten my wig and keep my brains from crackin'.

I was almost an hour into deep, wondrous dreamsville when I was awakened by the policewoman pacing the length and breadth of my bedchamber. When she saw my open eyes she leaned over and shouted "You don't answer your phone anymore? Jesus, I thought I'd find you dead up here with your throat cut . . . or with some groupie tart that followed you home from the club!"

"Sal," I started, "I'm shot, like, zombie city, walkin'-on-my-knuckles *beat*. I just crashed really hard."

With that, she threw herself onto the bed and started ballin' again. Suddenly I could see another long, sleepless night before me. This wasn't working. I needed to get some rest before we split for New York. But then Salli didn't want me goin' to New York. She drew me in a tightly locked embrace and wept into my chest. Fortunately for me, she must have cried herself to sleep, and I got back to my dreamless state of rest as well. When I came around to the land of the living again the sun was beaming brightly in through my window and the lady detective was nowhere to be seen.

# Chapter 42

I rang up Salli's cell to apologize for crashing so hard. She answered with "Look, Lars, I'm kinda busy right now. Can I call you later?"

"Sure," I told her, adding, "Oh, by the way, Mike Mallory paid me a visit yesterday and said . . ."

"Right," she interrupted. "I've just had that discussion with the brass here. I'll call you later," and I dug dial tone in my ear.

At loose ends, I decided to start thinking about what I had to pack for New York. What kind of weather should I be expecting? Looking through my clothes and pondering what to pack made me aware it was time to do a major load or two of laundry. And that brought me to the realization that I hadn't done any housekeeping since around the time Loose started his thing with the Art Pepper horn on Net Bid.

I carried a few loads of washing down to the laundry room in the basement only to discover I had no *gas meters* to feed the machines. I left my dirty vines in the washer and did a hot foot around to the dive to ask Syd, the day bartender, if he could front me some *geets*. About that time, the Blonde

One herself poked her golden locks out of the office, gave me a quick head-to-toe with somber visage. Checking my bare feet, faded blue shorts and torn tee shirt, she said, "You know I do try to maintain some kind of standard here. You are in violation of Blondy's dress code, so we are going to have to ask you to leave, now!"

Then I heard someone in her office snigger. Lieutenant Tom Cheatham? Blondy and Syd both erupted in laughter simultaneously and Lady said, "Give the bum some change so he'll go away." Then, smirking eyes on me she added, "Don't go away mad, Lars. You know I'm always impressed when you finally get around to doing you wash."

With the machines chugging away, I went back topside, put Dizzy's "Jambo Caribe" side on the box, picked up some of the clutter and scooped the cat's indoor toilet. After a run down the stairs to transfer things to the dryer, I came back and wiped the very visible layer of dust off my black piano and stereo equipment. I finished up with a quick push of the Hoover around the edges of the flat and a last descent to retrieve my clean togs.

Dumping the basket of stuff out on my bed, I fished out the dress shirts and hung them, so as not to have to spend time ironing. With that accomplished, I decided that I'd earned a break, so I loaded a few more Dizzy sides in the CD carousel and carried a couple Red Hooks out to the roof. Art and Yard were already there, stalking a group of pigeons that kept landing on the railing. It was a boringly typical California spring day, all sunshine and fleecy clouds with just a slight hint of cool breeze. An ocean going tug shoved a string of barges loaded with Von's Market trailers down the channel, probably headed for the grocery store on Catalina Island. I closed my peepers for a minute and pondered Salli Migiani's premonition about my coming to harm in New York.

Like clockwork, the phone commenced to warbling back in the house. It was the Lady Detective returning my call from earlier. Without preamble she informed me that her bold move had not been the boost to her career she had anticipated.

"I've been told to stick to the Jakob Rankovich murder, not to concern myself with Lucian's horn or anything else that might connect me to the docks unless I have a lead so solid that the feebs can't dispute it. My own lieutenant is talking down to me like I'm a cadet in training. This is so degrading, Lars, I hardly feel like doing anything at all.

"That plus my fear that you're going to be taken from me if you leave San Pedro. I am so depressed. I've even scheduled an appointment with the department shrink."

I told her that I was always here for her, but then she started talkin' about my canceling the New York gig again. "Sal," I said, "I'm here for you, but I've also got my career to consider. And I gave my word to Mike . . ."

"Fuck your word, Lars," she shouted. "You are so self centered and egotistical you don't realize that you are probably walking into a trap. I love you and I don't want to be investigating your death, or, even trying to explain it to some other detective three-thousand miles away."

"Sal," I shouted, "Listen to . . ."

"No, Mr. Star, you listen. I'm breakin' this off now, while you're still here. If you stay, or if you come back from New York, maybe we'll have something to continue." Then there was that irritating dial tone again.

I went back out on the roof. The pigeons had gotten discouraged and flown. My second beer had gone flat. The cats laid by me for a brief minute, but were soon distracted and disappeared somewhere out of human sight . I thought about Astrid, coming to New York to shop and to see me perform. I wished I could just get a permanent gig in Oslo, one that was strictly music and no connection to police, mysteries or missing saxophones. When the sun sunk behind the hills of the Palos Verdes Peninsula and the air turned chilly, I went inside and got ready for work.

# Chapter 43

A full week flew by with no haps, **nathen shaken**. Not a word on Loose's phantom horn, not a peep from Salli, not even a nod from Michael Mallory. Our nights at the Dive were average: a mix of tourists among the regulars. Blondy played her regal role, presiding over the premises from her back booth, greeting old friends and fans.

I talked to Astrid almost every night, planning how we'd storm New York and what we wanted to see while we had the time together. She told me she was getting tired of the Norwegian winters, and the problems of operating a tram through so much ice and snow. Astrid said she was more seriously considering a move to California where the weather could be predictably obnoxious, and especially because she missed me terribly much of the time and wanted to spend more of her life with me, possibly all of it.

Could Salli's premonition about her and I be that Astrid and I would come together to shut her out? That made much more sense than something unspeakable happinin' on the physical harm front. Whatever it meant, things had turned around now, with Astrid close to me though half-a-world away, and Salli at a cold distance while right in the neighborhood.

On Sunday around the crack of noon, Salli was scratching at my window. No phone call or announcement, she was just there. "Hey, Lars, can a girl come in? I wanted to spend some time with you before you leave for New York. I could take you to brunch?"

I jumped up, pulled on my blue shorts and ran around to the front door. Sal was already there. She rushed into my arms, pushed me back into my bedroom and body-slammed me into bed. Before I could catch a breath she was all over me.

"Oh, Lars, I've missed you so. I apologize for staying away for so long, I've been so depressed." She took my head between her hands, gave me a lingering kiss, before continuing. "The Rankovich murder investigation is going *nowhere*. They gave the Campbell murder to the Port Police, and the Lieutenant is liaising with the Port Police on Jeremy diStefani. They don't want me involved. I just know the answer to all of this is there at the port, but they won't listen to me; keep telling me that the port is off limits, it's so frustrating."

By 1:30 we were seated in a window booth at the Omelette and Waffle Shop. Mona, one of the owners, sat down across from us to ask me how things were going. We chatted for a few minutes about the problems of graffiti that had been plaguing our downtown area. Salli promised to put a word in the ears of some of her fellow officers and try to nudge them into keeping a closer eye on Gaffey Street in the early morning hours, when young gang-wannabe's often prowled with cans of spray paint to mark their territory like stray tom cats with bursting bladders.

San Pedro is a small town, even if it's surrounded by and incorporated into the big city of Los Angeles. Mona and her partner, Leslie, know most the locals that stop by to eat on a regular basis. Their Omelette and Waffle Shop is a sort of surrogate living room with a family feel for those of us that breakfast out almost as often as we eat home.

After breakfast, we took Sal's little utility truck up the coast and around the giant green rise of Palos Verdes, where we caught California's Highway One through the traffic of Santa Monica and Malibu Beach. Whatever might happen when I flew to New York, Salli and I would have our promised day in Santa Barbara for a shared memory.

It was a beautiful day, fleecy clouds scudding by over the ocean. White caps and occasional pockets of surfers dotted the coast from Zuma Beach through Ventura. The sharp purple outline of the Channel Islands; Anacapa, Santa Cruz and Santa Rosa, gave the illusion that we might be gazing over a large lake.

We had lunch at a fish house on Stern's Wharf, sat on the pier for a little while after we ate and watched sail boats returning to the yacht harbor. As the sun moved lower on the horizon, we strolled up State Street, through Santa Barbara's quaint Spanish style shopping district, where we found a small Martini bar. We ate fried calamari for a late evening snack with our Grey Goose Lemon Twist specials, along with frequent shared kisses, before we got back on the road.

Because of the late hour and Monday morning's close proximity, Salli opted to take the freeway back. The roadway was lonely and open through Camarillo, the town where Charlie Parker put in six months of recovery from a drug habit he never shook, and up the grade to Thousand Oaks. From Calabasas, the traffic increased in spite of the hour. As we reached the 405 Freeway back toward the coast, there seemed to be enough cars to make a rush hour. Ah, Los Angeles and our continuing love affair with the automobile. It made me happy I was not a driver anymore!

Entering San Pedro I realized that we'd been over 200-miles of roadway and through a full day without any mention of New York, impending tragedy, or future plans. We had lived a day in the *now*, like a pair of school kids on a dream date. The realization was, however, short lived. Pulling up 7th Street, approaching The Dive, dampness began to fill Salli's eyes, spilling over her cheeks as she stopped the car turned to me.

"I'm not coming up," she told me with a loud sniffle. "We'll say goodnight right here and if I do ever see you again, we'll start up fresh and new." Sobs wracked her body and she turned away. Through her tears she added. "At least I'll always have this perfect day in my memory. Oh god, this was such a perfect day. Oh, Lars."

I leaned across the center console, gently turned Salli toward me. With a light finger under her chin, I brought her face to mine for a goodnight kiss. Salli started to respond, but soon broke away shaking her head. "Please go now, Lars. I love you. I will always love you, but I can't take this right now. I have to leave and try to get some rest before tomorrow. I pray you'll have a safe flight, and that I'm wrong and we'll be together again . . ." And at that point she broke down completely. I tried to hold her, to comfort her, but she twisted away and asked me again to "please go."

Walking up my stairs, I found that I was crying too. It *had* been a perfect day, and yet I was already thinking about havin' a similar day hangin' in Central Park with Astrid.

# Chapter 44

Yard and Art's persistent nudging and licking woke me early Monday afternoon. They led me to the kitchen, where their kibble bowl was down to dregs and the water was low. It suddenly occurred to me that, as I'd been gone all Sunday, they hadn't had their usual can of tuna yesterday. No wonder they were after me!

I fed the boys, scooped their box, freshened their water, and then turned to the pantry thinking of my own rumbling tummy. I was still drug about my goodbyes with Salli and nothing sounded good to me. I finally put the espresso pot on and pulled open a tin of smoked herring, taking it all out to the patio to watch the ships go by.

Half way through my makeshift breakfast, I heard footsteps approaching over the roof's tarred surface. Michael Mallory pulled up a garden chair, dusted the seat with a pocket-handkerchief and sat opposite me.

"Briefing time," was his business-like greeting.

"And top o'the mornin' to you as well," I answered him.

"Let's keep this short and sweet," he countered, still all business. "We never had this meeting, I haven't been here, and

I won't be here long." He opened a brown leather briefcase, removed a manila folder of papers that he set in my lap. "You can look through these after I leave. The top sheet is a letter of introduction to the people you'll be meeting on the Hudson River. There's also a map and instructions on how to find the warehouse where Guido has his office, Guido's the man you'll be speaking with.

"The rest of the package is sealed in an envelope that you'll be giving him. He may just talk to you, or he may have a similar envelope for you to bring back. You'll be meeting with him this Thursday afternoon, after 2:00 pm. Just go to the address, walk in and tell them you are there to see Guido. That's all you need to do.

"Oh," he added. "They may ask you to come back again, or meet with someone else there before you come home. That's probably when they'll have papers for you to bring to me, if they do have some. I'll be seeing you in two weeks, when you return."

With that he stood, extended his hand and offered a smile. "And give my love to my brother. I know you two will get along very well. Like I said, he is a big fan of yours and he's anxious to hear your group in person. You'll like his club as well."

And with that, Mike Mallory was gone, out the fire door and down the stairs. I was contemplating a stroll over to the rail to see how furtively he might emerge onto Centre Street, when the door behind me opened again and Loose power-walked out.

"Lars, brother! New York is the thing!" he shouted as he stepped out on the roof. "I just got an e-mail from some cat in Brooklyn who thought he bought Art's Martin too! I think maybe when we go to New York, we'll get some good clues and you can solve this thing for me! Like, I'm counting on you, man, I know you can do it, baby!"

We talked a little over beers and Loose admitted that he was banking mucho on one paragraph from an instrument dealer who had bid nearly the same three large Loose had offered. To my mind, all it really told us was that someone was scamming the field, trying to cop as much as they could from as many folks as they could enlist to put up cold hard spondoolicks for something these punters lusted for, which might not even exist. How could I say this to Loose without sending him off the high board without a net?

"Awright, brother," I told him. "I'll meet with this cat or anyone else, if it will help, dude. I want to do right by you. I know what this axe means to you, babe." We shared a hug, I passed my man a beer and we sipped for a while in a contemplative mood. Yard and Art came out to school around our chairs, watch the pigeons and wrestle around in the sun.

"I'm not crazy about flying," Loose told me. "Like, I don't really grasp the concept, wind over the wings pulling us up into space."

I assured him I had flown to Europe and back many times, and the idea was solid. "Hey baby," I told him. "Like anything is cool if you can just believe. Like the Tinker Bell thing. If you believe strong enough, like, mountains will move out of your way and the religious cats will, like, lay palm tree branches at your feet, or whatever it is they do."

Loose was shakin' his head up and down, wide-eyed, at me. I felt like I was in some short story of Plum Woodhouse, telling Bertie Wooster that pigs could fly. Yard jumped up in my lap and spread himself out with his head on my knees. We sat in silence for a half hour or so, then, after two beers or more, Loose became all ebullient, telling me I was, like, some kind of Guru cat, all enlightened and knowing, who could solve the world's problems with a wink and a nod. I told him he was full of shit, that I wasn't any different than he was. But, he kept those intense peepers on me, like the cat that had just bet the estate and all the family jewels on Gumlegs in the fifth race.

As the sun began a descent behind the majestic rise of Palos Verdes, Loose finally excused himself and left me to contemplate the upcoming New York gig and my quality time with Astrid. I had about an hour of quiet fantasy to the tune of cat purrs before it was time to grab a quick bite and go to work for my last night before our East Coast gig. All my men would be joining me on stage this evening, a sort of "dress rehearsal" for our distant opening.

# Part II

## New York Bound

# Chapter 45

Blondy had chartered an airport van to pick us up on Tuesday morning. She was waiting at the curb when I emerged from the Channel View, the rest of the guys lined up opposite the Blonde One, bags in a straight line under the front window of Dave's Centre Street Diner, all except John who had booked a later flight to accommodate his wife and Trav, who'd phoned to say his sub cat would meet us at **Dig!**. Blondy was doin' the college football coach bit, tellin' the band that they were a world-class team, and they would make her proud, she just knew it! And, of course, we should all remember to plug her club as often as we could.

It was a chilly enough morning that I could see the Blonde One's breath as she spoke in the soft, rosy dawn light. The cool morning served a good reminder that we were traveling to a chillier climate. I had a coat and some sweaters in my bag, but was the only one waiting here in shirtsleeves, so I guessed that everyone was prepared.

The transport arrived, one of those blue-and-yellow jobs with advertising on every available inch of bodywork. The vehicle even had some kind of free-hanging hubcaps with

Pepsi logos that stood still as the wheels turned. I wondered if this guy delivered pizzas in his few minutes without a paying fare. Man, commercialism! Oh the humanity!

Blondy gave me a parting hug as I watched the driver lift my bag into the back of the gaudy vehicle. She assured me that Yard and Art would be well fed and loved in my absence.

For five men that had been hard at work on a bandstand less than five hours before, we were all remarkably awake and up. Conversations were spinning around in the enclosed space; talk about music, other musicians and the Big Apple itself. Each cat knew someone in New York he would have to look up and hang with.

Most of Loose's talk was about the gone alto. He told everyone about the dealer in Brooklyn that he'd be meeting, how I was going to glean clues from a meeting with the cat and set Loose's world aright! The others nodded their agreement, and then went back to their own thoughts and plans.

It seemed like the fastest airport trip I'd ever experienced. Before I knew it we were lined up at the Jet Blue counter, tipping bags onto the scale and heading through the metal detecting arbors. Long Beach is a small airport with the old fashioned roll-away loading stairs, and we stepped out onto the tarmac just as the sun was making its premier behind us, which caused the fuselage of the plane to light up with a sort of burnished halo. A good omen? Was some unseen god blessing our flight for us? Just another sign to me that Salli's fears were something beyond me and my band; nothing that should cause any serious worry.

Our jetliner had those little television screens on the headrests of every seat, just like the British Air craft I had flown the year before to Oslo. The guys thought these small viewers were cool. Not a big TV fan, I could take them or leave them, but the one channel I dug showed a tiny plane superimposed over a map of the U.S., keeping track of our progress mile by mile, fascinated me.

TV or no, I think each and every one of us was asleep shortly after the drink cart passed us down the aisle. In the window seat beside me, Loose was already making light Zs. I toasted Skoot, on my aisle side, we scarfed our gin-and-tonic breakfast with a bag of pretzels and I went on the nod myself. I woke up a couple times, checked the progress of our little craft on the screen and closed my eyes again. Minutes after the steward brought me around with a gentle reminder to raise my seatback, the pilot touched us down so gently I didn't realize we were taxiing home. Manhattan was spread out beyond my west-facing porthole, its tall buildings climbing to disappear into low gray clouds. I pulled out my pocket watch to check the time. Then I remembered that I was at least three hours off, so it had to be late afternoon. Were we facing rush hour traffic into town?

By the baggage carousel, a man with a light, coffee complexion in a dark uniform stood with a chalkboard, **Lars Lindstrom Sextet** neatly hand-lettered on its face. "Is this, like, from the club or our hotel," I asked him? The man cast a glance down toward his feet, gave those feet a light shuffle, and mumbled, "Got a call from a lady with a Master Card, jus' called herself Blondy. Said you'd be needin' a lift to the city, and you was to have special treatment."

This man's car had no advertising on the outside. It was a stretched out dark blue Lincoln with smooth gray leather on the seats and dark wood on the dash and door panels. All our bags fit in the massive trunk with room to spare. The interior had a deep backbench and rear facing captain's chairs backed up to the front seat. When the luggage was stowed, the driver turned to me and extended his hand.

"Name's Baxter. I'm a fan of yours, big time." We shook and he continued, "Like to ride up front with me? More comfortable ridin' shotgun than on a jump seat."

"Thanks, man. It'd be a pleasure." He held the door for me then walked around the big car and mounted his saddle.

"There's a copy of your latest CD in the glove box. Do you think the full band would mind signin' it for me?" I told him it would be a pleasure. I put my chicken scratch on the cover with an "All the best to Baxter," passed it through the slider to Dave in the driver side seat and watched our recording travel `round the limo. When it came back to me almost every centimeter of the booklet was covered with writing. Bax was beaming like a lighthouse on jumped-up power.

We sailed across the eastern boroughs and the Brooklyn Bridge in medium-weight traffic, but things slowed as we motored up the Henry Hudson Parkway. I watched Hoboken across the water change to Union City then Weehawken as we crawled toward the 96th Street exit. From 96th Street, we hung left on Broadway, then east on 107th Street.

Our digs here looked like just another ordinary brownstone from the outside. I double-checked the address to make sure we were at the right place. Baxter busied himself carrying bags up the steps and into the tiny lobby while the guys milled around, looking up and down the street in awe of where they were.

I slipped Baxter a twenty at the door. "Not necessary," he told me.

"It's cool, man, I've got a little favor . . . "

"Sure, brother, how can I help?" A big smile was spreading over his visage.

"Have you got any bookings for later this evening? I need to go back to the airport to meet a friend. She's arriving on Iceland Air around eight."

Bax slapped my hand, shouting, "You got it, my man! I could be back here just before seven, or . . . " I caught his searching appeal and nodded for him to continue. "Or I could wait while you get checked in then introduce you to this really *fine* chicken shack up on Lenox, just north of Central Park?"

"Sounds groovy," I told him. "They serve any fried fish?"

"Oh yeah," Bax crooned, "They got fried catfish with the spiciest hushpuppies north of Mississippi! And I got some friends there that'd love to meet you, includin' the cat runs the place. You go get yourself checked in there an' I'll be waitin."

The rest of the band was still millin' around the lobby while our statuesque redheaded host made some notes in her ledger. She spoke with an evocative Swedish accent.

"*Hej-hej*, I'm Barbro, you are Mr. Lindstrom?  Are you Swedish?" Her grin reached nearly ear-to-ear.

"Norwegian heritage mostly, but a bit of Skåne mixed in on my maternal grandmother's side," I confessed.

"Ah, Skåne," she laughed, "Well that is probably more Danish than Swedish. That's what they say over in Stockholm, anyway.

"And the rest of your party?  When will they be arriving?"

I told her we'd all be here by nine tonight. Barbro showed me a very pleasant room on the ground floor, then walked up the stairs to take the others to their spaces. I set my bag on the bed. That's when I noticed the guest book on the little sideboard. I opened it to find a collection of signatures that could have been a "who's who" of modern music. I recognized Art Farmer's scrawl, Horace Silver's fine hand, Jackie McLean and many others including Johnny Griffin, Martial Solal and Eddie Louis, men who resided and played in France. From Norway, I recognized organist Paal Wagenberg and guitarist Frode Kjekstad.

When I emerged from the building minutes later I must have had a look of awe across my face. Bax fed me back into the big Lincoln and pointed its nose out 110th Street toward Harlem.

# Chapter 46

Bax's chicken shack was all he had promised. We entered what appeared to be a narrow storefront with checkered curtains in the windows that flanked the doorway. The long room went some distance back to a counter separating the dining area from the kitchen. There were a dozen or so customers on wooden stools at a counter that ran along both the outside walls as well as a few round wooden tables in the room's center. Some of the cats greeted Bax as we went by, a few extending a hand for a coolly-*hip* slap or a high-five. I could hear the fat fryin' as we approached the back.

Bax ordered chicken with collard greens and some red beans. The cook, a big dude called Obi who was also the owner, told me that he used ham hocks to flavor the greens but he could make an order of beans without any meat in it, so I ordered catfish with red beans and rice. The beverage menu was limited, so Bax and I grabbed a couple Miller long necks, like the ones most of the clientele were sipping.

A pair of older gentlemen at one small table swilled Thunderbird wine from a bottle in a brown paper bag, but I don't believe they had bought it here, probably been carrying it around with them before they decided they were hungry.

While our chicken and catfish heated up in the grease, Bax turned to the room and announced me. "Hey guys, this is Lars Lindstrom, trumpet cat I been tellin' you'll about."

He was answered by a chorus of "Aw*reet*'s," "Cool's" and other similar greetings. Most the diner's occupants nodded heads to show that everything was cool and I was accepted. One very dark-complexioned cat wearing aging Levis and a raged Navy pea coat with a Musician Second Class chevron on the sleeve got up and came over to shake my hand. The Thunderbird drinkers raised bloodshot eyes to check out the scene, but couldn't quite connect, so remained silent.

Pea coat said, "Apologize for not recognizin' you *reet* off, brother. You do blow some *bad* horn!" That chorus behind him added assorted "Yeahs " and "A*men*'s."

Pea coat, who Bax introduced to me as Georgie, had played tenor sax and clarinet with a band aboard the Harry S. Truman after a couple tours of teaching at the Navy School of Music. He told me the teaching was cool and allowed him to play with some fantastic cats in his off duty time around DC, but he didn't re-up the second time after he had a taste of real warfare in the Middle East. A couple other gents there were players as well, though mainly just for small local gigs. None of them had permanent music work.

Bax introduced me to Pete, a youngish lookin' café-au-lait dude with serious dreadlocks that worked for him part-time keepin' the limo clean or driving when Bax wanted some time off. Bax asked Pete if he wanted to work a few hours over the next few days and Pete said, "You got it, Pops. My dance card was lookin' kinda thin anyway and I can sho' use the bread."

Then Bax turned to me. "You don't mind if I take you and your lady on a little tour of our city, do you? I'd like to show you around and we can use my personal car, so you ain't ridin' in the back. If it's okay, I'd like to bring my wife along too. She ain't as big a jazz fan as I am, but I know she'll like hangin' with you and your lady as much as I will."

"Cool, Bax," I answered. "But you gotta let me give you something for your time, baby."

"Bullshit." Was his curt reply. "Your Blondy lady a'ready paid me good for today. I dug you right away, bro, and hangin' with you, showin' you around New York is gonna be a solid kick for me."

"At least you can let me buy a nice lunch somewhere for you and your lady?" I took a pull on my Miller bottle and Bax did the same. When the bottles came down, Bax clinked his against mine and replied, "That's a deal, bro."

With that, Obi summoned us to the counter to pick up our food. I tried to pay for mine, but he kept sayin' "On the house, young man. We don't get celebrities in here that often." I argued that I wasn't really a celebrity, just a cat that liked to play music.

"*Awreet*," he answered. "You can send some other musician cats my way, say somethin' good about the food if you like it. That's what you can do, yeah."

Some of the regulars pushed tables close to Bax and mine. We started talkin' about where jazz music was headed, transitioned into one of those East Coast versus West Coast style discussions and went off into who each of us dug and who we wanted to hear more of.

Soon the food was gone and more beers arrived, uninvited but appreciated, as our bottles got low. Bax looked at his watch. "We need to be gettin' back to JFK pretty soon, m'man."

A thought crossed my head. John and his wife, Lacy, would be arriving just before Astrid's plane touched down. I checked and found John's cell phone number in my pocket, and then asked if I could use the phone. I offered to pay for the call. Obi said to just step into his office but Bax produced a cell from his coat pocket and handed it to me. "Just sit right here and make your call, man," he urged.

John answered on the second ring. He and Lacy had just deplaned and were on their way to the luggage pick-up. "Man, did you ever time that right," he told me. "I just had this thing out and turned it back on seconds before you rang."

I asked if they had arrangements for getting to the city. They hadn't, so I told them to sit tight. I'd meet them just after eight in the arrivals area for Iceland Air and other international flights. "I've got a very vouty limo here and I'm just comin' that way to pick up my lady-friend, Astrid, who's arriving from Norway. We've got plenty of room in the car and we can share some conversation."

"I don't care if you've got an old Fiat and we have to strap our bags on the roof," John replied. "Just saving the big bucks for cab fare is enough for me."

# Chapter 47

We encountered some traffic on the freeway-like road. The slow pace lent us occasional glimpses of the East River. Bax paid the toll and guided us through the Queen's Midtown Tunnel, then he circumnavigated most of Brooklyn. We pulled up at the terminal with a few minutes to spare to find John and Lacy waiting out front. John was pacing, Lacy was seated on a big crate that held John's bass drum and cymbals.

Bax and I loaded John's kit into the Lincoln's massive trunk. My friends got into the car with a burst of ooo's and ahh's. Bax told me where to find the car, in the closest short term parking area for limos and cabs. As he drove off, I went into the building to search out the arrival gate for Astrid's flight. A television monitor screen gave me a gate number, telling me the flight was about ten minutes behind schedule and should be touching down anytime. I picked up my pace toward the ramp where Astrid would soon be appearing.

I hadn't thought about customs and immigration, so my wait was longer than I had planned. I was directed to a lounge area outside foreign arrivals, where I parked my bottom on a hard plastic seat in view of the hallway coming out of the custom's inspection area. I quickly spotted my lady in the second wave of passengers that came out. Astrid wore black boots and a long gray coat that emphasized her long red hair as it cascaded onto her shoulders. She was resting a hip against the chrome cart bearing her suitcases, beckoning with those ice blue eyes. My fetching redhead extended her arms for a hug, which transitioned to a long kiss while traffic moved around us. In her high-heeled boots, the crown of the lady's red head came even with my eye level.

As I got my breathing back under control I explained about Bax and the waiting stretch limo. Astrid laughed. "Leave it to you," she said. "It's always a show, and I love it!"

We laced our fingers together on one set of hands while we each placed our other palms on the luggage cart pushing it forward. Astrid traveled light for a woman it seemed. She had one big case and one smaller one, so the cart was easy to maneuver. We made a game of steering the cart through the pneumatic doors and into the parking structure. Bax had found a good spot, quite close to where we entered the car park. Astrid took a step back to admire the limousine, and then moved forward to take Bax's hand as I introduced them. She gave him a peck on the cheek and verbally expressed her pleasure in meeting my driver and having his motor to take us to our digs.

"I know from past experience what a taxi can cost into the city," she told him. "And I love your *bil*!"

"Norwegian for auto," I told Bax. Astrid and I laughed along with our driver as I handed my girl into the back seat. "If it's cool with you," I told her, "Bax has invited us to take a tour of the city with him and his wife tomorrow."

"Oh, Bax, I'd love that," was her reply. She turned to me as I took my seat. "Lars, you are a treasure. You make friends of your fans wherever you go, and it is; how do you say? A *gas*, man."

We all laughed at that; John, Lacy, Bax, and myself. "You have hooked up with one hip lady," Lacy confided, which got Astrid laughing as well. Our gaiety set the mood for the ride back to Barbro's brownstone for wandering jazz minstrels. We all talked about things we wanted to see while we were in "the Apple." John and Lacy were looking forward to walking around Central Park and Greenwich Village. Astrid was curious about Harlem. When I mentioned the diner where Bax and I had lunched, Astrid said we had to take her there. She wanted to meet all my fans and followers as well as Bax's buddies.

We were enjoying our conversation so much I didn't even notice what the traffic was like, or what route we took. When we pulled up on 107th, I was surprised. It didn't seem like we'd been in the ride long enough to get across Brooklyn, Queens *and* Manhattan.

# Chapter 48

Astrid was impressed with our room, especially the guest book that all the boppers and swing legends had signed. Under her dark gray coat she wore a deep-green turtleneck and a skirt that almost matched her coat. She was even more attractive then I remembered from our last meeting. Although I was fond of Salli Migiani, Salli appeared plain and pale next to my Norwegian love.

We both took a minute to unpack and settle in. From the bottom of her suitcase, Astrid brought out a beautiful and heavy wool sweater, blue with dark gray and white patterns in the weave.

"This is for you," she told me with a wide grin. "I didn't know if you had anything to wear if the temperature should drop here."

"It's perfect," I told her, holding it in front of me and checking myself in the mirror on the wardrobe door. "And in my . . . " Astrid's voice joined mine and we finished the sentence in unison, "favorite colors."

The lady laughed. "I know, Man, that's why I chose it."

"I told you blue and gray were my favorite colors?" I was surprised.

"Lars, baby, you didn't have to say it. In the times we've been together, I've watched you. You always seem drawn to these colors. When you look at paintings, when we go shopping for clothes. I could just tell.

"So pull it on, mister. I want to go for a walk and check the neighborhood. I've been sitting on a plane and then in a car for the whole day now it seems like."

We shared another lingering kiss. Astrid stared up into my eyes. "I love you, you big lug!"

"*Big lug*?" I was laughing now. "Where did you learn an expression like *big lug*?"

"Watching American films, you silly" she confided. "I always loved Humphrey Bogart and Robert Mitchum. So is big lug not appropriate?"

I told her it was fine, it just caught me by surprise. With that, I eased into my new sweater. Astrid was still in her calf high black boots with the narrow three-inch heels. She slipped back into her overcoat of charcoal wool, took hold of my hand and we ventured out into the New York night. We stopped on the steps for another brief hug and kiss, and then pointed our toes towards Broadway.

The air did have a chill to it and I was glad Astrid had bought the sweater for me. With my arm around her, we snuggled up against the cold as we turned left onto Broadway. We had walked maybe three blocks when Astrid pointed to the corner on the other side of the pavement. On the ground floor of the building, a lengthy blue sign wrapped around the corner with orange neon letters that spelled "Tom's Restaurant."

"I've seen that place before. It's on one of your American TV shows that we get in Oslo! Do you ever watch **Seinfeld**?" She paused and looked up into my peepers. "No, you wouldn't as you don't have a television.

"I want to eat there while we're in the city," she purred. "Maybe we can have breakfast there tomorrow?"

Astrid steered me towards the crosswalk and we ambled over to look in the window. At a booth just behind the glass, Skoot, Loose and Dave were seated sipping coffee with well-cleaned plates in front of them. My girl pulled me to the door and we asked the guys if we could join them.

Everyone had hugs and greetings for Astrid. When they sat back down, Loose squeezed in with Skoot and Dave on one side of the table leaving the opposite bench for Astrid and me. We ordered coffee, regular for the lady and de-caf for me. Dave, Loose and Astrid talked excitedly about the television show that had often featured this very Bistro. Skoot and I were kinda out-of-it as neither of us were big TV fans, although I knew Skoot did have a large collection of Scandinavian and British comedy DVDs that he enjoyed watching.

Even though Barbro included a morning meal with our rooms, we all agreed to meet at Tom's again in the morning. In spite of our jetlag, we enjoyed conversation until our waitress was about ready to toss us out. When we started our meander back down Broadway to Barbro's place Astrid and I hung back from the others and took a slower pace. I enjoyed the intimacy as we strolled in step like school kids in the clutch of a mad crush.

# Chapter 49

Wednesday morning found Astrid and me retracing our steps from the night before, back to Tom's Restaurant. This morning my lady wore a long navy skirt that buttoned in front. The buttons were undone to just above her knees, showing dark stockings that disappeared into those same black boots. Her sweater was a sort of gunmetal blue that set her red hair off like flame.

The neighborhood looked different, somewhat brighter in the overcast morning light. Just around the corner from Tom's, on 112th Street, a cat had set up a sidewalk stand selling CDs. There were more peddlers along Broadway selling t-shirts, handbags, jewelry, and other items in a sort of carnival atmosphere.

Astrid and I were the first to arrive at Tom's. We asked the waitress for a large corner booth, explaining that we had at least five more in our party. Loose had said that he planned to invite John and Lacy if they were up early enough. It was after nine when Astrid and I had left, so chances are they would at least be available to talk to Loose.

The rest of our party straggled in, one at a time, as Astrid and I sipped our coffee. Skoot, a devoted breakfast fanatic, showed first. Loose and Dave showed next, followed closely by John and Lacy. Loose held forth for a while explaining how he'd contacted the musical instrument dealer that had also bid on Art Pepper's sax. They'd chatted for some time late last night and the man, Sol was his name, promised to come to our performance that night to confer with us.

"Us" I queried? "You're the one that bid on this phantom horn."

"But you're the detective," he voiced with confidence. "He'll have some questions for you, like, for sure."

I wasn't happy being drawn into Loose's plot, but I had promised to help, so there wasn't much I could say.

My thoughts were shattered by a loud laugh from my lady. "A man of so many talents," she chuckled. "Lars, you are one amazing cat!" She placed her hand over mine, gave a slight squeeze, and crushed her body into mine. She had summed it up as far as the others were concerned. Loose nodded his head with a satisfied smile while the band members buried their faces in their menus.

I ordered a lox and onion omelet with Hollandaise sauce and capers; Astrid opted for the Florentine. Loose had a large stack of hotcakes, Skoot decided my choice was cool and Dave had an order of sausage and eggs. John went all out with a corned beef omelet while his lady opted for a couple scrambled eggs with cottage cheese to comply with her diet.

Everyone was excited about how they might spend their day. Lots of plans and ideas were shared. Loose planned to accompany John and Lacy to Ground Zero with the idea of paying respects to the folks that had laid it down and left it there on September 11th of 2001. Skoot already had a list of CD stores from the phone book that he planned to hit in a search to expand his jazz collection.

Bax would be meeting Astrid and me soon for a tour of the city. Somewhere in my day, I had to find the warehouse along the Hudson where I would contact Mike Mallory's friend to make my inquiries and deliver his package. I was a bit nervous about my mission, mostly because I didn't want to involve Astrid, Bax, or any other friend into what might prove a dodgy enterprise. I'd have to come up with an excuse why I needed an hour on the waterfront to myself. Excusing myself to find the men's room, I found a pay phone in the back of the café and called the number Michael Mallory had given me.

# Chapter 50

After breakfast, we returned to Barbro's to wait for Bax. Astrid traded her skirt, boots and hose for jeans, jogging shoes and thick wooly socks. I was wearing a black turtleneck of my own under my blue oxford shirt, with my jeans and tennies. The sun had come out, but the temperature was still hovering below what felt like a comfort level to my West Coast soul. I slipped into my black leather jacket for extra warmth.

I had an appointment to meet someone named Guido at an unmarked warehouse near where Canal meets West Street. He had told me to just walk south toward Watt Street, come through the gate by the pier and look for the first open loading bay.

Bax and his wife, Tabitha, arrived in a white, *on* white, *in* white Eldorado. The ride looked shiny and brand new although I could tell by the lines the car was a few seasons older. Bax jumped out of the car and came around to hold the door for Astrid and myself, asking if we had any ideas of places we'd like to see.

"Could we cruise up Lenox Avenue?" Astrid asked in a little girl voice full of expectation. "Then maybe take a tour around Central Park?"

Bax chortled, "You're too easy, baby. We 'as gonna do that anyway."

"Just one bit of business," I interjected. "I need to talk to someone at a place on Canal and West around two."

Astrid leaned back slightly and looked me up and down. "A secret girlfriend?" She tried to give me serious, but broke into musical giggles.

"Uh, I promised a friend in Pedro that I'd bring these papers to this cat he's tight with and hold forth with him for a few choruses."

She put a finger to her cheek, resting her chin on her thumb and gave me more serious. "Sounds like one of your detective scenes to me, uh-huh." Her finger drummed the side of her face briefly. "Something to do with that saxophone Loose keeps yakkin' about?"

"Peripherally," I told her. Bax had closed his door and fastened his seat belt. He half turned to look at me over the seat back. I could feel the hot lights of an interrogation shinin' on me.

"A'right. Like, Loose's sax thing led me into some troubles on the docks back home. Lieutenant Tom," I looked at Baxter and gave some background for his benefit, "He's this cop that's tight with my boss, Blondy, who owns the club where we play. He repped me to this union cat that's, like, takin' heat over stuff bein' pilfered from the docks. The Lieutenant thinks it might somehow tie into Loose's thing because like, everything seems to take us back to the waterfront and the Longshore dudes, dig?"

"Do they think the saxophone might be here?" Bax asked.

"Man, I don't know," I answered. As Bax pulled into traffic, I told them all I knew about the case. While I talked, Astrid wound both her arms around mine that was closest and leaned into me with her head on my shoulder. Bax and Tabitha both made understanding noises and shot me the occasional question. When I finished, Bax said, "Sounds heavy, baby. I didn't know you was a gumshoe type cat."

I assured him that I wasn't really, although some people had me pegged that way. Then I sat back and relaxed as Bax started pointing places out to us; the original site of Minton's Playhouse, where bebop jazz was birthed by cats like Bird, Monk and Diz; Where the Cotton Club got its start, the Apollo Theater, and the building where former president Bill Clinton has his office.

From the top of Lenox, we moved over a couple blocks and headed back into town along Park Avenue. Bax was indicating for a right turn. I looked up and my jaw dropped. We were hangin' onto a street called Tito Puente Drive. I remembered that Astrid had one of those digital camera things in her bag, she had taken pictures of Barbro's brownstone and Tom's Restaurant, so I asked Bax if he could pull over briefly. When our luxury ride had come to a halt, I asked Astrid if she could take a snap of me by the street sign.

Bax parked it on a fire hydrant. Astrid and I got out and the lady posed me next to the pole, pointing up at the moniker of *El Rey*, the king of Latin jazz. She showed me the back of the camera, where my slightly comic image grinned back at me. She elbowed my ribs, chuckled and said, "You're so damn good looking, and photogenic too!"

We got back in the car. Bax pulled out into traffic for a couple blocks, then made a left where Malcolm X Boulevard entered the park and became Central Park Drive South. We did the slow cruise through this marvelous patch of green in the center of the skyward reaching city. We all got out and took a walk by the Turtle Pond and the Metropolitan Museum of Art. Astrid made me promise that we'd come back to spend time in the museum. Halfway through our walk in the park, the sky darkened and we heard the ominous rumblings of thunder in the distance. Bax suggested that we get back to the car as quick as we could. We were less than fifty feet from the Cadillac when the solid screen of water hit us full on.

I held my jacket aloft to protect Astrid's hair and face as we sprinted to the white chariot. All four of us fell into the vehicle amid peels of laughter. When Bax caught his breath, he said, "Well, it was gettin' on for lunch time anyway. Any suggestions?"

"Just an idea," I told him. "If anyone else is up for Chinese food?"

Bax and Tabitha nodded agreement as Astrid squeezed closer against my side. "There's like, this author cat I dig. Another musician, but, like, he plays and sings country stuff. He's, like, the only full-blooded Jew ever to play on the Grand Old Opera in Nashville, and he's, like, a really radical cat. He's even running for governor of Texas, if you can believe."

Bax gave out a loud guffaw. "Seen the cat on television," he told us. "Kinky somethin'. That guy is really a trip, things he says, he sure don't sound like no politician."

"Yeah, right," I agreed. "In his books he's always talkin' about a place called Big Wong's. Is there really such a spot?"

Tabitha spoke up. "Tha'd hafta be Big Wing Wong's, down on Mott Street in Chinatown. Yeah, it's real good. We been there a few times, *reet*, Bax baby?"

"*Root*," Bax agreed. "They serve some bad assed eats, and large portions too." He started up the Caddy and headed out of the park at Columbus Circle, then down Broadway and into Chinatown.

# Chapter 51

Lunch was a gasser city. We ordered some five or six dishes and everyone shared. Astrid took to Tabitha quickly and it was, like, old home week. Bax told about growing up in Harlem when times were less liberal. Tabitha talked about her school days in northern Alabama, before her family came up to New York. Astrid told them her perceptions of blacks in America as she attended school in Norway.

Coming up as I did in the Pasadena Boys Club Band, I had to tell them how I never saw any color line or discrepancy. The first I was aware of racial discrimination was when one of my band mates, a few years older then me, joined some group that took a bus through the south promoting equality, a Freedom Rider. My friend, Victor, described to me how crowds of white southerners mobbed the bus showering shouts of hate at the young people asking for equality for all folks. After that, I asked my parents about what was going on down there. My mother told me how, during World War II, when my father was stationed in Virginia, a bus driver sat for nearly half an hour without starting his bus because my mother wouldn't move to the front or place the black barrier card behind where she sat. He was, apparently, quite nasty toward this Yankee woman who wanted to give the niggers a leg-up. After that, I told them, I started noticing the newspapers and magazine, about the marches and sit-ins across the south. We all shook our head about the ignorance and bigotry of our fellow man.

Following green tea and fortune cookies, Bax drove us out to the Hudson River, dropping me off on West Street by the river's bank, promising to pick me up at the same location in just over an hour. In the mean time, Astrid and Tabitha would do some shopping in mid-town Manhattan. I waved goodbye with a solid helping of real anxiety and headed for the gate by the next intersection.

# Chapter 52

The dockside felt kinda creepy. A deep gray-blue sky overhead didn't help much. There was a guard shack by the gate, but no security man in evidence. I walked through, made tracks to the nearest finger that jutted into the Hudson River. A third of the way down the wharf, I found the open loading bay, but felt some hesitancy about just walkin' in. Something just didn't seem right. Was I being set-up for trouble?

Poking my head into the cavernous space I shouted a tentative "Hello?" I waited half a minute, and then took a few more hesitant steps and tried again, "Anyone here."

I thought I heard someone or something moving behind me, but before I could turn my head strange hands gripped my upper arms, pulling them close together behind my back. My elbows were lifted enough that I was bent forward as my captor started to force me forward. We marched from one large and mostly empty bay into a second with boxes piled high on palettes. As we moved past lanes and alleys between the stacks of goods, other men stepped out to close ranks behind us.

We finally emerged into a large open area where the troops formed into a tight circle around me. There were at least eight men, predominantly Caribbean Hispanics, a couple of bulked-up white muscle builders and one gentleman of color. One of the brown men clad in black jeans and a white singlet bearing a red circle with a line through it superimposed over Fidel Castro's image, took charge. He was staring at me, like a bad guy in a "B" western, but talking to his compatriots.

"Hey, guys, what have we got ourselves here? Looks like a trespasser to me. Maybe some kin'a spy. Whatta you'se think?"

As they all made agreeing noises and nodded toward their leader, I noticed that most of them were holding those big and ugly old-fashioned cargo hooks with the wooden grip on them. My tormentors staring circling me, moving in closer. A hook swung out to my left narrowly missing my shoulder. Men on either side lunged my way, again with their hooks swinging before them. The man in the anti-Castro shirt suddenly swooped in and grabbed my jacket collar, hoisting my feet off the ground and glaring at me. I managed to hang onto my envelope for Guido, but just barely.

"Hey, brother," I pleaded, "What ever you do, please don't hit me in the mouth, man, I'm a horn player! Please, man, can you put me down?"

"First," he replied, "You might wanna share with us what you're doin' here?"

"I'm here to talk to a cat named Guido, man. A friend on the West Coast asked me to give him some papers. Guido should be expectin' me."

"Right, horn man, so why doesn't you friend try usin' the US Mail? It's cheaper an' easier, an' no one gets hurt. So why you really here, man?"

"Hey, I been helpin' to check some irregularities on the docks, cool?" I gave them my best innocent face. I tried to do an eye contact thing with a few of these bad-ass dudes, but it was hard to move my head with my jacket pulling on my neck. The herd started advancing again. I closed my eyes in anticipation of some serious blows, and then I heard a loud voice that sounded like it was coming from the heavens.

"Aw, you'se guys. Ricky, Charlie, Whatta you doin' down theah?"

The young black man answered, "We found this strange dude sniffin' around the warehouse, we was just tryin' to find out who he is and what he's doin here."

"Well put 'im down," the big voice boomed. "I think he might be heah ta see me."

The anti-Castro cat abruptly let go of my jacket. It was such a surprise, I had trouble landing on my feet and remaining upright. I thought I might stumble forward and go crashing into a stack of palettes.

"Aw, Guido. We was havin' some fun w'this guy, okay?"

"No," the voice answered, "It ain't okay, Ricky, so now alla you'se get back t'woik."

I looked up and saw a short, heavy-set man in a well-tailored gray suit with wide chalk-stripes running up the fabric standing on a small landing at the top of a narrow staircase.

"You named Lars?" he aimed down at me. "Well com'on up, I been waitin' f' you'se."

I started up the stairway. Looking back down I noticed that my attackers seemed to be evaporating into thin air. Only their spokesman, Ricky, was left standing in the open space. Guido addressed him, "Ricky, why'nt you'se come up heah as well. I think you should be part o'this meetin'." Ricky started up the steps behind me, staring hard at where he put his feet, which I think was maybe just to avoid lookin' at me.

# Chapter 53

We were seated in a small office that also served as a sort of conference room. Large picture windows looked out over two warehouse bays from our perch just below the rafters. I could see the lift mechanism and roll cage of a tall, yellow forklift moving among the aisles. Now and then I'd spy one of the workers walking along the main corridor in the center as he directed the others, locating palettes that needed to be moved, or loaded onto waiting ships or trucks.

Guido sat behind a scarred oak desk, facing from the door that led to the narrow landing and steep stairs. When he had greeted me, his "Good t'meet cha," enveloped me in stale cigar and breath mints. His man, Ricky and I faced each other across a long table that stretched from just in front of Guido's desk towards the back wall and a bank of footlockers. Scraps of lettuce and breadcrumbs told me that the table also served as a place for the longies to eat lunch.

"So . . . whatta you'se got f'me," Guido barked when I'd settled into the plastic and chrome chair. "What's so special Mike sends me a courier, huh?" He laughed at his question, holding his palms out in front of his chest, wiggling his fingers and miming that I should hand over the goods.

"Oh, an' by d'way, please forgive my boys bein' a little rambunctious down there. They're really good fellows at heart, just like t' let off a bit'a steam."

I passed him the brown envelope I'd been entrusted with. Guido pulled out the papers, shuffled them and banged them on the tabletop to put them into perfect symmetry. He had a pair of cheap reading glasses on a silver chain around his neck, which he lifted and placed on his nose. I watched his lips moving slightly as he read through the information, thinking how I'd read somewhere that Abraham Lincoln had always read everything out loud.

As he digested the information, Guido would occasionally sigh, or hold his breath. From time to time he'd shake his head or nod as his eyes traveled the pages. When the full lot was face down in front of him, he shuffled the documents and squared them up once more, and then went back to skimming the pages for parts he wanted to review.

When he'd copped all there was on the pages and stored it in his cognitive cells, Guido straightened the pages again and placed them in a neat, squared stack exactly centered on the desk blotter in front of him. I dug he was an obsessive type, a detail cat.

Guido cleared his throat to make sure he had my full attention. Looking at me, he addressed his foreman first. "Ricky, put the knife away and quit cleanin' y'nails. You'se need t'listen up, heah?

"So, Mr. Lindstrom, how d'ya come to know our friend Mr. Mallory?" His peeps drilled hard into my face.

"It's a long story," I replied.

He made a theatrical event out of letting his glasses fall down to the chain around his neck, leaning his chair back and tenting finger in front of his chest. "I got time, Ricky, you got time?" He shot a glance at the other man who was nodding furiously, anything to please the boss. "Yeah, Mr. Lindstrom, tell us y'story."

I covered everything, from Loose's seein' the horn on Net Bid right up to the flight from Long Beach to New York. Guido sat back, rested his chin on his tented fingers and put forth an intermittent grunt or "hmm" to let me know he was still there, though his intent stare was enough. When I reached the part about Bobby Campbell bein' found dead in his office, he uttered his only full comment of "Not good." At the mention of Jeremy's car blowin', both the longshoremen emitted low whistles.

When I'd finished my recitation, I knocked the man my lobes for his take on the haps. Guido looked me up and down, placed his hands on the desk and folded his fingers together.

"First, I want you should know that I don't trust telephones. Mallory agrees wit' me on this. You'se neveh know whose is listenin', good guys, bad guys, g-men, whatevah. That's why you hand carried this to me." He lowered his head in the direction of the neat stack of paper on his desk.

"Also, in the brief phone conversations we did have, Mallory tells me you'se is some kinda clever detective. You snoop around a bit, and you'se's had some kinda luck wit' it. He mentioned somethin' about you savin' LA from a dirty bomb by dealin' wit' some terrorists last year. Didn't make the papers or the TV heah, far as I know, but I believe Mallory, he's a stand-up guy. I've worked wit' him on union stuff a few times, and I like d'guy."

"Mike's cool," I added just to show I was payin' attention.

"Yeah, cool! Dat's just what he is, real cool. But cool or no, dis thing's got him shaken.

"An' you wouldn't know, but Mallory knows. We had somethin' similar heah a yea' or so back. Containah's broken into and lots a' good beatin' feet in the night. The feds an' the city cops was lookin' into it, but they wasn't seein' nuttin'. They finally thought they was getting' close. They singled one crew for a closeah look. One guy, Elwood de Gier, they pegged f'the ringleader.

"They was just closin' in on'm, when de Gier, one of his crew an' a straight arrow type casual guy up an' vanished.

Some body parts washed up on the Jersey side'a the rivah a week-or-so later. One torso still in a bloody suit coat's got de Gier's drivers license, union card and security ID in it. The feds call it square, pilferage drops back to a more normal level and the shippers is happy again."

"Anyone ever run DNA or anything on the body? How were they so sure it was him." My inquisitive mind had to ask.

"Unfortunately, the feds had a lot on theah plate right then, post 9-11 an' all that. New York cops was stretched thin too. Heightened security all ovah town an' especially heah on the rivah. Feds said they'd wait an' see. The stealin' stopped, so they concluded that they had theah man. Simple as dat!"

We sat in silence for half a minute, then I asked Guido what he thought.

"At foist, I was just happy that the thievery had taper'd off. Made my life a lot easiah. Then the ol' rumah mill starts crankin' up. Elwood and his buddy hit the casual then took off. Maybe Elwood wasted his buddy *and* the casual. Or Elwood offed the casual cause he knew too much, after which he 'n his buddy cut up a couple winos so there'd be plenty of body parts to be found. You know how these guys can gossip over a few beers, or when time drags."

I took a small notebook out of my pocket, in case I had to remember some of this later. "You didn't put any stock in these rumors?" I asked.

"Not at foist," he replied. "But aftah a while . . . Ricky, tell'm what you'se was hearin'."

The dock foreman cleared his throat, looked at Guido, then across the table at me. "This Elwood dude an' his friend? They had a few buddies, drinkin' buddies on other crews, man. I was out at the local, buyin' drinks f'my crew an' this other group, they was sittin' in the next booth, talkin'. They was braggin' about how Elwood's crew had stuck it to the Port Authority an' made a bundle at the same time. They had a toast to him and chugged some Budweiser in his name. Then one of'm pipes up, says he's heard from ol' Elwood, that he's out in California an' runnin' the same scam, only he's changed his name."

"That's when I give Mallory a call." Guido interjected. "No de Gier listed out theah, but oddly enough, his thought-to-be dead partner *is* listed, operatin' cranes." The portly man's eyes traveled between Ricky and myself. "de Gier was a crane operator in Miami, 'fore he come to New York. His buddy was just muscle, heavy liftin', maybe runnin' the forklift. I try's to get a photo from Mallory. This guy, Billy Adrian was his name, he seems to be real camera shy. Only picture Mallory can come up with is from his ID card, and that's such a poor shot, it could be almost anybody white with long dark hair that we got. De Gier always wore his hair short, so whatta we have, really?"

"Anyone here have any photos of de Gier?" I asked.

Ricky gave me my answer. "One of his old crewmember buddies might, but if they do, they're not givin'm up to us."

"We got dick in the official jacket," Guido added. "Just an ID square that's as bad as what Mallory sent me from Califa'nia."

"Hasn't Mike Mallory or the feds questioned this guy?" I inquired.

"Oh, they got eyes on 'im aw'right, but he's a slippery one." Guido reshuffled the pages in front of him again, although they hadn't moved since he had stacked them before. "This diStefani kid, guy drove over the grenade? He was one of Adrian's guys, as was his girlfriend, this Frankov babe. It's drawin' our Billy Adrian friend a bit of heat, but so far no one's provin' anyt'ing."

"Do they know where this Billy Adrian was when Bobby Campbell bought it?" I looked between Guido and Ricky.

"Claims he was up on his crane most the night. His crew all back him up. They was unloadin' a big China Shippin' order. Great alibi. He' could'a climbed down, hit Campbell and gone back to work, but if five guys an' a lady back'im up, what can the feds do?"

"And when diStefani got blown up?" I asked.

"At home watchin' football wit' the guys on his crew, same guys vouched for him as on the other except the lady wasn't present. Adrian described the game in great detail to'm, claims he had a lotta money on the Raiders and the game was a close one, so he was focused on it."

"And if Adrian is really de Gier," I pondered, "then murder is something that comes easy to him, possibly even the murder of the cat whose identity he stole."

Guido let loose a low chuckle. "Ain't that a bitch? So, I'm gonna send some ideas back to Mallory, only I gotta think on dis a little. How long you'se gonna be around the city?"

I explained about my two-week gig up in Morningside Heights, invited Guido and Ricky to come to the club as my guest.

"Jazz," Guido spit out. "Too busy, makes me all confused. I like a little Frank, maybe Tony Bennett or Al Martino. An' I listen t'show tunes, but modern jazz, no t'anks!" With that, the heavy-set union man pulled some other papers over from the side of his desk, put his reading glasses back on his nose, squared the pages, and hunched over his reading material as though I was already gone.

Ricky stood and motioned toward the door. He then joined me and walked down the staircase close behind me. "I'll escort y'out," he said, "So you don't have t'run no more gauntlets through the guys."

I thanked him and we made our way, side by side, to the fence along West Street. Bax's limo was idling just across the boulevard where Watt Street dead ended.

# Chapter 54

Back in the limo, we cruised down to Battery Park. We got lucky and found a corner parking place, long enough to fit Bax's oversized ride. Donning our jackets once more, we strolled around 9-11's "Ground Zero." Tabitha took a turn at playing guide, pointing out where certain buildings used to be, and explaining how she and her sister, Cindy, had planned to come downtown for a bagel and some shopping that morning. They had gotten held up taking Cindy's son to school. He'd forgotten his homework assignment and they had to go back, then they had to put in time in the school office explaining young Carlo's tardiness. They were just heading into downtown, at about 94th Street when they saw the low flying airplanes, just before the smoke and fire caught their attention when the jetliners hit the tall towers.

That evening, they had both hugged Carlo, a precocious 12-year-old, and thanked him for forgetting his homework. "Baby," Tabitha had told him, "If you hadn't forgotten your papers, we might'a died in that street walkin' over to breakfast. You be the angel lookin' out fo' yo' mama an' me!"

Tabitha wanted to show us the bagel store, which had survived when buildings all around it had been set alight by falling debris. Looking at my pocket watch, I noticed that it was gettin' late. I wanted to make the club scene early, scope out the bandstand, do some sound checks and get to know the manager before we played.

"Like, we had a big lunch," I told everyone. "And I don't like to eat too much just before a gig. Maybe, if this place is still open, we could grab some bagels and lox for a hip snack before we head back uptown, which is somethin' we'll need to be doin' pretty soon."

"I was thinkin' jus' that, m'man," Bax added. "I think this is one of those 24-hour places. And their bagels are *killer diller*! We need to head down Vesey Street, right baby?"

"Yeah Bax baby, that's the spot." Tabitha hugged her husband's arm. Bax leaned over and gave her a kiss, and then we started walkin' again. The place wasn't far. Checkin' out the vacant spaces all around the tiny restaurant, I was amazed that the building it was in was still standing.

We found counter seats right behind the front window. The ladies told us what they wanted and Bax and I went to the counter to order. Astrid and I had lox, cream cheese, capers and red onion slices on our boiled bread, along with double espressos. I figured it would be a late night for both of us, so the strong coffee would be a help. Bax and Tabitha wanted jalapeño bagels coated with a combination of melted cheeses. They drank more green tea. When givin' Bax her order, Tabitha told him, "We need them anti-oxidants, baby. I know you love your coffee, but them anti-oxidants gonna save your life. You need'm jus' like I do."

In line at the counter, Bax gave up a nervous laugh. "Woman's always readin' them health magazine, *Prevention* an' like that."

"Tha's aw-*reet*, least she's thinkin' about you, lookin' out for you. Who knows, there might even be somethin' to it!"

Bax gave one of those deep-down heavy laughs. "You got that right, baby! I'm glad she cares much as she does. After twenty some years, it's a good feelin'. An' you know somethin'? I think I love her as much now as when I was jus' crazy about her an' she wasn't 'bout to give me the time a'day!

"It wasn't easy to win that lady's heart. I'll tell you about that some day if we find the time."

Then we were at the counter, a twenty-something in big black frame glasses askin' for our order. I was about to dismiss him as just another young consumer dude, when he did a double-take on me.

"You're that jazz trumpet player, aren't you? Something Lindstrom?" I smiled and nodded. "Man, my girlfriend just bought me your CD. I play some guitar, and I been listening since a was a kid, but, man, your group just blew me out to Mars or somewhere!"

I invited the young man to come up to **Dig!** for the show, tonight or whenever he and his lady could make it, told him his name was at the door until the gig ended or he showed.

"I just came on here, so tonight's not lookin' good," he told me. "But tomorrow's my day off. My girlfriend's too, so we'll be there early.

"Is it just you, or do you have some other cats with you?" he wanted to know.

"Brought my sextet cats from LA," I told him. He laid some young cat jargon on me that I couldn't quite make, but I'm pretty sure he was sayin' everything was mellow.

Back at the counter by the front glass, we all dug in. "This is so, so, uh, so New York!" Astrid announced, which drew chuckles from Bax and Tabitha. "And the bagels," she added. "I've only had some kind of commercial things they call bagels at the 7-11 in Oslo. These are so much better! So *real*!"

"Baby, I think bagels came from Germany originally," Bax told her.

"Well there you go," she answered. "Ever since they tried to occupy Norway in the 1940's we've been suspicious of anything German. So it took an American company like 7-11 to make us accept bagels!"

That got us all laughing again. It seemed that Astrid and I laughed a lot around these two Harlem folks. Bax and Tabitha knew how to live life! I admired them and I really enjoyed their company. I hoped maybe they might come out to San Pedro sometime, and our friendship would continue.

# Chapter 55

The limo dropped us at Barbro's place around half past six. Astrid checked out some American daytime TV while I showered and set out my clothes for the opening night. While she did the clean-up, dress-up thing, I went through my charts, tryin' to figure what tunes would get us the most attention if the jazz press was there.

By eight, a cab had dropped us in front of the club and I was layin' some words on Mike Mallory's brother, Mitch, and his *amigo*. They came on very effusive, sayin' how happy they were to have me there, what a frantic group I had and how they dug the sound. "Like some a' those ol' Blue Note sides from the late fifties, early sixties," Mitch declared. "Man, how I loved them ol' sides! An' you bringin' that good jazz sound back!"

A young brother was standin' by the dressing room door holdin' up a gianormous black bag that obviously was home to a contrabass fiddle. He introduced himself as Charles Wheeler, but said his friends all called him "Wheels." I laid a copy of our book on him and watched as he scoped some of the charts, givin' out the occasional "A'ight," and "Solid." "When Trav called me f'om Elay, he said it would be an easy gig and a fun one. Your tunes look good. Shouldn't have no trouble followin' you," he told me.

"Just curious," I asked Wheels, "How do you an' Trav know each other?"

"Yeah," he said, "We're cool. Like, I took some lessons from Trav when he was here at Julliard. We got to be tight. Even though he was older, he let my friends tag along, accepted us as musicians rather than just kids playin' 'round.

"So, like, we've stayed in touch. When I had an opportunity to play in Elay with a group, Trav put me an' a friend up for a week, wouldn't take no money from us. Really treated us like family!"

We had everyone on the stand by a little after eight, with our opening scheduled for nine. We ran through a couple numbers, had the sound man adjust the mikes and levels, and had time to all share a little taste before the curtain was to lift. Wheels fit in like he'd been with us from the start. His strong fingers gave us just the back-up we needed.

Over comped gin and tonics, the boys in the band told me about the great day they had experienced. Skoot bragged that he had spent over $300 on CD's he hadn't even known were in print. His best acquisition was a Japanese copy of Quincy Jones's "Explores the Music of Henry Mancini," with numerous solos by multi-reed man Roland Kirk. He had spent the day on busses and walking the neighborhoods combing shops for classic jazz recordings.

Loose had been calling folks who had dug his blog and e-mailed him tips on Art Pepper's saxophone. He was expecting at least one person to show for the performance that might have a lead for us. A Dutch lady, who someone at the local union hall had referred to Loose, told him that she had been expecting the horn to be shipped to her, but had heard nothing more after the first e-mail.

Just into my first chorus, nervous and looking out at a two-thirds filled room, I noticed Bax and Tabitha being seated at a front row table. They had brought an entourage as well, three other couples dressed in their finest vines. I recognized Obi and one of the other men from the chicken shack. They fell right into the groove, feet tapping and heads shakin' to the riff! Astrid turned her chair from the table she'd grabbed and joined the happy party with Tabitha, Bax and the others.

Sol, a chap who dealt in saxophones of all shapes and sizes was, apparently, the one who had promised Loose he would show at our performance. He had also been contacted that he had won the horn by default, as the high bidder had flaked; the man Loose had been talkin' to earlier on the blower.

The instrument dealer was right by the stage when it was break time.

The sax man had sent a cashier's check as payment, but he had never heard another word. There was no horn. Net Bid told him, "sorry, you have no recourse, the seller has been banned for illegal dealing. This is one of the ways we keep Net Bid safe for you."

Combing the Net Bid site and contacting other bidders, the sax dealer figured that Art Pepper's horn, if it existed at all, had been sold at least four times. Net Bid said their records showed that the horn had been delivered to the first high bidder, a Mr. Lucian Bezich. Net Bid denied any knowledge of a problem. But they had banned the man who had first listed the sax, so there was something to it.

A confidential call to a friend at Net Bid had produced some insider information that the horn might have been promised to a Japanese collector who, at the last minute, had tried to pledge three times the top bid price. Net Bid management had, of course, denied any such action.

Sol, as well, had been in touch with the lady from Holland, who played what she called "Dutch Swing." She had been assured that the horn was being shipped to her. She had wired the three thousand American dollars via Western Union.

I learned all about Sol and his shop later, of course. I spent my break with Astrid and our new friends talkin' about music and the old days in New York, when everyone who was anyone was *here*, and most of them were gettin' dangerously high and hidin' from the man.

Reclaimin' my space in the spotlight, I could dig that Loose was, like, solid shook by all of this. I asked him if he needed to sit out a set, but, ever the trooper, Loose said he'd be okay.

And he was, playin' some brilliant licks and kicks, sendin' the whole band to a higher level. It brought everyone up to their best. Astrid even commented on how we cooked at the end of the set, when we left the stand.

On our second break, Loose made a beeline for the bar to bond some more with his new friend. They shared a common misery over Art Pepper's phantom horn, plus an interest in old saxophones, and probably more. When the time came to fire up the groove again, Loose told me that he was going to spend the day tomorrow at Solly's Sax Shop in Brooklyn. Sol had a few horns he had to try out, including a King Super 20, like Charlie Parker favored, with a sterling silver neck and bell. He also had a couple 1909 Conn "Naked Lady" altos, slow in the action, but rumored to put forth a brilliant full sound. My sax man was anxious to try them all, and to share with Sol the misery of a horn bought but not delivered.

# Chapter 56

The next morning Barbro, being tuned in to musicians, kept the breakfast buffet open. Astrid and I stumbled down just after noon to find the rest of the guys seated at the table with plates full of goodies.

Everyone's critique of our opening night was positive. We were all pleased with the crowd, the way we had played and the reception we had received. We were, of course, confident that we could do even better for our second night, as we were now adjusted to the club and all.

I wanted to spend some time in the room, fine-tuning some of the charts and reading the local papers to see if anyone had covered our opening night, so I was pleased when Astrid announced that she was going into Manhattan with Tabitha to do some shopping. Bax had already promised to take us all up to Obi's restaurant later in the afternoon for some beer and grease. We had talked about later in the week, maybe drivin' up along the Hudson to West Point or someplace called Bear Mountain that was near the military academy. Astrid was very excited. She'd been to the city before, but never to the surrounding countryside. I was looking forward to it myself as it always knocked me out, like, *frantic city*, being around Astrid when she was bubblin' and happy!

I got into the music, tweaking' this arrangement, tryin' out some heavier chords on some other tunes. I ran down our program and went back to see if I could find any more improvements again and again until I lost track of time. It was close to five when Astrid came back to the room and told me Tabitha was waiting outside to take us up to the barbeque place in Harlem. Bax would be meeting us there.

Up on Lenox Avenue, Tabitha found a place to park right across the street from the chicken shack. We entered together to find that Obi had pushed a number of tables together and covered them with a bright white tablecloth. Three empty Miller bottles were spaced down the center of this newly created long board, each holding a burning candle.

Bax sat at the head of the table, holding forth before an assembly of our new Harlem friends. I recognized Georgie, the ex-Navy sax man and Bax's assistant, Pete. Pete's girlfriend, Lucille, was a stunner. She could have been a super model with her dark skin, reddish Afro and bright blue eyes. Georgie's wife was sweet, but rather shy. Georgie introduced her as Mildred, she shook our hands and blushed, not saying much after that.

The handful of day-drinking customers at the counter were all half turned, listening to Bax and takin' in this special scene. Bax stood and motioned us to his end of the table. He pulled out the chair to his right and held it for his wife as he motioned with his head that Astrid should be seated across from Tabitha. I drew out my lady's chair, seated her, then took the place next to her. Bax chuckled. In a wild and frantic put-on British accent, Obi said, "Good, good. I didn't want my guests of honor sitting below the salt!" At that, the entire assemblage laughed.

A lady I hadn't seen before came from the back carryin' two bottles of wine, one red and one white. Another woman followed holdin' a tray full of crystal-stemmed glasses.

Bax introduced the ladies, Obi's sister, Grace and their cousin, Sammy. The woman with the tray of glassware smiled, tittered and said, "Don't ask me how I got that nickname! It's too long of a story."

Bax added, "She don't like to talk about it. Sammy had an ol' boyfriend said she reminded him a' that witch lady used to be on television." At which Sammy gave forth a long "Baaaxxx!"

The girls disappeared back behind the counter. Bax asked who wanted which wine. A couple of the guys asked for their usual Miller beer and Obi told them, "You know where the cooler is. You be drinkin' beer, y'all can get it yourself."

Bax started pouring wine and passin' the glasses along, then, when everyone had a drink in front of them, he proposed a toast "To good friends, great food and excellent, very *vouty* jazz!"

Sammy and Grace returned. This time they were bringing loaded down platters, one of fried chicken, the other, catfish. As Bax started loading up plates and passing them around, Grace and Sammy went back to the kitchen again to emerge with bowls of country-fried potatoes and coleslaw. "You'all can help yourselves to the salad and potatoes," Grace told us wiping her hands on her apron. Then Sammy arrived again with another pair of smaller bowls that she set in the center of the table. "Hush-puppies," she announced. "One up toward Baxter's end of the table is full o'peppers and extra spicy. The other one is jus' a little bit hot."

Obi told them, "Y`all take them seats that's open down the table, girls. We cain't start without you." Grace made a little face, like she wasn't sure she belonged with the customers, but Sammy steered her to a chair, taking the other empty place across from their cousin.

The dinner was fantastic! Astrid smiled and marveled all through it. Alvin, one of Obi's regulars, who was both a jazz fan and a history buff told us how Harlem had originally been designed as a slick new neighborhood for white folks a long time ago. The developers had designed fine wide boulevards and, for the time, the most modern buildings. Somehow, over a couple generations, the Nuevo-riche had moved on to bigger, better and newer places and Harlem became a very classy haven for Americans of color coming to New York. "Yeah, black folks," he added to counter some mutterings from the peanut gallery, "But tha's not what they called us back then." At this amendment to his story, the nay-sayers nodded agreement. They were satisfied.

Alvin's story went on as he told us about the old Cecil Hotel on 118th Street where, sometime in the 1930's Henry Minton had opened a bar called Minton's Playhouse. Minton himself originally played saxophone there. During the war, Minton helped down-and-outs, as well as black musicians returning from the war. Minton's hosted jam sessions that drew a mixed-race crowd. Everyone was welcome and jazzmen from all the big bands, black or white joined in the fray. It was here at Minton's Playhouse that Thelonius Monk hooked up with Dizzy, Bird and "Klook" Clarke, birthing a new music they called "be-bop." It was here as well that white composer Neil Hefti heard the music and started arranging this new style for various big bands.

Cats played on the stage at Minton's from nine in the evening until four in the morning, with the greatest jams coming after the other clubs closed and headliners from venues both uptown and downtown brought their axes to join in. At four, when the bar officially closed, the music would move down to another room in the hotel basement, where the jam was spread all morning and sometimes into the afternoon.

Alvin also told us tales about other Harlem jazz landmarks, like Small's Paradise and the Cotton Club, and how racially mixed clubs became accepted further  downtown in the basement clubs of 52nd Street, places like the 'Duces, Birdland, and the Famous Door.

The time flew by. More wine was opened, plates were cleaned and the conversation continued to sparkle. Others at the table added bits and pieces to Alvin's recounting of Harlem history; anecdotes from parents or grandparents who had been a part of the scene.

There was one of those neon-encircled clocks on the wall, big numbered face inside a circle of glowing blues and pinks. Watchin' the hands move closer to eight, I started getting' nervous and fidgety. Bax noticed and rapped a fork on the side of his wineglass that produced a lovely clear C# tone.

"Folks," he announced, "I move that we temporarily adjourn this meetin'. I got a limo client gonna be needin' a ride down to **Dig!** in the very near future. May I suggest that you all find your way down there as well?"

When Astrid and I stood, everyone else in the restaurant stood as well. All the folks, regulars at the counter as well as our tablemates had hugs for Astrid and handshakes for me. They were all chuffed up as Astrid passed out cheek kisses to all who hugged her. We both told them all what a pleasure it had been for us.

As Bax handed us into his waiting limo, Astrid slid close to me on the seat and, in Norwegian, she told me, "Du ha' den **Coolest** venner og jazzviftene i det hele verden!" *You have the coolest friends and fans in the whole world!*

"Secrets back there?" Bax asked as he buckled up in the driver's seat.

"I was just telling Lasse," she announced, "how enriched my life has become in the time since I met him. I never dreamed I would get to know such wonderful people or have so much fun!" Then looking me up and down, she told me. "I may very soon be ready to take you up on that offer to move to America. Especially if you can keep getting jobs that bring us back to New York every now-and-then."

# Chapter 57

I did a quick change back at Barbro's while Bax idled the big Lincoln at the curb. I invited the band to join us as Bax had plenty of room for the short ride. We were all excited about the evening and the events of the day. Loose had spent the day in Brooklyn, Skoot had checked out more record and bookstores. John and his wife had taken a tour bus around the area while Dave had made his own historical walking tour.

We pulled up in front of **Dig!** about twenty minutes before nine, plenty of time to get everything together.

Walking in, I almost lost it. The room was packed, like, wall-to-wall people. Mitch Mallory appeared at my side sporting the biggest grin I'd ever seen. He put a fatherly arm around my shoulder as he walked with me toward the bandstand.

"I've got some extra help comin' in," he told me. "We've just seated the last unreserved table and I'm gonna need a doorman to start filterin' the fans. I'm anticipatin' a line down 110th Street. Man, I'm gonna send a very expensive bottle of booze to Brother Mike for sendin' you here! This could be one of our most successful bookin's!"

I suspected Bax was at least partially responsible. He had been mobilizing his many friends and acquaintances. Then again, I had to thank Blondy. If she hadn't booked Bax's limo to pick us up . . . And how had she known about Bax? Was he referred to her? Did she pick his name out of a phone book?

No, I thought, Blondy just somehow knows all the right people. Chance wouldn't enter into it. Whatever it was, I was thankful! Wonderful new friends and fans, an extremely cool gig, and quality time to share with my Astrid. I could send Blondy a bottle of expensive booze . . . but it would be wasted, I thought. Sellin' booze was her *game*, and she wasn't that much of a drinker anyway. Maybe I should send some flowers. I'd ask Astrid later.

Dave approved of the new chords I'd substituted and he dug the new arrangements as well. After my initial nerves, I got into the swing of it and we cooked our butts off!

The crowd showed us their love and appreciation. Mitch came over on our first break and asked if we could do an extra hour, for which he would compensate us generously. He had so many people waiting to get in and he didn't want to disappoint anyone.

At the end of the evening, Mitch thanked us profusely as he pressed extra bread into our hands. He also told us that he'd recognized a columnist from the *Times* as well as someone from *Jazz Times* in the audience.

# Chapter 58

Back in our room Astrid made love to me with such abandon I thought she might love me to death! We both dropped, exhausted, into sleep. When we awoke, around noon, we were still lying in the pose we'd fallen out in.

We'd told Bax the night before that we had planned a day on our own, walking around and drenching ourselves in the local atmosphere. We started off with breakfast courtesy of Barbro, followed by a walk down Broadway.

Astrid insisted I put a five-dollar bill in the hat of a street musician, a very cool tenorman, a ways down the road. We spoke with African and Caribbean illegals selling shirts, jewelry and curios along the boulevard. Farther down Broadway, we caught a bus into Times Square. From there, we took the subway under the river to Hoboken, New Jersey.

There wasn't that much to see in Jersey, so we hopped on a ferryboat back to Manhattan. From the Battery, we walked until we located Tabitha's favorite bagel shop. We shared bagels and espressos before finding a bus back to the upper-west side.

We had about an hour to grab a quick nap at Barbro's before Bax was due to take us all back to **Dig!** We made the scene again, and then laid in each other's arms until it was time to get dressed and hit the club. Astrid brought out another stunning outfit, this one with a mint green blouse that once again highlighted her stunning red locks. The skirt and jacket were more earth tones. Her stockings, a darker, coffee shade. As she dressed, I started singing the old Count Basie tune "Shiny Stocking." My lady gave me one of those head down, questioning looks, then stood and shut-me-up by putting her tongue in my mouth.

**Dig!** wasn't quite as packed as the night before, but they were definitely doing a good business. Again, the crowd was receptive and provided the inspiration to give them all we had. Loose was playing a King saxophone with a silver bell outside and a gold wash within. His buddy Sol sat front row center keeping an eye on Loose and the horn. We quit at the proper time tonight. There had been a line outside for a while, but everyone got in without an extra set. Mitch and his partner were, once again, very pleased with the turnout, and said they had added an extra bonus on our salary.

After work, we put in a wake-up call with Barbro for 10 am. We went right to sleep in each other's arms, anticipating a great day to come with Bax and Tabitha.

# Chapter 59

Barbro's breakfast spread was amazing. She had set out some of that pink Shrimp salad, exactly like the one I'd had the year before in Oslo. I had a large second helping, at which Astrid laughed and told me that it was such a common recipe around the Norwegian coast. I replied that it was one of my most loved breakfast dishes. She promised me that if we ever married, she would make it for me every morning until I couldn't stand it anymore.

Bax and Tabitha came in to join us for a second cup of coffee. Barbro wouldn't accept any payment for their coffee, saying they, too, were special guests. Bax had parked just a couple of blocks down 107th on Amsterdam Avenue. Barbro brought us all some home made cinnamon *Wienerbrød*, a sort of Scandinavian pastry.

By 11:30, we had hit the highway, headed up through the city. We crossed the Hudson River from somewhere in the Bronx. On the Jersey side, we picked up the Palisade Parkway, heading north with a spectacular view of the Hudson on our right. Just before the highway took us back into New York State, it veered left, away from the water and into wild, frantic, wooded, green hills. Astrid was makin' little girl gleeful noises all the way, squeezin' my hand or my shoulder at each new marvel. She loved the boats on the Hudson and the fjord-like shoreline. Bax and Tabitha kept up a runnin' dialogue; our friends the tour guides, and we were all happy to be together, and glad that Blondy had once more brought a blessing into my life!

Before we knew it, we saw the big green sign that told us we were entering Bear Mountain State Park. "Do you think we'll see some bears?" Astrid asked in a voice as full of excitement as any ten-year-old. Bax laughed. "You never know," was his answer.

At the road's junction with Highway 6, we pulled off the expressway and found a roadside rest where we could stop the car and walk around. We did see some bears, but I got the feeling it was a sort of "set-up" show for the tourists. It was, however, enough to make Astrid excited and short-of-breath. They had polar bears in the far north of Norway, but very few bears around the Oslo area, if any at all.

Back in the Cadillac, we continued on through the West Point academy, just a series of building and bronze plaques actually. We didn't see any cadet cats. From there, we continued north to Highway 84, where we turned east across the river, heading back toward the Apple on Highway 9, down the east bank of the river.

We stopped in Yonkers and had dinner at a very ordinary coffee shop, and were back at Barbro's by 7:30 in the evening.

It was another exceptional night at **Dig!**. Like the night before, all the tables were filled and all the patrons were satisfied. Mitch once again praised our music. It seemed like everything in the world was right. I hadn't heard anything back from Guido, but conspiracy and crime were farthest from my mind as Astrid and I snuggled together in our Morningside Heights bed.

After Barbro's fabulous breakfast buffet the next day, Astrid and I caught a bus to Central Park. It was a beautiful, clear afternoon with bright sun and a slight breeze. The temperature had risen to almost comfortable and in our jackets we walked, skipped and ran through the park, childlike and lacking any cares.

We had made plans to dine with John and Lacy at a fancy place they'd discovered midtown called "Felidia Ristorante," so we returned to our room around 5:30 to put on some fancier *drapes*. John had said it was an amazing Italian place with a phenomenal wine list and authentic Northern Italian cuisine, although the master chef, Fortunato Nicotra, was from the area around Trieste on the border of Croatia. He and Lacy agreed that there was nothing quite like it in Los Angeles. Lacy had told Astrid that she heard a rumor about Julia Childs learning some of her cooking skills from the restaurant's owner.

I put on the one dark suit I had brought along with a blue oxford shirt. Astrid surprised me with kind of an abstract art tie she had found when she and Tabitha were out shopping. It had some soft blues and greens under a Picasso-esque golden trumpet. I didn't ask, but I had to assume it was probably the most expensive neckwear I'd ever worn.

# Chapter 60

Back in San Pedro, it was pure luck that Salli Migiani happened to be the only detective in the squad room at 2:30 on a Thursday afternoon. She was finishing up some dull and monotonous paperwork regarding an old case scheduled to come to trial soon when the phone rang.

The smoky female voice on the line claimed to have information about a container load of high-end stereos that were about to disappear from Berth 231 on Terminal Island. She said she was a Longshore clerk, and she had heard of the crackdown on pilferage. The voice told Salli she didn't want to be suspected of "ratting out" her co-workers, so Salli should come alone to meet with her. "You are a plain-clothes officer, right?" They could meet at the entrance to the Evergreen Container Facility on Terminal Way and she would pass on all the information she had, along with copies of the manifest and a list of the men involved in the scam.

Salli told the woman she would be there in twenty minutes, no more, to please wait. She made a quick call to her lieutenant to let him know where she was headed, but only got his voice mail. She left a detailed message and decided to take her own private car so as to be less conspicuous.

Luck was with her again in the form of extremely light traffic on John Gibson Boulevard, putting her onto the Vincent Thomas Bridge in record time. She raced around a couple slow trucks that were laboring up the western rise of the span, and then put her BMW into the outside lane to grab the exit on the other side of the channel.

As Salli was cresting the hump of the bridge's span, another vehicle appeared in her mirror. What looked like an older dark-colored Chevy truck, probably a Blazer, rocketed towards her, pulled alongside in the fast- lane and tried to cut her off sharply. Salli braked in time to miss the Blazer, but the truck slowed as well, staying beside her and crowding her small sport utility into the bridge's steel railing. Sparks flew as her vehicle scraped the green painted supports and the lady detective forced her wheel over fighting for purchase in her lane.

The heavier American truck fought back and the two motors wavered like nearly matched arm wrestlers bouncing first off the support pillars then off the concrete center divider. The BMW managed to hold its own almost to the Ferry Street exit, but at the bridge's eastern terminus, where the lanes widened slightly, the aging Blazer swung out and back, hitting Salli squarely and sending her small ride through the chain-link fence and over the embankment into the container loading facility some 70 feet below.

The Blazer sped on towards Long Beach, overtaking another caravan of large trucks and weaving in and out of the light island traffic.

# Chapter 61

John had already booked us a taxi. The driver took us down Broadway, past Columbus Circle. We turned eastward on 58th Street. Lacy and Astrid pointed out Bergdorf Goodman on our right and FAO Schwarz to the left of us just before we crossed Park Avenue. The girls also noted that Bloomingdale's was just a block up 3rd Avenue. They spoke briefly of taking a day to shop together down in this area.

Our cabbie dropped us between 2nd and 3rd, right in front of the elegantly decorated eatery. Walking in, we dug that the eatery was divided over two levels. We were seated up the elegant, maroon-carpeted stairs in a sort of greenhouse window overlooking the avenue. John chose a red wine for us from the list and we sat back to dip crusty bread in the olive oil and vinegar while we talked about our New York experiences.

The menu was mind-boggling, so many delicious choices. Astrid put a hand over mine and rubbed her head on my shoulder. "I know you don't eat meat," she said, "but would you mind terribly if I had the pan roasted duck breast?"

"Hey, babe," I told her. "You're your own person, I'm not here to change you."

"I don't care what you *non-meat-eaters* think," Lacy announced, "but I'm ordering venison loin in raspberry sauce. It sounds *so* good."

John told us he might be less adventurous, but he was having his favorite artichoke and cheese ravioli in marinara sauce. I told him that sounded good to me, so we made it two ravioli dinners after the ladies had ordered their meat dishes.

The sommelier was right behind our waiter with John's choice of red. He poured a small taste into my drummer's glass, clicked his heal, and stood at attention while John made a show of swirling his glass and taking a small sip. My man nodded that the *vino* passed muster and a big smile broke out on the wine steward's mug. Our smiling sommelier poured generous helpings of the joy juice for us all; ladies first, set the jug on the table, then clicked his heels and shimmered into the background like Bertie Wooster's man, Jeeves.

The pasta was so fine that even a culinary bum like me, whose idea of Italian cuisine was frozen pizzas and Charles Shaw Merlot, which we called "Two-Buck Chuck," was impressed! John poured us more of his good wine as the ladies took small bites and chatted about shopping in the Apple. John asked for small samples from each of the girl's plates and they all made yummy noises. I sat there thinkin' that if I ate all the time the way I'd been feedin' my face around New York, I'd end up lookin' like Sidney Greenstreet with a horn!

John whispered something to our waiter as the second bottle of wine arrived. Just after the man cleared our well-cleaned plates, another man arrived with four servings of Tiramisu, elegantly presented with squiggles of chocolate sauce dripped around the plate. As it was Sunday evening, we had the night off, and time to down a second coffee behind the rich Italian sweet.

After our coffee, Lacy suggested we sample the *Grappa*, a sort of strong Italian brandy. Our wine steward was back with a selection of after-dinner libations, a number of which sounded too tempting to pass up.

Three more rounds of liqueurs washed us into the cab our waiter summoned. Lacy and Astrid started talking about drinking songs. Soon John's and my thunderous voices joined the ladies in songs, poorly sung because none of us knew the words beyond the person who would suggest a number. Feelin' bad for what our poor driver had to endure, I slipped him an extra twenty for the tip. We poured into Barbro's laughing and were soon off to the Land of Nod.

# Chapter 62

It was well past noon on Monday when Astrid and I poked our heads out looking for Breakfast. We sat for a while first sipping strong coffee. Like, *hangoversville!* About the time we were ready to face some food, Skoot and Loose came in for some java.

"You look a bit drug," Skoot said, checking both Astrid's face and my own as he sat opposite us. "Did a little imbibing last night, did we?"

I told him about our ultra-vouty meal of the previous dark, adding, "We probably should have passed on the sample tray of different flavors of Grappa."

"I think the pear was my favorite," Astrid added. "It must be a funny sight, those pear trees over in Italy with all those bottles hanging on them as the pears grow in the bottles!"

"What!" Loose exclaimed. "Bottles on trees? Pears in bottles? Like, clue me baby. Where you been flyin' out to?"

We explained to Loose how Italian pear brandy came in bottles with the fruit inside, just like that tequila in Mexico that has the worm in it, except it would be hard to get the pear *inside* after it was full grown. "So, like, they go to the tree with all this tiny baby fruit on it, they hang the bottles so the pears grow in'm. Then, when the brandy is ready, they bottle it with the fruit from the same tree, dig?"

"Sampling trays of different brandies after a big meal with lot'sa wine," Skoot tisked, "What you need is some hair-of-the-dog-city, Arizona, m'man! And I think I know just the place!"

"We were gonna invite you to come with us anyway," Loose added, "cause we know you dig brewpubs. Now it looks like there's a really good reason."

"Like, we made a couple great find," Skoot told us. "Before the amber nectar is discussed, however, a stiffer riff to entertain your mind. Like, last night Loose an' me decided to scope out what **Dig!** has goin' beside *our* gig. So we grabbed a cab and jumped to the scene."

"Man, we caught the all high flip out mother to end all mother of grooves!" Loose chimed in. "Outer *voutesphere!*"

"Like, you remember Barbara Sfraga," Skoot asked?

"Yeah," I told him, "brilliant songbird with a style that's really pushin' Shakespeare on the vocal scene. I've dug her work. She is really movin' on and *on*."

"Well, you missed her *new* action last night, bro. Barbara was at **Dig!** and she knocked everyone out with a group called **Center Search Quest**. Mala Waldron, Mal's kid, was blowin' keys and singin' too." Skoot's peeps were lit up like, he must have been solid *sent* by this tribe. "The bass cat was a tall poet dude named Christopher and they were being drivin' by an amazing skin and cymbal man they called T.A."

Loose added, "Allen Won was settin' fourth some beautimous sax riffs out front. Man, I wish you guys could have **been** there."

"So, you say it was *frantic city*? I mean Barbara is *always* full of surprises."

"Reet, man," Skoot went on, "But this was really a *shift of the riff*. Like, it's difficult to describe, dig? Can't put a label on it. It was heavy jazz, right in the pocket, but there was so much more! It's like I was watchin' some kinda musical show written by Dali and Garcia Lorca, and cast by Monk himself, dig? They were explaining *real life* with bits of poetry, plenty plenty soul, and things that elude my brain to draw a picture for you. It was *sound theater* showing the world the perfect high, Dig?"

I made a mental note to catch Barbara and Center Search Quest at my first opportunity. Maybe I could get another gig in Mother Gotham soon, with a couple extra days to check the scene, or meet Astrid here again soon for a little holiday after I finished helpin' Loose find his horn.

Ms. Sfraga, jazz deity that she is, never ceases to amaze with her unique individual styling. Set her in the middle of a surreal straight-ahead group of cats like Skoot and Loose were layin' on my lobes, and I could hardly imagine the results, but it would have to swing like a garden gate!

"So, like, you said a couple great finds?" I reminded my sax-cats.

"Yeah," Skoot told us. "On a much more mundane level, there's a real voot-o-reeny brew pub way down Broadway, like, right off Times Square. We went walkin' around Times Square yesterday, y'know? They always say if you stand there long enough, you'll meet everyone you ever knew"

"Yeah," Loose chimed in, "Only we didn't see *anyone* we knew. An' we walked around there for hours, checking the big light-up signs and things."

"Anyway," Skoot resumed, "We were diggin' on this street cat, blowin' some heavy tenor for chump-change on a little triangle of sidewalk where Broadway crosses 7th Avenue and 42nd Street. I let my eyes wander after this gorgeous young chick and, low and behold, she's walkin' past the building with a sign out front says *Times Square Brewery*.

"So I pull on Loose's coat and tell him, like, cast thy peepers down yonder boulevard. He doesn't cop to it right away, but then he sees the sign and we start movin' our feet in the new direction.

"We arrive in front of the place and, like, it's massive! Three-stories of microbrewery hangin' right before our thirsty faces!"

Skoot did a quick Groucho with his eyebrows and mimed flicking ash off a cigar, then continued.

"Well, like, the first two levels are mostly eatery, like righteous American fare, nothin' fancy. But when we reach the top of the stairs! There's all the beer tanks and gear with a long bar down the side wall."

On our way out, I tapped on John's door to invite him and his wife to join us, but John told me they needed to stay in and rest a while longer, so Astrid and I followed Skoot and Loose to the subway station, where we caught a train to Times Square.

Coming up from the underground Astrid hugged me close to her and told me, *soto voce*, that the total circus atmosphere of this place never ceased to make her marvel. "I've heard that there are places like this, all lit up in Tokyo, but this is the only place like it I've seen," she confessed.

We made our way down Broadway, turned onto 42nd, and there it was, the Times Square Brewery.

Ever the historian, Skoot told us, "Legend has it that these guys started in a condemned industrial building, but they were finally forced out when the building was torn down, so they relocated here. Word on the street is they brought a good following from the original place."

The restaurant floors had a healthy lunch crowd for a Monday, but the numbers thinned as we reached the upper deck. Wheels was at the bar with a nearly full glass in front of him.

"Had a hard time holdin' all these stools f'you'all," he told us with a big grin. "As you can see, I fought'm all off so good, they got scared an' split."

We did the fist-bang greeting thing, Astrid hugged Wheels and then took the stool next to him and the rest of us spread ourselves down the board on either side of them.

"I recommend the English Style Pale Ale," Skoot told me. I nodded, trusting my friend. At one time, Skoot used to brew his own beer, so he knew of what he spoke. Wheels said he always favored a dark beer. "Dark beer for a dark cat," he grinned nodding his head in time to the solid funk on the bar's stereo. Loose agreed that the Northern England Brown Ale "swung like a temple bell in an earthquake!" Astrid said she would stick with Pilsner, like what they usually served back in Oslo.

The attendant brought our drinks and we started talkin' about how the gig was goin' and what we'd seen of the city. When we mentioned the chicken shack up in Harlem and our friend Baxter, Wheels' eyes lit up.

"A'ight man, I know that cat Bax. We hired him f'my little brother's wedding, take him and his lady to the reception. And, if I'm recallin' right, it was Bax's buddy catered the reception, Yeah, man, if you goin' up there again, take me with you, *reet?*"

Astrid was served first, naturally. As the other glasses were set before us, she took a sip. "For a micro brew, this Pilsner isn't very impressive," she announced. "If they served something like this in Oslo, they'd have nothing but tourists. No Norwegian would drink this stuff, especially at the price they're charging!"

The bartender took a step back and looked around the room to see if anyone had overheard my lady. Eyeballin' that he was cool with the crowd, he rushed forward to offer baby a choice of some other brew for a replacement

"Hey, Pale Ale is pretty good," Skoot interjected. My red hat nodded that Pale Ale would fill the bill while Wheels and Loose drank deep, clinked their glasses together and the bass player said, "S'ok m'man. Don't worry about it. Anyone can do Pilsner, it's these English brews that count."

For a refill, Astrid joined Skoot and me knockin' back the ale. After three or four rounds, we all decide to walk around Time Square and look at the signs. I left the bartender another generous tip as I felt slightly embarrassed by my lady's frankness, although I had sampled her first beer and I agreed with her heartily.

We ambled around the famous square, checked out Skoot's busker from the previous day and grabbed the train back uptown. We reached **Dig!** with about five minutes for a quick sound check before we kicked off the night with Loose's "Horn Gone Blues."

# Chapter 63

Our mood was high as we finished a killer diller gaggle of tunes with some of Monk's "Bemsha Swing," but it didn't last long. Leavin' the stand we saw Loose's buddy Sol pushing through the crowd to reach us. He was clearly upset, wringing his hands as his eyes jumped around the room.

"Lucian, Lucian," he cried. "What is happening? I went home tonight, sat down with my family to supper and the phone rings. The cops tell me to meet them at my shop right away, someone has driven a stolen car through my front window."

My curiosity was peaked as Loose hugged his friend and asked him how bad it was. "Terrible, terrible," moaned Sol. "Three of my finest horns crushed beyond repair! One was that very expensive Yanagisawa baritone that Skoot had just tried out yesterday, and one of my King's as well as a Selmer Mark VI tenor worth seven, maybe eight grand."

I had to ask, "Does it appear to be an accident?"

"No," he wailed. "Cops say it was a robbery, they called it 'smash-and-grab'. People in the brownstone across Bedford said they saw two men and two cars. The first car jumped the curb and flew right into my store front, the second one, a jeep thing, pulled up to the curb behind it, then the two men ran into my shop and started carryin' things out!"

By now the rest of the band was around us in a circle. Skoot asked, "Do you know what they took?"

"That's the strange part," Sol told us. "They took another old Martin alto saxophone, a newer model than the Art Pepper horn, and they took two old brown Martin sax cases from the back. Oy, and the mess they made! They opened cases and just dropped the horns on the floor. They smashed a display case, a big glass square with a new Yamaha tenor in it. The horn looks like it was hit by a truck as well.

"And sopranos, they took four nice soprano saxes, all brand new expensive models, I just don't understand it!"

"Think this could be related to the business with the Art Pepper horn?" asked my piano-man Dave. "I mean, like, why would they take empty Martin cases?"

"Oy," Sol replied, "And one of the Martin cases had a priceless old Conn in it! They threw the horn against the wall, major damage to this poor ol' sax, and they take the case? What is this?"

Loose was now looking stunned. "Are you serious," he asked? "Why would they do something like this?"

"I might have brought this on myself," Sol was shakin' his head. "Remember I said I sent a cashier's check? Well I got a good friend at my bank, went to school with me. I got him to look into things for me and he found that my check hadn't been cashed yet. It wasn't easy, but somehow, he got the word out that the payment was no good, kinda like stopping payment. When the money showed up in some company's deposit, they refused to honor it. Believe me, it cost me a few bucks to do it, but it saved me plenty. Well, I thought it saved me plenty, now? What do I know?

"It might'a put me on these guy's list somewhere. I was thinkin' one crooked man, what could he do? Now, I'm thinkin', Sol, you were crazy. You don't realize who you're dealin' with." The horn dealer raised upward empty palms in front of his body in a gesture of surrender.

"So, Mr. Lindstrom," he looked up at me.

"Lars, man, I'm just Lars"

"Okay, Lars, your musicians here have told me you are sort of a detective. Maybe you can come around tomorrow, look at my place, tell me what you think?"

"Hey," I replied, "Really, the cops are much better equipped to deal with this sort of . . ."

"Cops tell me, Solly, they say, we've filled a report. Just send it to your insurance and they'll pay off. 'You aren't investigating, lookin' for the bad guys?' I ask. They tell me they'll check with pawnshops, like that and keep an eye open for the horns. 'What about the thieves, I ask?' 'Solly,' they tell me, ' . . . do you know how many break-ins we get every day around Brooklyn? There isn't time. If we're lucky and they're as dumb as most crooks, we'll get'm behind bars before long, what can we say'?"

"Did they find fingerprints? Any other evidence?" I asked.

"They said these guys must'a been wearin' gloves. Not a print on the hot car, nothin' they could find on the horns they'd handled. All the neighbors saw was black pants, big black coats with the collars turned up and black baseball hats."

I noticed that Dave was looking at his wristwatch. It was time to jump back on the stand for another set. I told Sol I'd give him a call the next day, picked up my horn stepped into the spotlight.

# Chapter 64

We finished the night as best we could, but the heart had gone out of Loose's playing. He had some good ideas, but not a lot of fire in his horn. Seeing his mood, I gave him a solo spot in the last set, had him play "The Thrill is Gone." His mood put real feeling into the ballad; a sort of outlet for the pain he felt in empathy with his friend. He sounded out so much real depression at our audience I had to fire off a couple really up and happy cookers to bring them back before closing. We ended our night with the calypso-rhythmed "Barbados Carnival" penned by bassist Chris White for Dizzy's band. I did my best on the vocal, hopin' it might cheer things a little.

At ten the next morning, I got up, dressed, and went out in the hall to phone the number Sol had given me. We agreed to meet at his shop around noon. Sol instructed me where to get on and off the subway to reach him.

I tried to steal quietly back into the room to prepare for the day, but Astrid awoke anyway, so we went out to the buffet to have breakfast. Over coffee, eggs, Swedish waffles and shrimp salad, Astrid said she was going with me. I explained that I could be dealing with murderers or, at the least, ruthless thieves. While I would love to have her company and was confident that she would be a help in spotting clues or patterns, I didn't want the wrong sort of people making our association and thereby putting her in danger as a way to get to me or Loose. My lady argued that if anyone was watching, they had probably already made the connection, so what more danger could she be in? In the end, John and Lacy had come into the breakfast room and Lacy was excited about the big stores we had driven by the night before. Lacy convinced Astrid that this would be a perfect day to go shopping. Astrid quickly got in the spirit and offered to invite Tabitha, and offer her gas money if she could drive us.

At a little past eleven, I ankled out to the Cathedral Park subway station and caught the "B" Line heading toward Brooklyn under the heart of Manhattan and the East River. It was an interesting ride, a great opportunity for people watching. All sorts of interesting characters got on and off as I rode; young folks with piercings and tats, a tall cat with a Mohawk hairstyle carryin' a guitar case, some leather boys and some cats and chicks who must have been living rough judging from their layers of clothes and unwashed appearance. All in all, about like the waterfront in San Pedro, 'cept they're much happier in Pedro 'cuz the temperature rarely drops below 68 degrees.

I exited the underground at Newkirk Avenue, and then hoofed it for about three blocks. Sol's Saxophone Shop was easy to spot. A crew of glass men shuffled around out front, two men tuggin' at the corners of a large sheet of temporary plywood while others unfastened padding and straps from a sheet of window glass. Sol stood in the doorway wringing his hands and muttering. When he saw me coming down the road, he shot forth with his hand extended.

"Mr. uh, Lars, I'm so glad to see you. My god, this window, cleaning up, its costing me a fortune. I should have let them keep the money," he moaned, "It would have been cheaper."

"Right, Pops," I told him, "But then you couldn't collect the insurance. Won't your policy cover most of this cleanup and repair?"

"Oy," he shouted. "Those bastards will pay some of it, maybe most of it, but I'll be fighting with them all the way, believe me! I've dealt with insurance men before, and I always lose unless I involve my lawyer. And then I still lose, 'cause I gotta pay the lawyer when it's all done!"

I motioned toward the store with my head, "So let's take a look inside, man. Clue me to what they did and lay the damages on me, like, all you know."

Sol turned on his heels and led me inside, muttering all the while about prices, values and modern injustices. Once inside, the man turned to his right, throwing out his hands like a model on "The-Price-Is-Right," presenting the wreckage behind the plywood that was being pried loose from the outside.

A carpenter knelt down, nearly finished with the low front wall that would support the large display window. He was putting new pieces of flooring on the platform that would once again hold up instruments on display. Mangled black expandable grating hung in pieces on either side of the opening, the bottom half of one side bent out at an improbable angle where the intruding vehicle had pushed it aside. A plastic Buick hood ornament hung from the twisted metal.

Two bent and crushed saxophones rested atop a glass display case filled with flutes, sax mouthpieces, ligatures and other woodwind player's paraphernalia. The glass had been swept up, but the stove-in framework of a five-foot high freestanding showcase hunched over in the room's center. A chrome saxophone stand remained inside, but the featured horn was long gone.

In the back room, instrument cases that had been rudely pulled off their shelves had been re-stacked against the opposite wall. Another flattened silver alto sax lay atop the pile of damaged cases. It was obvious that Sol's intruders had accomplished monumental damage in the very short time witnesses could place them there.

I went through the cases that had been thrown down, opened each one and looked inside for any small clue that could have been left behind. Sol stood behind me, left elbow on his right palm and his chin in his other hand, closely watchin' my every move. Had he been smiling, he would have resembled the late Jack Benny with his thoughtful pose.

I found varying levels of damage: separated tongue and groove corners, ripped black velvet lining, wooden sides shattered with what must have been some heavy rage. I examined the horns that had been returned to less damaged cases. Some had keys and levers twisted or snapped off. Others suffered scratched lacquer or small dents.

Toward the bottom of the pile, in an old non-descript black box, I found an older Martin alto, gold color, but lacking the distinctive modern styling touches of the Art Pepper horn. As I picked it up to check for damage, something caught my eye. There was a piece of paper or cardboard jammed in between the bell and the body of the horn, where a forked bracket connected the two. I pushed it through with my little finger to discover our first real clue.

"Sol, baby, check this out," I aimed over my shoulder as I removed my handkerchief from my jeans pocket to pick up the familiar matchbook from the floor. "I think this proves a definite connection for us. Have you got any plastic zip-lock Baggies?"

"What is it, what have you found?" Sol spoke the words quickly, full of agitation.

"It's a souvenir matchbox, a few years old cause we stopped orderin' matches to give out customers some six years ago when California banned smoking in bars. It's from the club where I play in San Pedro." I held it up between two cloth-covered fingers to show Sol Blondy's old headshot over the slanting text that was the Dive's logo.

"I would say that whoever your visitors were, they not only wanted to let you know about the connection, but I think they also wanted to tell us that they know Lucian and I are here in New York as well."

Sol took a few steps to a chest of drawers under a workman's bench where a saxophone laid partially dissected awaiting a new set of pads. He tried a couple drawers before he found a box of small plastic bags. He turned and held a bag open for me. I dropped the matchbook inside and pressed the ribbed ridges together to seal the sack.

"So are you taking this new evidence to the police here, already?" Sol wanted to know. I told him honestly, that the New York Police probably wouldn't care. "I think I'd better serve you if I send this to a friend of mine in Los Angeles. My friend, a police lieutenant named Tom Cheatham thinks the saxophone scam ties in with an organized gang that is also stealing cargo from the docks in the Port of Los Angeles, and possibly here on the east coast as well. Lieutenant Tom is working closely with the FBI in their investigation, although I doubt if he's told them his suspicions about the Art Pepper horn yet. This may be the one piece of the puzzle that will tie it all together. It certainly proves that we're not just dealing with a cranky loner playin' Internet games."

Sol voiced his agreement and suggested we go two doors down to a little neighborhood bagel place where we could talk about it over a good cup of coffee.

# Chapter 65

Over espressos, Sol talked about the music business, how tough it was to compete with new big-box chain stores springing up everywhere.

"I'm just lucky I specialize. If I was just selling horns and general music supplies, I would have been out of work ten years ago, believe me. The Internet is what saved me, that and my knowin' so much about classic saxes."

The old sax man raised his cup, took a sip and continued, "I had earlier started goin' to garage sales and thrift stores with my wife; that was a kinda hobby for her. I start to notice people giving horns away! Gran'dad's classic Selmer Cigar Cutter, a very rare and sought-after instrument, they got it out by the curb with no price. I ask 'How much,' they tell me make an offer.

"Well, I've only got forty-nine bucks in cash on me, so I offer forty-nine, and these people are all over me with praise and thank yous.

"By the way, did you want a little pastry or something? I'm feelin' a little peckish." Sol went up to the register and came back with a couple pieces of Baklava. He set the plastic dish in the center of the table saying, "Enjoy! Enjoy!" Then he continued his story.

"So anyway, I put this tenor sax in my store window. Within a month, I'm offered four grand, just like that." The small man shrugged and made an apologetic face at me. "So I start goin' to estate sales, garage sales, thrift shops, swap meets. I find some saxophones for a fair price, where I can still make a buck, but I find lots more that people just want me to take off their hands! Nobody knows the value of these old saxophones anymore, they're just more baggage to these families! 'My son played it in school, but he got tired of it,' 'it was my dad's and since he's gone, it's just takin' up space in the attic,' all these sad tales I'm hearin'."

Sol took a bite of his Baklava. With his mouth full, he went on. "About this time, my son says, 'Pop, I should build you a web-site on the Internet.' What did I know of computers? I told him sure, knock yourself out. Then the surprise comes, from all over American and Europe, people are e-mailin' me, asking 'Can you get me a Mark VI bari with a low 'A',' 'Can you find me an old King Zephyr tenor in good playable condition?' All these customers I've never met!" He swallowed and took a sip of coffee and another nibble at his pastry. I'd almost finished both the coffee and the dessert.

"Well, I've been repairin' and rebuildin' saxophones for years. Guy I bought this store from? I was his sax tech until he retired and offered the place to me, so now I've got so much saxophone business, which I like anyway, I can afford to lose the other part of the store. I stopped carryin' trumpets and violins, I passed my school band rental stuff to a competitor who's strugglin' and I'm happy bein' the saxophone man. At least I was 'til this shit started. I'm sorry, I'm just ranting on. Forgive me."

"It's cool," I told him. "The background run-down is helpful, Pops."

He pushed his chair back. "I'm takin' up too much of your time," he told me. "Let's go back to the shop."

In his store, Sol asked how much I wanted to look into things for him. "Hey," I replied, "This is kind of a hobby thing for me, Gates. I'd feel like a bad guy myself if I took money. I can't promise anything, anyway. I'll just nose around and if my efforts do the dance for you, like, bring you to *hapsville* with the gig, that's all that matters. Like, I'm not a detective, man, I'm a musician! And I don't like seeing other music cats like you and Loose getting' burned down!"

# Chapter 66

Tuesday we hooked up with Bax and Tabitha again. We swung by a mailbox, so I could get the Blondy's matchbook from Sol's off to Tom, and then headed out to have a look at some of Long Island. Bax steered his big beautiful piece of Detroit history down the Westside Highway, which became Joe DiMaggio Highway before it crossed the harbor into Brooklyn. From the bridge we had a great shot at Lady Liberty out across the water.

We stayed on the coast road, around past Coney Island. Just before the Naval Air Station, after Bax stopped to pay a toll, we turned right down a peninsula that took us to Rockaway Beach. Once again, he wouldn't hear of our contributing anything.

We got out at the strand there, took off our shoes in spite of the cold, and walked on the sand. Astrid found some colorful shells that she kept putting in my coat pockets until they were nearly full. When we turned back toward the car, Tabitha shot Astrid a wild look and said, "Last one to the Caddie is a *hopeless square!*"

We all took off running. About halfway back, I was feelin' it, not used to heavy exercise. Bax had stopped and sat down to catch his breath, so I did a halt for myself and we walked the rest of the way. When we caught up with the girls they were still laughin' as they each were was tryin' to catch their own wind.

Back in Bax's ride, I emptied the shells from my pocket into a plastic shopping bag I found on the floor. Astrid and I sat back, her body hard against mine, and listened to our native guides tell us about the landscape. Tabitha pointed out Fire Island, just across a small bay. Then the road went inland, with thick woods all around us and an occasional glimpse of water. The strip of land we were motoring along was growing thinner, often presenting water on both sides of us. Bax announced that we had almost reached lands end and, at a place called Hither Hills State Park, we turned around to head back.

Around half-past-three, we stopped at a quaint little fish house that extended over the water of Hampton Bay on wood pilings. Tabitha said we had to try the lobster; it was the very best in the world. We feasted on lobster, baked potatoes and coleslaw, but I maneuvered to grab the check and scored. Bax argued a little, but he let me buy them dinner. "Believe me," I told him. "We owe you a few meals, brother."

Highway 495 took us straight back to the 59th Street Bridge and Manhattan. We negotiated some rush hour traffic, but made it back before Bax's Caddie turned into a pumpkin. Astrid and I had time for a shower and a drink before the show. We hit **Dig!** early and grabbed us a couple gin and tonics.

# Chapter 67

Halfway through our **Dig!** gig, and we were still seein' new faces every night. I awoke Wednesday feelin' *aw-reet* with the world! Much of my new found groovitude was wakin' up next to Astrid, but I couldn't deny how totally *voot* it felt getting' my name out in the Apple.

Astrid rolled her body into mine and kissed me good morning then pressed her head into my chest and wrapped arms around me. I started thinkin' it was time to make the legal move with her, ring the chapel bells of joy, and set up the proverbial little cottage in the 'burbs. We were both too up there in years to hear the pitter patter of anything but little cat-fuzzed feet, but that was cool, Astrid already had a daughter, and I was just a big kid myself.

Over coffee and pastry, I told her I had *legal eyes*, asked her if she would consider middle-aislin' it with me. "Oh, Lars," she cried, "It is so nice of you to ask, but . . ."

"But what?" my mind went racin' ahead. Was all this happiness just a fantasy of mine?

"Lars, baby," she told me in melancholy tones, "marriage is a big step, especially when I have a home and a good job in Norway, and you're a jazz musician. Oh dear, how do I say this. I don't want to hurt you, but I've seen how you live, day-to-day, gig-to-gig. I'll bet you don't even have a savings account. How can you support a wife?" She took my hands in hers, staring deep into my green orbs. "I'd like to move to California, if I could find a job there and be nearer to you. Then we could see if we could make it together. One step at a time, baby, and we'll see where our love takes us. *Jeg elske du!*

"I do love you, you know, very deeply," Astrid's eyes did the misty thing and she snuffled once. "I'm not interested in any other. You are the perfect lover for me and I find so much to love about you." She wiped her eyes with her palms. "Oh Lasse," she moaned. "Lets just give this some time, please. Just let me think about it." Then Astrid got up and moved quickly back to our room.

As my eyes followed her, I noticed Barbro by the doorway. "You had a phone call earlier," she told me. "I took down the number and told the man you'd call him back." I recognized the number. It was Sol's shop in Brooklyn. I made the call and found he had more information for me. He wanted me to come by at two this afternoon to meet someone and talk.

Back in our room, I asked Astrid if she wanted to ride the subway to Brooklyn with me when I went to see Solly. "It's okay," she told me. "Tabitha wants to take Lacy and I to see some museums. I'll see you later this afternoon and we'll grab a simple dinner. Maybe we could walk around the corner to Tom's again."

# Chapter 68

I shuffled to the subway stop feelin' blue and drug. Here was the old capitalist thing again rearin' its ugly head. My first wife had split over short bread, although lookin' back, that wasn't really such a bad thing. Her head was never on quite straight, she wasn't really that into the music and she said my friends creeped her out. All-in-all, I was much happier when she split.

As I hit the platform, the "B" train was breakin' through the tunnel at me. I got to Sol's place early to find him heating a big sax pad over a Bunsen burner. He pressed the pad into a low B♭ key on a Mark VI tenor, and then looked up at me. Sol wiped his hand on a stained leather apron then extended it to me.

"My friend will be picking up this saxophone in a few minutes," he said. "I think you'll find him interesting to talk with. He was a longshoreman here for a while as a day job."

I pulled up a wooden stool next to Sol and we hit a few pleasantries; weather, how's the family, how's the gig and that rap. While I was describing a table of high-rollin' Italians who had parked themselves ringside last night and kept sending up drinks and tips I hear an electronic "bong" from the wall above our heads.

"That'll be Kennedy," Sol announced. He went to the shop briefly and came back with a coffee-and-cream skinned dude of some seven feet with a big natural blond afro. The man's vines looked classy and expensive. His silk tie was barely wide enough to cover the buttons on his ivory-colored silk shirt. Below his baggy brown trousers, he had highly shined two-tone wing-tip shoes of chocolate and bright white.

He smiled and we slapped hands. "So you that frantic trumpet cat glommin' all the ink these last few brights. Daddy, I am into your sound, heavy-duty! My name is Kennedy, Kennedy Bourké. I was born th'day John Kennedy got his ticket punched, and my mom idolized the man and his brother, so she named me for both of them brothers."

"I haven't tried it yet," Sol interjected, "but I've finished the pad job on your tenor." He tightened a screw that held the low B$^b$ key mechanism in place and handed the horn to Kennedy. The tall man picked it up, and blew a few mean, frantic licks, including a chorus of Bird's "Donna Lee," then brought the brass horn down from his chops and exclaimed, "*Cool!*" He wet the reed, ran some scales down to the bottom, unhooked the axe from his neck strap and set it in an open case on the workbench. To Sol, he said, "Pops, you a miracle worker! No one else ever gon' touch my horn cause, daddy, you the only sax man I trust!"

Then Kennedy turned to me. "So I hear you been diggin' on some uncool doin's on the dockside, king. I put in some time out there as a casual, while I was doin' time at the Manhattan School. It's scut work, but the pay was *grandiose.*"

"How'd you get a day job like that," I asked with genuine curiosity? "That's a long way from musician's kicks, babe."

"Yeah I know," came my answer. "I grew up 'round the Big Sleazy, dig? Like, *Vieux Carré City.* My dad, he'd aw'ready split our crib, but he had a shoeshine stand on Canal, so I'd go see him often. He always said, Kenny, boy, you don't wanna scuffle like me. You get you a real job. From then on he keep introducin' me to his customers who worked on the riverside. Finally, one of'm brought me down t'the union hall and I started doin' casual work.

"But the music was always my *first lady*, y'dig? I put in two years, seven months an' fou' days a'sweatin' on them docks, til I saved the daddy green to get inta school here in New York. 'Fore I come here, the union gave me a recommendation that got me onta the docks on the Hudson and East Rivers."

I jumped right into the head of the riff. "You ever meet a guy named Elwood de Gier? Or his pals?"

Kennedy's head started to nod up and down to a slow jivey rhythm. "The Woodman's Gang," he spoke. "Oh yeah, I remember the Woodmans. I got the feelin' those boys carried some serious prejudice in their hearts. Wouldn't talk to me. Matter of fact, they didn't talk much to nobody outsid'a they own circle."

"Were they known as the Woodman's Gang around the docks?" I asked.

"Gossip tagged'm that," the tall man told me, "Wasn't nothin' official. But they was some bad boys, I'll tell you!

"When I first arrived here, didn't know no one, I walked inta a meetin' they was havin' in Warehouse 48. I'm bein' friendly and copasetic, just tryin' to fit in, new kid on the block an' all that. One of'm, cat had two first names, Billy somethin', he's talkin' nice to me if a bit condescending. While he's talkin', three of his crew come up behind me and take me down, start kickin' me, callin' me names an' sayin' their crew wants nothin' t'do wit me. When I tell my boss, he say just steer clear those boys. He says they'll lie and stick together, bully some others into lying with them and I'll never prove they hit me. After that, I mind my own business around that crew, but I keep hearin' thangs about them being like the mob, maybe even killin' peoples what get in they way. Bad News City!"

Solly had told the man what had happened to his shop. I added that I thought the Woodman might be involved, and I told him the story of Loose and Art Pepper's phantom alto. Sol added his experiences in the arrangement. When the tale had been fully told, Kennedy put his face into incredulous mode.

"Thought I dug some fresh paint and new glass, pops," he told Sol. "Didn't know someone had tried to boost y'r shop, though." Deep thought painted his demeanor for a few bars, and then he asked, "Why you think it be Elwood. Word on the street is he and two other a'tha Woodmans died in some work accident."

I told Kennedy about my experience in the Pedro warehouse, when Loose was summoned to cop his sax. And I took the story through my meetings with Mallory and Guido. By now Kennedy had found his own stool and was sitting across from us, his head still bobbin' as he heard me out.

"Riff is definitely in a solid minor key, m'man," he told me. "If de Gier and his buddy is still on the field, then anything is possible. I got the impression those boys would sell they own grandmothers to a pimp an' then ask'm to grant they friends freebies every Saturday night! Bad, bad jive."

Kennedy's eyes glazed as he had another deep think. "Sorry I cain't help you more, pops," he said as he came back to the conscious world. "But maybe my ol' bossman can. You can find him 'most every day at the end of shift at a little hole-in-the-wall called **The Dockside**, right where Pine Street runs into the East River. I don't know the street address, but you cain't miss it. Dudes name is Anthony. Big Sicilian guy, I mean, short, y'know, but big around, dark hair, dark eyes set, like, way back in his skull, man. Looks like a weight freak, real menacing, fat, double neck, but t'dude's really a sweetheart. You can say I turned you on to him. I think he can help you."

With that said, Kennedy followed Sol out to the register and ran a gold card through to pay for his horn repairs.

# Chapter 69

I had a little nod at Barbro's when I got back from Brooklyn. I don't remember what I was dreamin', but I was woken up by a flushing toilet, feeling solid platinum!

"Oh, you're back from Dreamsville," Astrid stated as she came out of the bathroom. "Give me a minute to freshen-up and we'll take that walk to Tom's. Or do you have some other place you'd like to try?"

"Why don't we just do some strollin' around the neighborhood and see what we find?" I suggested. "We haven't taken the time to really scope the local scene yet."

Astrid threaded an arm around me, pulled our bodies together, and then turned her face up to mine. "You're not mad at me?"

"Why should I be mad at you," I asked?

"I was afraid maybe I hurt your pride this morning," she told me. "I didn't mean to be unkind. I just never looked that far ahead. Like, to your serious *legal eyes*," she burned me down with a frantic, ***off-for-moon-city*** smile. "I'm just enjoying these wonderful feelings we're sharing; like a school affair thing. I just know I want to be near you as much as I can."

We ambled down 112th, moving together like two people in a slow sack race. Our feet took us south down Broadway, past some interesting cafes and bistros. We watched people, pigeons and places go by. At 106th, we turned eastward. Amsterdam Avenue looked interesting, so we hung a left uptown and kept to our tortoise pace. I thought we might go all the way to Columbia University and look around, but between 110th and 111th, the smell of curry wafted towards us from a storefront. The sign announced *The Bengal Café*.

Astrid looked at me. I turned to her, met her gaze, and we boogied, arm-and-arm through the portal where a man of medium height man in a cranberry turban showed us to a back booth. Sitting down, we both burst out laughing like loose-wigged hopheads.

Our be-turbaned wallah brought us large bottles of Kingfisher lager and deep-fried cheese poori bread with a few small silver bowls of dipping sauces. Astrid was craving Chicken Tikka Masala, and I decided to try the less spicy Seafood Biryani. I think the meal was exceptional, but I must confess that I was paying more attention to my *shape-in-a-drape* dinner partner than to the food I put in my mouth. We joked, giggled, shared unspoken affection and another large lager through our curries and out into the evening air.

When we walked into **Dig!**, Kennedy was ensconced at the bar. I noticed he had his tenor case by the barstool. I introduced Astrid, they hugged and Kennedy and I did the hand slap thing again.

With greeting rituals out of the way, Kennedy asked, "Mind if I sit in for one number? I had the night off, so I swung by, and I was thinkin' I sho' would like to put on my résumé that I played with yo' band."

I kept my face straight and told him "No."

Then, before his falling chops hit the deck, I added, "You can sit in for more than one tune, m'man. Do the night with us and I'll be honored."

His "Aw-reet!" was so loud that heads turned around us.

I led Kennedy to the bandstand and made introductions all around. Wheels and Kennedy already knew each other and had gigged together a few *blacks* ago. Since my sax players both blew E♭ horns, I loaned Kennedy my book, which was in his key, to scope the chords and the charts. He knew most the tunes already, the standards and jazz classics. We kicked it off with Coltrane's "Giant Steps," just to get Kennedy jump-started. It was our best sounding night yet. I was almost ready to call Blondy and ask if she could afford one more regular.

# Chapter 70

My second meeting with Guido the next day flowed more smoothly than the first. His man, Ricky, was waiting at the gate to welcome me in the light rain. He was dressed in cowboy boots and a cheap, green, plastic poncho. Ricky's blue "Mets" cap was dripping, but it seemed to keep the water out of his eyes. Entering the warehouse, he momentarily removed his sky piece and shook the drips from the cloth. A little more water wouldn't hurt this place, there were already damp tracks from a forklift and watery boot prints heading in all directions across the concrete.

The short and wide figure that was Guido waited, leaning forward on the railing outside his mezzanine office and chewing the stub of a long dead stogie. Today his suit was gray sharkskin. The black brogues on his feet told of the extent to which he might do any heavy work in the dockside environment.

For this meeting, the conference table had been pushed back against the wall and two of the plastic folding chairs set before his desk for a more intimate chat. Guido rolled his black high-back leather throne rearward and opened the bottom right drawer on his wide desk. He came back up with a half-full bottle of Black Jack Daniels.

"How's about a little eye opener while we chats," he asked? Although it was just past noon, which was, like, first thing in the morning for me, I accepted his hospitality.

"Ricky, would you'se mind findin' us a couple a clean glasses while you're up?" The team leader rummaged briefly in a cabinet at the back of the room. I noticed a small sink and a grubby looking coffee maker by where Ricky was doin' his search. He returned with a pair of old, water-spotted Flintstone jelly jars.

Guido poured generous shots for the two of us, well past Fred's naval. Ricky sat to my right and didn't seem to notice that he wasn't offered a drink. Must be the pecking order here. Ricky probably had his own bottle hidden in his workspace.

I swallowed some of Guido's liquor, then hit him with a shot across the bow to catch him off guard. "You didn't tell me that de Gier and his buds had a sort of gang goin' here. What did they call themselves? The Woodmen or some handle like that?"

Guido knocked back a healthy slug from his own booze, and then told me, "Yeah, well, that's the problem. We could never prove nuttin' except they was a very exclusive crowd. They didn't mix, but they always came to work on time, volunteered for a bunch of overtime, seemed like model workers until the feds started lookin' at 'em." Guido leaned back and tented his fingers, touching them briefly to the tip of his nose.

"There's a lot of idle talk goes 'round a place like this. If I listened to all of it, it would drive me nuts, y'know? This bunch is a gang, this guy's seein' his pals ol' lady on the sly, the night crew is sellin' the Brooklyn Bridge to the guys on the day shift. Too much bullshit to waste my time on. They looked good on the outside, they got the job done. How'm I s'pose to know dat there's rot inside'm?"

Nice save, but thin. I continued. "So is there still gang activity on the waterfront?"

"Gang activity," the wide man pondered. "How does one describe gang activity. Some people say labor unions are just a big legalized gang." Now the union boss seemed to be waffling.

"I've got crews that stick pretty tight, I got a few very open and friendly crews, I got plenty a' guys in the middle just do the job and go home. Some of the groups get together at a local cocktail place after work and don't welcome other groups or casuals into their party. Some guys might meet after work at a secret opium den fa' all I know or care. Long as the job gets done and no hassles come back on me or the union. So if we're done playin' twenty-questions, I got some papers you'se can take back to Mallory." He handed me a 9x12 brown envelope, sealed with wide beige plastic tape.

"Now," he told me, "just for your own rather rude curiosity, I'll tell ya' that we are still havin' some problems." He tipped more amber liquid into his makeshift whiskey glass and motioned toward mine. I nodded that it was cool, he poured and continued his soliloquy.

"Gang activity? I couldn't say. But the level of goods beatin' feet is risin' again, almost as bad as two years ago before our friends did a floater. From what folks are tellin' me off-the-record, the containers gettin' looted all belong to companies that refuse to dole out protection monies. The feds can't pin it to any one crew, but they can't eliminate any either. Maybe it's what you'se'd call a gang. The government boys call it racketeering and they're makin' life hell around here, al'ays pullin' crews off the job for more questions. I'll tell ya, I'm fed up with it, but what can I do?

"Maybe Mallory's got some ideas. I'd love t'hear'm!"

Guido tipped back his jelly jar and emptied it, then stared out his office window at empty space or distant thoughts. Still doin' the distant gaze thing, he spoke again. "Mallory says you'se do some kinda detective work. Says you saved the LA harbor from some kinda terrorist bomb."

He turned back towards me, refilled his glass without offering me any. "Anything you'se could find to help us, I'm open minded, y'know? I'd like to find the bad apples and get'm outta here so's to take the heat off me."

I watched Guido return the Jack Daniels to his bottom drawer, slip his reading glasses back on his nose and return his attention to his desktop. I had been dismissed. I finished my drink and followed Ricky out to the gate. I still had some time before Bax was to return. I hoofed a couple blocks along the riverfront, keepin' my orbs focused on the side streets that passed under the Joe DiMaggio Highway on my left, in search of Pine.

The **Dockside Pub** was easy to spot. It was an old, freestanding square of nondescript stucco surrounded by asphalt, sitting in the shadow of the elevated I-478 highway. The parking area was full of big pick-ups and urban assault lorries most of them bearing longshore union decals or bumper stickers.

Even as my eyes adjusted to the twilight of the tiny room, Anthony's large form jumped out before my very eyes, unmistakable. I approached the table where he was holdin' forth about some longshore-groupie hooker who used to come service the docks "in the good old days." I spoke his name and he turned his head to me. His eyes were just slightly crossed, givin' the impression that he was lookin' at someone just behind my left shoulder.

Anthony confirmed what Kennedy and Guido had already told me. The others in his crowded booth of drinkers testified and punctuated with affirmative nods. I asked Anthony why no one had said anything about their believing Elwood was still alive and scammin'. He replied, "The creep ain't our problem anymore. We was glad to see the back side of'em.

"An' give my best to Kennedy. He was a good worker and I wish I still had him workin' for me."

I emerged from the semi-darkness to find Bax and the girls waiting, the Caddie's wipers slapping at the increased volume of rain on Pine Street.

# Chapter 71

Since the sky didn't seem ready to clear anytime soon, we decided to make this our day for museums. The Museum of Modern Art was on our way to Central Park, so we stopped there first. I discovered that Astrid and I had much the same taste in painting, and she was very knowledgeable about art history and styles.

We spent an hour or so in the downtown gallery then headed into the park and the Metropolitan Museum of Art. By late afternoon, when we emerged, the sky had cleared. Bax suggested a pizzeria-*o'rooney* nearby. We left the Caddie parked by the Met and made tracks out to the boulevard for pizza and beer. For our good fortune, the place not only had thick crust pies with a very spicy sauce, but they also had Red Hook Ale on draft! We all hung for a while when the food was finished, drinking ale and basking in the warm glow of love and friendship.

Back at **Dig!**, Wheels brought word that Kennedy still felt like he was levitating from the night before. Everyone sent salutations back via Wheels to tell Kennedy how we had all enjoyed his contribution and held his playing in very high esteem. I passed along the greeting from his former boss, Anthony. I had already expressed to Kennedy that, if he ever made it to LA, I wanted him to come perform with us at Blondy's, and maybe I could get him some other gigs in Southern California as well.

Wheels and Kennedy had done some righteous jammin' since their reunion the previous dark. They were talkin' about puttin' a group together, serious East Coast style, and layin' down some bad hard bop. By late in the bright, when they had established their ideas, they had put in calls to a few of the up-and-comin' piano stars who sounded to them like they might have a feeling for what they had in mind to make a world-class ensemble.

Loose had spent the day with Sol again, over in Brooklyn. Although he lusted after the Art Pepper Martin, Loose had fallen in love with the King saxophone that sported the sterling neck and bell. He swore that, if he didn't get the Martin axe, and could somehow recover financially, he'd buy this other horn, favored by The Bird. Skoot laughed and reminded Lucian that, "Yardbird got a sound like no other out of the King, but he had sounded almost as good playin' a plastic sax, cause *he was Charlie Parker*, and none other."

We sensed a less serious crowd in this *almost* Friday party atmosphere, so we had some fun. We ran down some of our Slim Gaillard tunes, like "Laguna O-Rooney" and "Cement Mixer." We also revived an humorous old Louis Prima and Sam Butera song, "There'll Be No Next Time," the musical story of a man who keeps makin' the same mistakes. The last time we'd played and sang it had been almost a year ago at Blondy's when Jerry Butera, a blues-playin' cousin or nephew of Sam's had sat in with us. The audience broke up over it, they *righteously* dug it, although the band members said on break that it wasn't quite the same without Jerry's drumming behind it.

At last call, everyone was smilin' and happy, band and listeners alike. Mitch Mallory came to the stage as we were summin' up the last chorus of "Straight No Chaser," on which

I had again sung the Gene McDaniel's lyrics. The impresario grabbed the mic and told the remaining drinkers and revelers that he, personally, had never had such a fun evening, and he hoped they had enjoyed it as much as he had, at which the room erupted into applause, whistles and shouts of "Right on," "Yeah, Baby," and "Aw-*right*!" Mitch had more to say, but he was drowned out by the riotous shouting and clapping. Finally, the club owner gave up, put the microphone back in the holder and came around to shake each of our hands and thank us one at a time.

# Chapter 72

Earlier in the week, Bax and Tabitha had hinted that, when our eyelids lifted into Friday daylight, they had "something special" planned for us. John and Lacy were curious, so Bax had said they were invited as well.

Eleven in the bright found John, the ladies and I on the steps in front of Barbro's where the long dark limo drew us in and swung us away up Amsterdam Avenue towards Harlem. John and his lady put it down on the jump seat style captain's chairs, Tabitha and I book-marked my lovely Astrid for the short ride. Our chariot hung a ralph on Martin Luther King Boulevard, then another on Malcolm X, where Bax copped a space across from a series of yellow and blue awnings, each bearing a script moniker: "Sylvia's."

We jaywalked the thoroughfare, passed between some thin trees just coming into bloom and through a portal in the middle of the block. We had entered a huge restaurant. Sylvia herself was there to greet us.

"Bax, honey, you been stayin' away for too long," she told him. "And who are your good-lookin' friends?"

Bax introduced us all around. Sylvia shook hands with John and I, gave abbreviated hugs to our ladies. As she hugged Tabitha, she asked her, "What did you think of that new shampoo I gave you to try?"

"Sylvia, baby, it was just marvelous," Tabitha replied, then turning to us she said, "Sylvia has launched her own brand of cosmetics and hair care products. She is just a wonder!"

When a handsome young brother had seated us and handed us menus proclaiming *Sylvia's Soul Food*, Bax told us about our hosts.

"You all are occupyin' a landmark in African-American owned businesses." He patted Tabitha's hand, gave it a loving squeeze and continued, "Herbert and Sylvia started this place in 1962. It was just one small storefront with maybe enough tables for thirty people. Lord could that girl cook! She prepared such wholesome and good tastin' dishes, and at very fair prices, with the whole family pitchin' in. I don't know how they survived those early years, but they gott'm a following from Harlem and other parts of the city.

"Well, as you saw out front, they now have most of the block, and there's tables enough for hundreds of diners!"

Coffees arrived all around. Good strong coffee, and tasty as well. Bax stirred cream and sugar into his, and then continued. "Sylvia's grub got so popular that about ten years ago, she had to start her own line of soulfood products, included pre-seasoned vegetables, special spices, cornbread mix and her own special recipe pancake mix as well. You can buy her products now all over the country; cookbooks on how to prepare her dishes, as well. She's even opened a second restaurant down in Atlanta."

"Don't forget her son, Van," Tabitha added. "He the brains that got started buyin' up the block and seriously expandin' the place."

"That's right," Bax agreed. "And you'll see folks from all over the planet in here now days; all different nationalities and cultures. They *all* love our Harlem soul food."

At that, plates started arriving; pancakes, eggs, sausage and some killer potatoes! We all dug in and *dug* it. For the next half hour, our conversation was limited to "ooo's," "ahh's" and comments on how *reet* and satisfyin' everything was.

While we tantalized our taste buds on Sylvia's home cookin', the room filled to capacity with the lunch crowd. When the plates had been relieved of their victuals by our hungry selves, and coffee's refilled, we all talked about what we might see in the remaining afternoon. Lacy mentioned that she'd been curious about Lady Liberty since she was a child. When they had talked about the Lady in the Harbor in school, she had always imagined herself standing in the narrow balcony around the statue's torch, looking down on the water and the city from that lofty and precarious perch.

"People can get up to that torch and go outside above the water," Astrid asked, eyes wide?

"Not any more," Bax told her. "But at one time, you could climb a narrow stairway right to the top of the monument's arm. I think the metal got weak with age, or somethin'. They stopped lettin' folks up there many years back."

"I think you can still go up to the lady's crown," Tabitha added. "There's windows up there 'top of her head you can look out."

That made our decision for us. We were headed for Bedloe's Island in New York Harbor to visit the turquoise-hued copper-skinned lady of steel that France had presented to America as a gift over a century ago.

At the register leaving Sylvia's, I dug that they were selling a book for kiddies, "Growing Up Sylvia." One of Sylvia's daughters, Brenda, had written the story. I marveled out loud at what this one family had achieved. The girl who was runnin' Bax's card told me, "It jus' took love, family and hard work, sir. Love of God, love of family, the love of our friends and customers, and a' course love of work." Like, Sylvia and her people were right in there!

I got my head around that pretty good. These were solid citizen type folks, the kind of people that made up the best things about our democratic experiment. They had a stone grand little dive here, and I was seriously **boxed**, like, in a chilled, groove way over it.

Bax pointed our chariot straight ahead down Malcolm X. Most of our conversation centered around Sylvia's and the frantic repast we'd all just dug and devoured. I was so into how everyone was layin' it straight on what a solid *gas* Sylvia's had been, that I didn't even cop how we got to the battery and the water's edge.

Bax copped a commercial space for the limo, paid the toll and we made tracks towards a long line of tourists. After winding through this queue of Clydes from around the world, we were funneled into a massive white canvas tent to wait for the next round of tour boats to Staten Island and the Lady. The air had a fresh salt tang in it as we flew over the chop and swell. A couple times, spray from the wind over the water would toss a hint of iodine mist into our faces, but it was as cool as the water itself.

On the dwarf island, we fell in with a flock of cornfeds from a tour bus crowd, headin' up the walkway. A small dirty-blonde ranger chick in green threads lined-us-up for the march then laid the tale on us, with names, dates and historical haps. She led us to an elevator that sent us up through the building that supported the statue. From the rooftop landing, we entered the Lady's copper gown and started up the metal steps.

It was, like, really warm and close inside Lady Liberty. We serpentined upward as I dug the greenish red walls closing in around me. I was Panic City, seriously wigged by the first landing platform. My eyes were darting and I was dripping sweat. John commented that I wasn't lookin' so good.

"Like, I think I'm getting' behind that closterphobia thing, man. My world feels like it's seriously shrinkin'! Like, I hate to burn down the scene, but I think I'm gonna make tracks for the open air."

"Yeah," John agreed. "I feel kinda freaky myself. How's about you ladies, shall we call this one off?"

Astrid and Lacy both told us we were just wiggin' out. They were determined to get to the Lady's crown and look out. We told them we'd meet them back on solid terra firma, like down where we could pull up a big piece of lawn and watch the boats. Bax told us that he'd make the scene up to Miss Liberty's sky piece and keep an eye out for the ladies.

"That's cool," Astrid said, giving me a minor squeeze. "Look up from time to time, *Lasse*. Maybe you'll see me waving from the window up there." The girls were as determined as I was shaky, so John and I followed our trail of breadcrumbs back to the elevator and motored it down to the surrounding parkland.

I fell out for a slow count while John was diggin' the harbor kicks. He nudged me awake when the girls were comin' out of the monument and we got to our feet to welcome them back.

# Chapter 73

The wind had picked up and the boat ride back from Bedloe's Island was an outright chill. Our feet on the firmament of Manhattan, John suggested a sandwich shop he'd discovered near Ground Zero where they made some nutty pastrami, French dipped beef and Po' Boy sandwiches. "I know they've got fried oyster, not Kosher, but they kinda look the other way, and other seafood subs for you, Lars," Lacy told me. "And you won't believe the side dishes! Macaroni salad, coleslaw, home-style potato salad, and its all so good!"

Of course our limo owner hosts knew the place and quickly put down that it was a straight up *gasser*. And that's just what it was. The sign above this frantic old-style deli was lettered in both English and Hebrew. The inside smelled like a very vouty Thanksgiving kitchen; food smells to knock back a smile under your olfactory senses!

My Po' Boy grooved with spices straight out of the Crescent City, strictly Cajon-*o-rooney*. The green pea salad I'd selected was the perfect compliment. I was stone knockin' back my chops around these Cajon-kosher kicks. Astrid was cooing over one of those Po' Boys that did the *Dagwood* bit with a little of every meat and cheese in the house. Everyone was gassed by the groovitude of this quick repast. The sandwiches were so fat that we all ended up baggin' what we couldn't scoff here and now for a later snack.

Bax laid it on us that he had, like, back-to-back nuptial scenes on his dance card for the morrow. Tabitha told us that Sunday, one of them would come for us early. They had eyes to throw a ball for us at their pad over in the Bronx before Astrid's plane left."Like, I had pinned it that you were strictly a Harlem stud, Bax," I stated as a half question.

"Born and bred," he replied, "Though my folks came up from somewhere on the Alabama-Florida line. And my Tabby was born in Georgia and schooled in South Carolina." He smiled over at his bride. Tabitha beamed back at him.

"When I had paid my dues and business started happening easy, you know, with the grease comin' in, we moved across the river. Traded our Brownstone apartment for a house to give our children some room to grow in.

"House seems a bit empty now, with them mostly grown and gone, but we're still stickin', and the mortgage is nearly paid off, so we might just stay there into our golden times, dig?"

I told Bax my lobes were diggin' his words in a major key as we passed Columbus Circle once more, headed uptown. Broadway was becomin' some familiar action by this time. I was startin' to dig it as a natural groove. These mean streets were black-to-white against my home turf of Pedro, but it was cool. I had found some warm feelin's and straight up lovin' folks here that I'd keep in my wig with, like, heavy feelin's and a warm groove.

Friday traffic was light and my introspections were brought up short as the limo set down in front of Barbro's. Lacy and John told Bax they'd catch him Monday for our journey to the airport, and they split. Astrid and I lingered for a few just standin' around through idle words to delay our friend's departure. Tabitha copped to it right away.

"Yeah, baby," she told my lady. "We gonna miss you too. I think maybe I can talk Bax into happenin' by for the early set tonight, though. We'll see you in a few hours."

With that, we said our goodbyes and made our bird inside for a shower and a brief rest before show time.

# Chapter 74

When Astrid and I entered **Dig!** that evening, the club had one of my favorite Gene Ammons sides on the box, "Gentle Jug." The record was all ballads, and played as only the Jug could *sound* a slow tune. Mitch saw us come in, greeted us with a loud, "There you go, dad, you got it all," and went over to turn off the disc player. I told him to leave it for a cut or two, that I was diggin' it. The proprietor gave an affirmative nod and went back to his drink, which was already in progress.

I led my *main day charge* to the small, boarded floor in front of the stage, and held her close. We swung a slow dance together that went right through the quiet between tracks for couple of songs. When we opened our eyes, the band along with Lacy, Bax and Tabitha were standing at the edge of the small square of hardboards. They broke into applause, Astrid gave a girlish curtsey in their direction and I felt heat on my face, like I had just been busted for somethin' really uncool. By this time, others at the bar and various tables had joined in the clapping.

When the thunder of all those hands died away, the band and I claimed the stage, ran through a quick sound check and jumped straight into Parker's "Donna Lee." Astrid and my friends had staked a claim on the center ringside table and Mitch had joined them along with a tray of complementary cocktails. I could see their heads and bodies boppin' to our beat. Almost through the duce of weeks and not a bad night yet! This whole New York deal had me on some kinda freakish high.

Bax and Tabitha ended up hangin' almost through the second set. When they excused themselves, Mitch stayed tight with the ladies and kept the juice flowin'. Mitch's partner, Ruben, joined them as we cut out for our second break. Ruben brought champagne along and set the bubbly-juice all around the small table to offer a toast.

"My partner's brother asked me to take a chance on a group of California cats I'd hardly heard of," he said raising his glass. "Here's to you, Lars, and all your worthy studs that blow with you. You've brought me a fine crowd for the past couple weeks, and I am *very* glad I listened to my partner and took the gamble. Here's to your continued success!"

We raised our glasses, and when I looked around, my peeps dug that the waiters had poured for the full room! Everyone was in on the goodwill thing. My head was wigged out on some distant star. I was wishin' Bax had hung long enough to see this.

My ravishing regal redhead psyched me out. "Bax and Tabby knew about the champagne," she told me. "They said to tell you they wished that they could have stayed, but they both have quite a full day tomorrow. Their thoughts are here with us though. They're like, how would you say? *Good people!*"

# Chapter 75

On Saturday Astrid and I decided to groove behind a slow and mellow kick, just the two of us. We got up early, beating the rest of our caravan to the breakfast bar. We did a quick scarf of the offered fare and got in the wind before the others showed. We walked east along 110th to Morningside Park, where we copped a bench for a few beats and watched the squirrels makin' tracks up one tree and down another. We also dug a pair of *hippie-dippies* lightin' up right out in front of the world. I told Astrid they would probably burn themselves down if they couldn't show more cool than that, and we fell out of the park onto Manhattan Avenue then rounded a traffic circle thing over Central Park North.

We took our time strollin' over the grassy knolls and dales in a light mist that kept threatening serious rain, but didn't deliver. By noonish, a pale sun broke through on our parade. I was feelin' lushed to all ends, but I hadn't had a taste since last night's gig.

Astrid and I mooned around the green lawns like a pair of Minnesota Clydes. We held hands, chased each other around the trees, stopped for kisses on every other bench and even fed the ducks some crusts we'd bagged at breakfast just in case. It was one of those brights where I wished we could hold back the dawn *and* the evening before it!

Somewhere around Central Park Lake, we must have got our heads turned around. We thought we were headed downtown, maybe take in Greenwich Village, but found ourselves staring across the Harlem Meer. So we split from the greenery onto 5th Avenue and made tracks back to Tito Puente Way and over to Park Avenue. Within a few blocks we found a neighborhood tavern that offered lunch and an international selection of beers and ales.

Mellowed out behind some *sweet* cheese sandwiches, French fries and three or four brews, we backtracked to 110th Street and Morningside Park. The young hippies had cut out and left our bench to the squirrels, so we reclaimed our place and necked like horny teens until the wind came up salty and the air turned cold. The vote was unanimous for a quick boogie home to Barbro's, where our necking could resume and maybe even become more serious in the privacy. Leavin' the green space, we dug a pair of clipsters who looked like they had eyes to boost someone. We gave them plenty of space as we split from the park.

# Chapter 76

I held Astrid very close in the cab cuttin' out for the gig that evening. I was already sensing the lonely I'd be strung out under by this time tomorrow when my fine chick was in the wind for her fjord-side homeland. Inside the club, I was semi-drug just leaving her side to mount the bandstand. I put it off til the last minute.

While I was diggin' on the mellow kicks of just holdin' Astrid, in walked Wheels holdin' forth with a cat as tall as himself, wearing jeans and a long-sleeve t-shirt tie-died in bright yellows, greens and reds. The cat had a halo of thick dread-locks surrounding a long, thin face with large brown eyes. My peepers popped and my brain asked me, "Is this real?" The dude with Wheels almost looked like an *anti*-travel poster for a Caribbean island.

Dread-locks waved his hand around as he talked, his voice loud and free. As he pitched his riff to my bass man, I saw that Wheels was steering the man right for Astrid's and my table.

"Here you go, man," he interrupted Dread-locks soliloquy. "Set your eyes on my main man, Lars Lindstrom. Lars, this is my Jamaican buddy, Jam-Man Jenkins. Jam-Man plucks bass strings with '**Jah's Turtles**,' a local reggae band."

The Jam-Man held out a fist. I touched it with my own, and then shared a low high five with the dude.

"I met Jam-Man on the docks," Wheels explained. "He was a kindred spirit, another musician giggin' as a casual to support his musical hang-ups." Jam-Man stretched his narrow face into a wide grin full of large tea-colored teeth.

"Ya, dat be me, mon. I put me back to da loads an' pay me dues all fa' da joy a' da music and d' love of Jah." He did a rapid bobble-head as he talked.

"Thought you might wanna talk with Jam," Wheels told me. "He laid some interestin' news on me the other day when I was cluein' him about Sol's break-in and Loose's horn."

Jam-Man's head was still waggin'. "Ya mon, we be talkin' an' I remember somet'*ing* in me head. Wheels, he t'ink it might be help*in*' ya' mon."

"Jam was in a bar near the docks," Wheels continued. "He was with some other islander friends knockin' back some Red Stripe. They had laid claim to a booth near the back, an' the survivin' Woodmen were on the bench right behind them. Jam knows these cats, cause they often go out of their way to offend any brothers workin' longshore; name-callin', pickin' unfair fights, or just cruel practical jokes, dig?"

"We be for*ward*in' into de bar aftah dees bahd man sittin' down a'ready." Jam-Man told me with wide eyes lookin' serious at me. "Dey be into what dey say*in*', an' don' even pay attention to notice I and my friends sittin' dere."

Wheels took over again. "So, like Jam's in the corner of one of those horseshoe booths, sittin' real close to this other bunch. He couldn't help but overhear these studs goin' on about a big score coming in soon to a dockside near them! They're holdin' forth about some of the latest and fastest computers, a large shipment of these new babies. So, like, who's going to miss fifty or so from a damaged container? Their plan was to swing the crane and knock the box against a bollard *after* they've helped themselves to these new latest-and-greatest babes, burnin' down the container after they got theirs to make sure they didn't damage what would soon be a bonus for themselves. They would all swear the box was 'received in damaged condition,' and fill out the appropriate paperwork for the *insurance.*

"The interesting part is, Jam-Man remembers all the who-ha from when Elwood disappeared," Wheels added.

Jam-Man's head started its cool nod again. "Elwood a va-*ry* bahd mon. He t'reaten me mo' dan once, oh yeas! So I va-*ry* su'prised when dees mon say-in dat Elwood be comin to see dem de *nex'* week. Elwood s'pose to be dead is thinkin' I. But say dem dat he's liv-*an* in California and dey be send-en him his tribute ev'ry job dey be do-*an.* Say I, somet'in not righteous here, but Jam-Man do'n want be jammed up in it, no. "

I asked Jam-Man if he would talk to Guido; tell him what he'd heard. His reply was, "Say I, Jam-Man do'n wan' no-ting to do talk-*an* to policeman. Jam-Man stay away from policeman, an' pray I de policeman stay away from Jam-Man!"

Wheels said, however, that Jam-Man would be aw*'reet* with it if I told Guido, the cops, or whoever, as long as he wasn't dragged into it, just let Jam remain as a kind of an "unnamed source." I figured that if need be I could always let slip the name if they needed testimony to prosecute. Hopefully, just the lead Jam-Man had given us would be enough to move the case forward.

In the corner of my peripheral vision, I noticed Mitch lookin' nervous and pacin' by the small stage, so I told Wheels it was time and excused us adding, "Hope you can stick around to dig a set or two Jam."

"Oh ya," the big man told me. "Wheels, he be *I's wheels,* so I be heah, sure!" I gave Astrid a squeeze and a peck and apologized for not givin' her my full attention.

We played a solid set and when I called union and returned to our table Jam-Man was entertaining my lady with tales of growing up around Port Antonio, Jamaica.

"Ya, fine lady, swear I," he was sayin', "My fatha, he drive de boat fa' Mr. Errol, an' dat's de trut'. Mr. Errol, he die befo'

I born, but I and I feel like I know d'man from what me fatha tell me all 'bout him."

Astrid smiled my way and clued me. "Jam-Man says he grew up on the small island where Errol Flynn lived! His family worked for the actor, and for his widow after Flynn died."

I noticed Jam-Man was avoiding eye contact with me, so I think his tale could have been a put on for Astrid's sake. When I stared him down, he grinned and quickly changed directions.

"I likes jazz too, mon," he laid on me. "I and I play some jazz back in Kingston, when I go-*an* to school."

"That's cool," I told him. "Hope you're enjoyin' the show."

"Mo-*ah* den dat," he said, layin' both hands flat on the table. "I's bass be in Wheels wheels, mon. He say-*an* to me, maybe I can sit in an' jam wit you for a song."

I added another "Cool!" to the exchange, then invited him to go get his axe. The big Rasta man returned in a flash draggin' a big amplifier and a classic Fender bass with no case.

Wheels said, "Mind if I sit one out, pops? I got eyes for the fine brown frame a' that waitress been servin' us. She should have a break a' her own comin' soon.

"Like, I've sounded on her before. She wasn't diggin' my kicks, but now that she's knocked her lobes to me playin' behind your nutty little group, maybe I can make some moves on her."

I wished Wheels some luck then turned all my attention to Astrid, ignoring the draught Mitch had sent me. Jam was busy settin' up his kit and the rest of the cats were holdin' down the brass rail at the bar.

Dave was the first one back on the stand when our break was over. He held a confab with Jam-Man featuring a lot of head nodding. They brought John into the discussion, tappin' out some beats on the edge of the baby grand. As I took the stand, Dave suggested we try the Beatles number, "Ob-la-dee, Ob-la-Da." It sounded reet to me so I gave it the green.

Jam-Man's heavy basement rhythm started us off with John poundin' an island beat behind him. We were soon into a rousing Reggae version of the classic rock tune, all of us glidin' on the strong boomin' beat. Our sonic kicks even brought a handful of dancers up to the floor.

The folks on the boards requested an encore. Others around the room shouted agreement, so we jammed an easy B♭ blues to a slow Caribbean bounce, a solid, frantic crowd-pleaser! The dancers loved it as well as the others, many of whom were rockin' in their seats to the powerful rhythm.

For a moment, I was out there, flyin' beyond worries and troubles. Then Wheels came back on stage, Jam-Man lifted his amp out of the way and we got our old groove back, cookin' like a two-ton commercial oven.

We ended with the ballad, "Deep in a Dream of You." And it all came back to me. In one more bright an' a black, we'd be in the air and in the wind, motivin' homeward. Astrid was set to fly out tomorrow at eight in the twilight. This dream was movin' into history, and I was left with my humdrum life and Loose's missing horn caper. That and the accompanying bring-down of the longshore caper I was scopin' for Mike Mallory and Lieutenant Tom.

I was momentarily drug, but a smile from Astrid brought me around. Let tomorrow bring the bad jazz, tonight my most beautiful and favorite shape on the planet was here with me. Like they say, "Dig these mellow kicks in the *right now!*"

I eyeballed that Wheels was getting' tight with his waitress, which added to my happy dues. This moment was a heavy one, bringin' lots of joy. It would make for some frantic memories for all of us.

# Chapter 77

Sunday morning found us scoffin' a quick morning meal then waiting for Bax out on the Avenue. When the familiar Lincoln pulled to the curb, it was Bax's man, Pete, who jumped out and held the rear door for us.

"Bax and Tab be getting' everything ready up at the house," he told us. "They asked if I could bring you round before I swung by to pick up my customers for today. Since the weddin' is in the Bronx as well, it ain't really out of my way," he smiled as he handed my Astrid into her seat.

Soon we were purrin' our way up Lenox Avenue through the heart of the new Harlem. There was a highway sign telling us we were headed toward Yankee Stadium, but near water, Pete put us onto the Harlem River Parkway, and soon afterwards swung onto I-95 for a short stretch. He then caught the Henry Hudson Parkway. We motored north with the Hudson on one side and some very vouty parkland on the other. When we crossed the Harlem River, the parkland diminished like an A$^\flat$ chord confirming a major resonance. We left the parkway just before more parkland, headed west on the greenery's border to Palisade Avenue and went back toward the Hudson on a small horseshoe spur called River Road. Pete slotted us into a wide driveway beside a large Cape Cod style house.

The limosine business must be a hot kick. Bax's digs was like a jive king's castle. Two stories coated in bright white with dark green trim and vented shutters; it looked like an advertisement for the American square's dream. The fat lawn stretched out at its forecourt could have been a city park in some bergs.

Bax came around the side of the gianormous structure and waved us back toward the stretch. "Tabitha isn't quite ready yet," he told us. "She's been at work all morning whippin' up some dishes for the barbeque. Why don't I give you a little tour of the neighborhood?"

Bax held the door for my lady and me, then parked his frame on the jump seat. "Wave Hill," he called over his shoulder to Pete, and the motor did its move-ahead thing.

We *leroyed* back onto the Palisades Avenue, held forth for some blocks then *ralphed* it onto 252nd Street. As the houses and parkland passed our window, Bax spoke with heavy pride about his borough.

"Bronx has had some very well-known citizens over the years," he told us. "Folks like Edgar Allen Poe, Mark Twain and Teddy Roosevelt. Did you know this area was the birthplace of break dancing? Salsa too, they claim."

Bax explained how it was a very old and well-seasoned area, settled by a Swedish sea captain, Jonas Bronck in 1639. As he was relating Bronck's story, Pete pulled up in front of another mansion thing.

"This is Wave Hill," he explained. "This has been the home to some frantic cats over the years. Samuel Clemens, *Mark Twain*, lived here first. Later it was home to Teddy Roosevelt. Closer to our times, conductor Arturo Toscanini called it his pad."

Pete put the ride in gear again, into the land of the greed heads. Blowin' through a main drag, Bax pointed out a big restaurant, Giovanni's, that advertised "live jazz." "They mix some nutty drinks there," he told us, "And serve some grand Italian dishes with the jazz."

We cruised past Yankee Stadium and Bax checked his wrist. "Guess we can head back now." He nodded to himself and continued. "Tabitha should be cool by now." With that, we slid it back to the west and Palisades Avenue.

# Chapter 78

The inside of Bax and Tabitha's pad was more palatial then its skin foretold. The front hall did its thing around a staircase that brought Mississippi riverboats to mind. The décor and furniture was a bit square to my taste, too fat and Early American, but lookin' at the digs left no doubt; Bax's story was great! From the back balcony on the upper deck, we had as good a view across the Hudson as my rooftop back home gave of the LA Harbor Channel. Tabitha told us that the green cliffs on the other side were the Jersey Palisades. Between here and there, a couple really stickin' cats were fightin' the wind in sleek white sailboats, the smallest of which had to be fifty-feet or more.

Below us, in a killer-diller back yard that sloped toward the water, Bax was puttin' flames to coal-like lumps in a modern "Sharper Image" type barbeque cooker. A nearby picnic table was piled high with potato salad, Cole-slaw, French bread loaves and a makeshift wet bar. Bax had stacks of steaks, whole chickens and raw fish on the end closest to the flame machine.

The day was sunny but with a serious chill in the air just the same. I guess it was an East Coast thing. We all decked-up in sweaters. I was draped in the new blue-gray number Astrid had brought me from Fjords-Ville.

Our lunch proved to be, like, a very vooty feast like some ancient Roman Bacchanal. Casual conversation ruled the downside of noon. Tabitha proudly opened an ice chest filled with imported Rignes Beer for Astrid and me.

"One of the caterers that Bax works with scored it for us, ain't that right Bax honey?" Bax laughed and did the agreement thing with a nod of his wig.

I knocked the caps off four green bottles and we toasted our friendship with our brews from the north. Tabitha and Astrid got serious about the Norwegian beer, but after our primo bottles, Bax poured his second cup from a an aged flask of single-malt and I lushed myself over to the blue British gin jug.

I think we all ate too much. I know we all drank too heartily. After supper and with more strong drinks, we lined up fancy red-striped lounge chairs facing the river where we told childhood stories and watched more sailboats cutting trails in the smooth green water.

Bax's man, Pete, came down the lawn eventually to break up the party. He told Bax the wedding had gone fine, the celebrants were at the reception and he had at least three hours to get Astrid to the airport on time before he needed to return and take the honeymooners to their hotel in Connecticut.

Pete drove us all across the Bronx, side-trackin' to skirt the New York Botanical Gardens, which Bax explained covered over 250 acres, and was worth seein', maybe the next time we came to town. Astrid and I agreed that it was a plan. From there we caught the Cross Bronx Expressway, crossed more water and passed through places with names like Flushing, Jamaica and South Ozone Park. Astrid had turned quiet as Queens flashed by our window, huggin' my arm tight into her side. I glanced down and saw a tear drawing a line down her cheek.

"I really don't want to leave you," she whispered to me. "I don't want to go back home. How long will we be apart this time? When will we get to see each other again?"

I had no pat answers for my great sweet swinging groove double-clutching high non-stop pine-top go of all double swings in beauty, but I hoped we would see each other again soon. "I'm gonna look for some Europe gigs this summer," I told her, though I knew Blondy wouldn't be happy if I took off for a month or more to tour Scandinavia.

At the Air Iceland gate, we clung to each other for four or five minutes; no words and lots of lingering kisses. We were interrupted by Bax touching my shoulder, then touching his wrist-bound timepiece.

"Sorry, man," he said. "I gotta get you back to **Dig!** for your last show and I gotta get this limo back in service for our honeymooners."

Astrid and I kissed once more and I watched her eyes leaking as she turned and knocked me another kiss from the departure gate.

My peeps were spillin' trails of moisture, too, as Pete pointed the motor's nose back to Manhattan. Bax and Tabitha gave me some space to dig on my temporary loss. I think Tabby had nodded off, her head on Bax's shoulder.

"I'm gonna try and get-by for at least one set this evening, man," the limo man told me. "We are gonna miss you both, pops. Tabitha and me haven't enjoyed anyone's company this much in a long time, and I want you to know we'll be keepin' both you and Astrid in our hearts and in our prayers."

I tried to answer, but now my face was doin' some serious leakin'. I got my head and my voice together as we made the turn off Broadway and told them that both Astrid and myself felt the same, and would miss hangin' with them.

I jumped out in front of the club. Bax, Tabitha and Pete all bailed from the limo as well. My friends both gave tough, serious hugs and Pete extended his hand.

"Been a pleasure drivin' you out, pops," Pete told me. I held the door for the limo folks as they got back inside. Tabitha kissed my cheek, and the big vehicle roared to life, leavin' me at the curb.  Entering **Dig!** I dug that Sol was holdin' forth with Loose, talking excitedly and waving his hands around as they talked.  Up on the stand, Sol's Charlie Parker model King Super 20 alto was set up on Loose's sax stand.  They passed me, headed to the bar, Loose's arm around the small man's shoulders.  Skoot and Dave were already ensconced at the bar, gin glasses half-full, or half-empty, depending on how you looked at it.

# Chapter 79

Our final black of the gig gave us a house as crowded as our second night at **Dig!** had been; wall-to-wall fans all charged with energy. I recognized faces in the crowd both from previous shows and from places Bax had taken us. Jam-Man was at the bar with some Rastafarian friends. Georgie, the ex-Navy tenor cat, held down a table with some of the faces I'd met at the chicken shack in Harlem. Kennedy was parked at the bar groovin' to our tunes. Mitch comped the band a few rounds of libation as he beamed over the crowd of drinkers fillin' his club.

Bax and Tabitha were there by break time, pulling up chairs at the already tight "chicken shack" table to join their friends. We did a lot of smilin' and back-slappin' through the breaks then shared another round of goodbye hugs.

When the crowd began to thin and the barman gave last call I was down. In spite of Mitch's effusive praise and promises that he would have us back soon I was feelin' stone drug. I knew I was facin' a night at Barbro's alone in an empty bed that would still resonate with the aura of my special redheaded *frøken*.

I survived the night although I didn't sleep well. Longshoremen and saxophone thieves threatened in my dreams. I got hung up pondering the distance between San Pedro and Oslo, counting sea miles, flight hours and other measurements of the distance separating Astrid from me.

Around nine-thirty, I stumbled out to join the band in the breakfast room, my bags packed and standin' by the door. The rest of the cats were sailin' in dreamland, rushed and lushed on the success of our East Coast adventure and anxious to blow another chorus. I momentarily caught a contact high from their wigged-out mood, but it faded when Bax pulled up for our final airport ride.

It was a gray day, depressing and blustery. Rain started lightly sprinkling crossing the East River. By mid-town Brooklyn, it was sendin' down big buckets, cats-and-dogs city! My peeps were threatenin' to join the deluge.

In the airport terminal, I left the guys in the Jet Blue waiting area to find a quiet bar. At the Flight Deck Lounge, I scoffed an early liquid lunch of gin and lemon twists. When I shuffled back to the Jet Blue area, there were only minutes remaining to boarding time. Loose and Skoot tried to lure me into their conversation, something about how the current Republican administration was tryin' to do away with the pitiful funding for the arts that remained. I was righteously lushed. I just sat and stared ahead at the counter where a cat and a chick in Jet Blue drapes were checkin' their list.

Once onboard the bird and belted to the chair, I tried to clear my head, but my wig wasn't ready to do straight. I was on the aisle, my horns safely stowed under my seat, John and Lacy between me and the porthole.

The stew chick brought me two small bottles of gin with a bag of mini pretzels and a bottle of tonic water. The fermented juniper berries juiced me into a black hole of slumber. When John shook me and laid it on me that we were over California and about ready to raise the seat backs, I was momentarily unsure of where I was. The tinny voice of the cabin steward spewing forth the words about our approach to Long Beach brought events back into focus. I was homeward bound, just me and the band, no Astrid. The unopened bottle of tonic rested in the pouch on the chair ahead of me. It was time *get with it* back at Blondy's; back to my humdrum life, problems of dockside pilferage and Loose's lost horn. Beyond the aircraft's metal skin, the voice assured us, it was "three-forty local time, sunny and seventy-eight degrees," but that dark cloud of funk was still hangin' over my present life.

# Part III

## Back On
## the Left Coast

# Chapter 80

We emerged into the bright sunshine, my peeps burnin' from the smog and glare, my back achin' from some eight hours of sleepin' scrunched into a weird pose. I fell in line at the baggage claim area with the rest of my troop, tryin' to concentrate on the flow of assorted cases and carryalls.

My wig was unfocused by shouts and scuffling that sounded like it was just behind the wall where the plane's luggage contents were emerging. The wall shook as something on the other side collided with it. A couple more dull thuds vibrated off the barrier and the belt carryin' suitcases ground to a halt. A determined looking head and a pair of hands poked through the flaps where suitcases marched through from the back. Fingers clawed at the rubber belt trying to make purchase for a crawl forward, but the man couldn't seem to get a grip and he disappeared back into the small opening.

As the waiting passengers began to chatter, speculating on what was happening a phalanx of cops, both uniformed and plain clothes, appeared around the side dragging a man in handcuffs in their midst. A voice behind me called my name.

I turned to find Lieutenant Tom Cheatham and his detective, Carl-something, approaching me in quickstep. "First," Tom told me, his eyes not quite able to lock on mine; "I've got some bad news for you." The police cats steered me to a nearby concrete bench and sat me down. Tom stood over me, a fatherly hand on my shoulder.

"Salli Migiani drove her car off the Vincent Thomas Bridge just after you left. We're pretty sure someone forced her off the road, but we don't have any concrete evidence as yet. I know she was fond of you and you seemed to be good friends. I have to tell you that I don't think she suffered. Her car landed on its roof near the channel's edge, landed so hard that her seatbelt snapped causing her to fracture her skull and snap her neck.

"I wanted to let you know earlier, but Pearl told me not to bother you while you were doing your New York appearance. She said it would be soon enough when you returned and she didn't want anything spoiling your appearance back there."

"Hey man, I appreciate that," I told him. "It's, like a real drag, I mean, yeah, I really had eyes for Salli. Like, she was a really *in there* chick, a very smart lady goin' through some tough changes. Now, the toughest change of all." My damn eyes were threatenin' to leak on me big time, probably cause I was still feelin' somewhat lushed. I started to express what a drag I found the whole enchilada, but I lost it after a few words. I was shakin' my wig and cryin' like a rug rat. Tom put his arm further around my shoulder and told me it was cool, then steered me toward a bench where I could park it.

"You're probably wondering about the commotion back there," he tipped his head toward the baggage claim area. "We received a tip from Mr. Mallory that one of his loyal employees had overheard another longshoreman talking about planting a bomb at Long Beach Airport to kill passengers emerging from a certain Jet Blue flight. Remembering that Pearl had said you were flying Jet Blue back from New York, I ran the flight numbers and decided we had better check out your return.

"I contacted Long Beach, asked them to meet me here with a security team, and sure enough, here is this guy with a small bag of plastic explosive going through suitcases as he off-loaded them from the plane. We kept an eye on him, watched as he dug around in some of the bags, and then followed him back here, where he was unloading bags onto the conveyer belt. The Long Beach S.W.A.T. guys grabbed him and neutralized the bags he had booby-trapped. They're going through all the bags from the flight though, so they don't have an unfortunate incident to explain later."

I brought my eyes back under control, blew my nose in my handkerchief and told Tom "Thanks."

"You missed Salli's funeral I'm afraid," Tom laid on me. "She had a lot of fellow officers at Harbor View for the funeral, at least as many as your friend Officer McCaffery had last year. Her wake was held at Blondy's, just like Morgan McCaffery's. It was a great send-off and everyone had good things to say about her. Salli was a very professional officer and one of the most talented detectives I ever worked with!"

I quickly clued Tom into Jam-Man's words about Elwood checkin' in with his boys from California. Tom found it very interesting, and invited me to one of the department's FBI briefings to relay the tale. As Tom spoke, we heard the baggage belt start to move again. I got to my unstable feet and started in that general direction. After just four-or-five steps, however, Salli's former partner, Carl, came at me with the familiar green canvas bag that held my kit. I switched my horns to my other arm, took the proffered case and followed Tom and Carl to a waiting slick-back panda sporting the Los Angeles City Seal.

# Chapter 81

Blondy was waiting at the Dive's door with a big hug for me when we rolled up. "Com'on in and have a little taste before you head up the stairs," she told me. "Tell Mother Wendy all about New York and the club you were holdin' forth in."

Syd, the day bartender, was headin' for Blondy's favorite table with a tray of martinis as we came through the door. There were the typical Monday afternoon regulars in the dimly lighted room. A couple of "happy hour" suits from the Chamber of Commerce just up the street, five longshoremen, the two regular day-drinkers and a secretary from across the street ensconced at the bar.

"I'm really sorry about Salli," Blondy told me taking both my hands in hers when we were seated. "I know she was special to you and, even if your true love is that lady you met in Oslo, I know Salli's buyin' it must hit you hard, baby." I told her that she had it all, straight up.

"I want you to just relax tonight," she added, "you and the band. I've got this young kid who looks like she' going to turn into a monster star soon. Her name is Sara, Sara Gazarek. She's a student at USC right now, but she already has developed quite a unique style and sound. Sara has a trio of her classmates at SC to back her and I think you'll dig the show." I told Lady that was *reet* with me, that I might fall by to dig this chick, but right now I was anxious to re-bond with my boys.

"Art's been my love for the past weeks," the Lady told me, "but Yard has been a little pill! He kisses up to me until I get the can open, and then he acts like I'm not there. And, if I don't keep a close eye on him, Yard will bully Art and try to steal Art's grub as well!"

I knew that Yard could be kinda single minded at times, so I couldn't defend his actions, but I assured the Blonde One that Yard did love her. "He does the same to me," I confided. Blondy nodded her head and signaled the bar for another round, although I probably didn't need it.

As I nursed my second martini, I clued-in my blonde boss on Bax, Tabitha, Sol, Wheels and Kennedy, tellin' her what I grand time we'd all had. "Maybe next time, Mother Wendy needs to come along as your roadie," she commented, looking away wistfully. "I've never been to New York, but I've always wanted to see it."

# Chapter 82

As the days flew by, the band cats and I got back into the regular routine of life. It might have been all in my skull, but it seemed as though our New York experience had left us all sounding better than ever, although it was a bring down that right here in our home town, we didn't draw anywhere near the crowd we'd gotten used to in the Apple.

I'd met with Mike Mallory out at the union office building on Harbor Boulevard, relayed the envelope, told him the news from Guido and the haps that Elwood de Gier might be alive and cookin' up some bad news here in the Los Angeles Harbor. I punctuated the story with what I'd dug from Jam-Man, Kennedy and Anthony. Mike listened, took some notes on a legal pad, and thanked me for all my help, then dismissed me. I'd done my gig and done my head and now I was yesterday's fish-wrapper.

Joe Migiani had showed up for a Friday show and introduced himself. He was a short, fit man, dark curly hair and olive complexioned. Joe was draped in khaki slacks, a hooded gray Port of Los Angeles sweatshirt and a heavy cloak of *down-and-out*. He invited me to share his small table at the intermission. I told him how sorry I was about Salli's murder. After thankin' me for the CDs I had given him, he locked orbs with me. "You made my baby-girl Salli very happy in her last weeks on earth," he laid on me, doin' major serious. "I want to thank you for that as well. Salli thought of you as a very special friend and I'm sure you cared for her as well. I believe that the time she spent with you was finally helping her to get over the hurt of her earlier failed marriage. I like to think that, if she had lived, I might have had a jazz star as a son-in-law." Joe Migiani smiled and extended his hand. I laid some firm skin on Joe and nodded to the Blonde One, signalin' that she should maybe comp his drinks. Blondy winked back that she understood. She knew Joe was Salli's old man and he wouldn't get a bill for his tab.

Through it all, Loose was, like, permanently drug. There was no new news on Art Pepper's alto or the Net Bid auction. No one was phonin' or emailin' any fresh gen on the subject. It looked like the horn had become a lost cause.

Astrid called me almost every night and between the two of us, we were turnin' some serious wheels for Ma Bell and Norwegian Telecom. Even with a continent and an ocean between us we were connectin' in a nutty mellow groove, our romance makin' a great story. Astrid told me that if she could find the smallest little excuse, she'd be here knockin' on my door in an eye-blink.

It was in the confines of this mixed bag that I took myself down to the dive on a Wednesday afternoon, lookin' to share some company with the Blonde One. My Lady was kinda distracted like, helpin' Syd stock the bar and listening to me with one ear, but I sipped some serious suds and did the puppy routine at her skirts, pullin' on her coat about my down state.

Blondy was just headed back behind the oak counter when a man in blue shorts and a white golf shirt with the Fed-Ex logo over his left breast did a fast shuffle into the bar. He caught my conscious thing because I didn't see any package, or the little, flat brown pad thing they always carry to scarf your signature for whatever they brought. As he drew near us, this cat drew an ugly little gun from the waistband of his abbreviated trousers, pointing it at the Lady.

Weird! Blondy fainted when she dug the rod in his hand, or at least she appeared to fall out. Her eyes had done a frantic fade into her skull with only the whites showin'. I moved into the bar area, trying to catch her or break her fall to the duckboards. The Fed-Ex stud took another step towards us. His visage did confused slidin' into seriously pissed off. He pushed me out of the way and made a grab for the lady, but Blondy suddenly came alive. Straightening up very quickly, the Blonde One came around the corner from the end of the bar with a Louisville Slugger, which she swung upwards, connecting right between the Fed-Ex man's hairy thighs. He rendered a loud half-cry, half-moan as his body sagged. The man's small gun went off in rhythm with his collapsing knees, deflating a miniature Budweiser blimp that hung from the ceiling and breakin' the glass on the framed face of Jayne Mansfield. As the man lurched forward in pain, Blondy brought the oak bat up again. She took a wide stance, like a serious cricketer before the wickets and swung, leanin' in with all her weight behind it. The bat caught Mr. Fed-Ex solid on his left ear, sending him, unconscious, to the floor.

Syd already had his cell phone out and 911 on the line. A car must have been in the neighborhood as sirens cut in before the bar man had even disconnected from the call. He did not, however, fold the handset closed. Instead, he casually asked Blondy for Lieutenant Tom's number and keyed it in as she called it out. When someone answered, Blondy took the phone in one hand and brought it to her ear, keeping her slugger poised over the motionless figure with the other.

The blues were there with our would-be attacker cuffed on the linoleum within minutes. Blondy kept her bat poised anyway, takin' no chances. She only relaxed her stance when Tom Cheatham walked calmly through the door. The Lieutenant rolled Fed-Ex over with the toe of a well-shined black oxford. Lady threw a half-finished beer in the comatose man's face, bringing his eyes wide. A moment of struggling made our captive painfully aware of his prisoner status. He stopped his struggling but clammed it at the same time. Not even a name, rank or serial number. Tom instructed the uniforms to take him to the Harbor Division lock-up, and then turned his attention to the Blonde One and me.

The Lieutenant took copious notes as we relayed the haps to him. We covered it two-or-three times, Tom wearin' his cop face, not relatin' to Blondy as the friend or lover I usually dug there. My Mother Wendy tossed serious right back at him as we burned it up with our chart of the scene.

Then the big cop closed his notebook, shook my hand and took Blondy in his arms, apologizing for doin' his job and radiatin' frantic concern for the Lady's well being.

He spoke to someone briefly on a hand-held radio, and then told us that they had found no delivery van of any kind outside, no Fed-Ex, UPS or DHL was in the neighborhood. Because of this, headquarters suspected that our arrestee was a phony, an imposter, and most definitely a criminal. I couldn't have agreed more.

Tom hung in for another half-hour, then said he had to get back to work. He promised Blondy he'd return as soon as he could. When Tom was out the door, Lady asked me if I would please hang with her for a while. She would never cop to bein' scared, though I could tell she was. I played it like we both just needed some company and shared a few drinks with her until Tom returned some two hours later.

# Chapter 83

When I returned for work in the evening, the Dive was nearly empty. Blondy was holdin' down her favorite booth in the back corner. I sashayed over to check on the Lady, as her stare seemed kinda weirded out. Assuming the opposite bench, I could see her eyes were red, not the kind of red that comes from cryin', but the shade left by close encounters with Mexican agriculture. Blondy was wasted and sailin'!

On the stand, Dave was cuttin' out on the box, Loose on the loose wig beside him as they blew a nutty duet. They were gettin' close to Lennie Tristano and Lee Konitz, warmin' up with their fast jam, soundin' like that pair who had put down some very existential riffs at an earlier time, like, late forties or so.

At the bar, the three leftover drinkers appeared too far in the bag to notice, leavin' only me and the Blonde One to witness this powerful creation. Blondy tossed three fingers of popcorn in her mouth from the red plastic basket next to her empty martini glass on the table.

"Maybe you should feature these two once in a while, baby," Blondy spoke, a touch more loudly than usual. "They are a stone gas!"

"Speaking of stoned," I offered back. "Are you gonna be okay?"

Her retort? "Okay, baby I am cruisin' the voutesphere! I am out there in Coolsville! I am feelin' no pa . . . Okay, truth time, I'm tryin' not to feel any pain, but it ain't workin.

"First they threaten to torch my club, then they murder one of the cops suppose to be protectin' me, and now they send some weak-willied hit man to do me . . ."

Lady spaced for a few bars, after which she added, "A hit man who could now be sporting a righteous concussion, from what Tom 's been sayin' . . ."

"Babe," I interrupted, "you don't know that he was here to waste you. Maybe he was after me, or maybe he just blew by to offer a warning, try to kinda freak you out so Tom or I might back off this dock thing."

"Back off what," she shouted. "I ain't doin' nothin' accept lettin' you work here. Maybe you're bringin' all this grief on my head! I should lose you and just have Dave and Loose play here every night."

"Loose," I reminded her, "is mostly the reason all this is happenin'. He's the cat went lookin' for some old, magic saxophone and drew us this heat!"

Lady tried to change the subject. "Lars, baby, I'm starvin'. Have we got time to fall-out to the Beach City Grill for a quick bite of chocolate?"

"That'd be the weed talkin'," I answered. "Munchies-City!"

"Yeah well," she tossed back at me. "Anyway, we *do* have time. I own this place and I say the others can kick-off the jam while you take me out for one of those *Death by Chocolate* desserts. Whata'ya say?"

Roundin' the corner onto 6th Street, Blondy fumbled in her bag and came out with a badly rolled joint that dwarfed her little finger. "Gotta light?" she asked. I told her that I think she was probably carryin' enough of a load for one black. She didn't need to do up any more.

"But Lars," she wailed, "I'm still feelin' *pain*. I don't want to be feelin' *pain*, man."

I pulled the number from her lips, dropped it back into her handbag and gave her a sideways hug. "Me thinks the Lady is gettin' too drug by things, Depression-City. Listen, we'll scarf some chocolate, go back to the Dive, and you can either relax and mellow out to the tunes, or leave Ruthie in charge and go home to cop some rest"

"No can do, pardner," was the Blonde One's smug reply. "Tom's comin' back later to clue me about our intruder and his condition, like, when he clocks out of the cop shop."

I turned Blondy to face me and held her at arms length, lookin' into her eyes. "You're, like, out there behind a Mexican farm's worth of high and lushed as well, and you've got a date with a brass-covered cop? Lady, some times I wonder!"

"It's copasetic, baby," she replied. "Tom's vice, but he knows I like a little buzz now and then."

"Little buzz?" I looked her up and down. "Girl, you need to chill out. You are, like, on some kinda freakish high!"

"Oh *posh*," the Blonde One giggled. "Is posh the word I wanted?" She punched my shoulder lightly, did a left-face maneuver and started walkin' again, a big grin sittin' wide on her pretty mug. "Know what, I'm startin' to groove, like feelin' way better. Thanks, Lars. You're good for me, babe. You do know how to get me laughin'."

Blondy got her fudge-covered chocolate cake. I nibbled at a wedge of blueberry cheesecake. We joked and laughed through our oversized sweet dishes and coffees. The blonde's joy, however, rang false, like she was doin' a stage number to try and ease me up off her. I did my best to avoid heavy talk. She'd be gettin' enough bring down soon, when she rendezvoused with the Lieutenant.

# Chapter 84

David and Loose held onto their Tristano-esque bag through the first set. They were on a solid ball of a kick and, as people started to find their way into the club, the musicians spread their good news to one and all. We ran over "Lennie's Pennies," which is a challenge for me each time we play it with it's fast pace, unusual rhythmic pattern and unique progression of chords. Give me Trane's "Giant Steps" any day. That pyramidal progression I can deal with! We also tried "Bop Goes the Leesel," a much more fun riff to ride.

We were summing up the last chorus when Lieutenant Tom strolled through the door, hands in his pockets and badge clipped to his belt. He signaled me to join him as soon as I could get away, then made feet for Lady and her booth. Blondy shot Tom a sloppy grin and signaled Ruth for more martinis for all of us. Tom slid in beside the Blonde One wearing a concerned face.

I arrived on the opposite side of their table in time to hear Blondy in an angry tone telling Tom he had no right to lecture her, she was over twenty-one and would do as she pleased, damn it! She punctuated her reprimand by sluggin' down half of her cocktail in one swallow.

"How do we save this lovely lady from herself?" Tom asked me quite rhetorically. Then to Blondy, he said, "Hey kid, its okay. I'm not judging you or bustin' your chops, as Lars might say. I'm just concerned. I don't want you to hurt yourself."

Lady grinned at that and asked Tom, "You wanna toke a little smoke with me?"

Tom shook his head, shooting me a "what are we gonna do with this chick" face. Blondy faked a minor pout, took another, more reasonable sip from her glass, her face brightening. "So, like what's your story, man? What's the haps with Fed-Ex man? How about a toast to Fed-Ex man goin' down." When she saw we weren't raising our glasses, she tried on "pout" again, but soon forgot it and rubbed her blonde locks against Tom's shoulder, her eyes half closed.

"Our well concussed FedEx shooter," Tom began, when Blondy had straightened up, "just happened to be a member of the same crane crew as Adrian, Billie and the late Jeremy diStefani. They took him to a local hospital ward, where they could keep an eye on him, Vance was his name."

"Was?" I queried as I picked up on the past tense thing.

"Was," Tom repeated. "Vance refused to say anything to us when he came around. He ignored the officers sent to interrogate him, like they didn't exist. He told the nurse who came in to check on him that he wanted his attorney there, right now, pronto. When the nurse told him he'd have to speak with us, he told the woman 'You tell them, I ain't talkin' to pigs!' And that's all we got from him.

"When the doctor was finished, he told us that the man had a slight concussion and very swollen nuts, but otherwise our prisoner checked out okay. He seemed a bit confused talking to the medic, but he damn well knew who we were and wanted nothing to do with us."

Blondy told us, with a serious mug, "I thought I hit him harder than that. I'm gonna have to go to batting practice. Lars, you wanna play ball with me?" she giggled.

"Right," Tom continued, "so anyway, since our man didn't have any life-threatening injuries, we put him in a jail van with two uniformed sheriff's deputies. They were suppose to accompany him to the downtown lockup and process him in. The feds requested we put him there and give them a crack at him as well and we complied.

"The ambulance left San Pedro, headed downtown, I guess these deputies have a set route they follow. They exited the 10 freeway to take Central Avenue, then Alameda to the jail. Between 7th and 6th, in downtown L.A., that's a pretty crumby semi-industrial area right off the Nickel, they found trouble. Central runs sort of a diagonal there and the alleys intersect at a forty-five-degree angle. Coming up Central, the alleys meet the boulevard jigged away from their view. Midway through that block, a small white sedan comes flying out of the blind alley, going way too fast for that area. The sedan rammed the left rear quarter panel of the sheriff's van and spun it around a couple times."

"You mean our perp bought it in a fender-bender?" Blondy was incredulous.

"That's just the start," Tom told us. "It gets more weird. We think our man was still alive at that point. One of the deputies started to get out of the van to have words with the driver of the car that hit them. Before his boots hit the ground, the white car erupted in a ball of flame, lighting up the night and igniting the sheriff's van as well.

"We found that one deputy about thirty feet from the van, he apparently tried to run clear, but his uniform was already in flames. The force of the explosion threw him forward.

"When our forensics team arrived on scene, they told us that the woman driving the white sedan had an exploding vest on, like the suicide bombers wear in the Middle East. She had donned a military-style camo vest rigged with about seven pounds of plastic explosive gel, they're saying, enough to take out a locomotive!"

Blondy let loose a loud whistle as my jaw hit the Formica. Dave was signaling me from the stage that break time was over. When I noticed, I just shook my head, and the band went on without me. I was all hung up on Tom's tale, and I think he wanted me to know how it ended.

"If that isn't sufficient to catch your interest," he went on with a deadpan expression, "how about this. The white car was registered to . . . Tah dah! None other than Jeremy diStefani's former squeeze, Billie Frankov. The early word from the lab is that Billie was most likely our bomber. Another one from Adrian's dockside team. And, one of the guys said it appears she may not have been a willing accomplice. They found a concrete block that looks like it might have been clamped onto the accelerator with rubber straps. Of course, they have to look at that further, at this point its just speculation. The rubber straps were badly melted."

I'm not sure how Blondy was takin' all this in her boxed "peace and love" state, but it wasn't layin' a feeling of cozy security on my head. This new murder was puttin' me through some serious changes. We were dealing with some twisted *motha* studs that had a hook for doin' serious harm, and it was makin' me real hincty. I swung from the scene feelin' really low and brung down.

# Chapter 85

I was brought from my much-needed slumbers before the clock had even struck noon. Blondy was on the horn, and she didn't sound very solid. "How about a little somethin' to break your fast?" She asked.

"Frantic," I replied. "Can we hit, like, Pacific Diner for a change?" I thought I heard a gagging sound over the line, after which the lady's voice came back with, "Don't think I could face solid food this morning. I was thinkin' of ordering out some eggs and potatoes for you and Tom. I've already got coffee on, and Tom called to say he's got some more of the story for us. Shall we say forty minutes?"

An invitation I couldn't refuse. I took a quick five in the rain-room, found a semi-clean shirt and pair of socks, and set my feet to waltzing over the stairway boards. I booked into the Dive to find Blondy tippin' a heavy dose of Southern Comfort into her coffee mug. "You don't wanna share this little secret with Tom, okay?" she told me, hidin' the bottle behind her bench, then stirrin' cream and Splenda into her morning cuppa.

"Reet," I told her, "Solid." I drew fingers across my lips like a zipper. I sampled my own coffee then joined the blonde one in the tense silence.

After five of watchin' the Lady do hangdog, the quiet was broken by the deliveryman from Dave's Diner. He brought Styrofoam containers out of an insulated pouch, placing them on the table as Blondy signed the check and slipped the cat an extra five in long green.

The food man almost did a head-on with Tom as the former was bookin' and the latter was makin' his entrance. Syd brought another mug for Tom, and the lieutenant started opening containers and spoonin' food onto his paper plate. I picked up a plastic fork, gave it a disdainful stare, and Syd rushed over bringing us all real silverware from behind the bar. Tom and I tucked into the nourishment while Blondy sipped her super-charged coffee and watched.

"You're not eating?" Tom asked politely. "Already ate," Blondy lied.

When the paper plates held nothin' but grease stains, Tom brought forth his notebook and started the meeting. "That bomb yesterday killed two deputies and our suspect," he told us. "But it looks like Billie Frankov cashed in sometime earlier. They performed her autopsy at seven-thirty this morning. Her charred skull had two holes in it and contained at least one nine-millimeter round that could be identified. On the remains of her right foot, she had burnt up bits of a tennis shoe. The tennis shoe bore traces of the same rubber strapping that they found on the gas pedal."

The Blonde One's already shaky face went a shade further toward green as she said, "Oh my God! That poor woman!"

"Don't think she was little miss innocence," I reminded Lady.

"Surely not innocent," Tom added, "but a victim just the same. There wasn't much blood in evidence in her car, so we have to assume Ms. Frankov was shot elsewhere and was already dead when they buckled the seat belt on her.

"Which would indicate that we have a leak in the system, LAPD, Sheriff's Department or San Pedro Hospital, we don't know as yet. Somehow, someone knew we were taking Vance to the county lockup and they knew the route we would use. They killed Billie, drove her body to the alley in the downtown area and waited for us, all on very short notice. It appears that they strapped on the suicide vest, fastened her foot and the cement block onto the accelerator and waited. They had to have had a lookout, probably with a walkie-talkie or a cell phone stationed down the road, closer to the freeway. The vest was rigged with some kind of rip chord. When they knew the van was coming, they started the engine, pulled a wedge of some kind from under Billie's foot and slammed the car into gear. As she sped off toward Central Avenue, they had the trigger chord tied off with enough rope so it would pull the pin as she entered the street. We know that because we found the rope, with the pin still attached tied to the hinge of a dumpster in the alley. The rope must have gathered sufficient tension that it flew back into the alley mouth when the pin released."

"These are some heavy, heavy *mothas*!" escaped my mouth before I could catch myself. "You got that right, Pancho." Was Blondy's reply.

"As you probably are aware," Tom went on. "We put out an all points for William Adrian, but he has vanished completely. Putting out a listing on his license plates proved a dead end when a dog walker found his car tags in a trash can down on the promenade.

"The port cops already had a bulletin out for his arrest. They had gone to his job site, but he wasn't there, so they called the union. The Brotherhood of Longshoremen said he had called in sick two days before. As yet, they had not returned him to the duty roster. A trip to Adrian's address revealed that he had left in quite a hurry. The apartment is a wreck, clothes, shoes and other things scattered everywhere. His razor and toothbrush were conspicuously absent from the bathroom. They found a large gap on the clothes rack in his closet, drawers pulled out of his dresser, dumped on floor and scattered.

"DMV records had told them that William Adrian owned only one vehicle, a dark blue 2002 Corvette. From what you, Lars, and Michael Mallory had told me, I ran the name Elwood de Gier through the system. There was no driver's license listed, but we turned up a 1987 Chevrolet Blazer, color black registered in that name. The Blazer tags are the ones that were found on the channel walkway. I shared that information with both the port boys and the feds, putting us all on the same page."

"You said his license tags turned up in a trash can, could he still have his old New York plates? Or de Gier's? " I asked.

"That's some good thinking, Lars," Tom told me as he brought up his cell phone from his belt. The policeman hit a speed-dial number and relayed my idea to someone on the other end. When he closed his phone, he said. "We're pretty sure he's driving the old full-size Chevy Blazer that's registered to Elwood de Gier. They impounded Adrian's corvette as soon as they couldn't locate him. So now they'll be watching closely for Chevy trucks with New York tags. Feds can probably even get that number from New York. I hope this is the charm."

"Could he have fled the state?" Blondy asked.

"Don't think so. If he fled the state, who plotted the bomb to take Billie Frankov and this man Vance out?" Tom stared off across the bar for a minute, then added, "I think Elwood, Bill Adrian, who-ever it is, he's still close by, maybe even hiding out right under our noses here in San Pedro."

# Chapter 86

Tom had to get back to work. Six seemingly related murders, three of them lawmen, had put this case right at the top of every agency's priority list. As it was definitely related to racketeering and grand theft at four major U.S. ports, the FBI was assuming the lead, but Tom had put himself in charge on the local murders. *The Man* takes a special interest when the dead are their own. Every officer in both the Los Angeles Police Department and the Los Angeles County Sheriff's Office were on full alert to catch Billy Adrian.

After Tom's departure, Blondy brought her Southern Comfort bottle back to the table, poured a healthy taste into my mug and her own, and signaled Syd to top-off our coffees.

"That familiar ol' dog is sheddin' enough hair to bury ol' Mother Wendy this mornin'," Blondy told me, not lookin' me in the eye, more focused on the table and the hot cup between her hands. "And you know I hate to drink alone."

"S'cool, kid," I told her. "My bright is in need of a little boost. This whole riff is becomin' a real 24-carat bring-down!"

We sipped coffee and Comfort in a mellow silence. Some color started returnin' to Lady's face as the caffeine and lush-juice kicked into her system. After a time, the blonde one patted the empty space beside her on the other side of the booth. I pushed my cup across the Formica and took my frame to her side. Blondy gave me a tight hug and held on for a long time. When she let go of me, I could see her eyes were damp.

"These cats are burnin' down my world," she choked.

Lady was on a solid come down. "Take it slow," I told her. "Don't let yourself get strung out on these negative kicks. This too shall pass, and the scene will swing again, kid. Swing like a garden gate."

The blonde one gave a negative shake of her golden head and added another slug of joy juice to her mocha java.

"Hey, com'on babe," I put a reassuring arm around her and gave a squeeze. "Tom's gonna fall-in on this, Babe, you know he's layin' it on straight. Puttin' jive-*motha* bad guys in the slam is what he does, like his solid full-time gig. You said yourself that he' good at it. Like, we've probably bottomed-out here already. Skies will be nothin' but blue from here kid, dig it!"

Blondy was comin' around. She knocked me that frantic smile of hers. "Thanks, Lars. Maybe I *am* over-reacting. It's just all such a vicious scene. I think I'd rather be locked in that shipping box with the Arabs again than this waiting for the next down chorus of mayhem and jive-turkey-shit to fall on me."

And on that note, entered a very effusive Loose, windmillin' his arms around and shouting my name. "Hey, Lars, Lars, baby, it's on again! I'm gonna get my magic axe. Dude just called me at home! We can meet with him tomorrow and cop the prize!"

"There you go!" I greeted him as Loose slid into the seat opposite of us and started drummin' an excited paradiddle on the Formica with his fingers.

Blondy sent forth a frantic groan, poured more juice into her nearly empty cup and took a long hit. "This is just what I needed today," she lamented. "Can you cats take your heads somewhere else for this rap? I got work to do."

I looked over at my alto player, watched him bouncing on the red suede like an oversized orange-and-black Tigger. I patted Blondy's hand, got up and pulled Loose free of the booth. "Let's hit my rooftop," I laid on him. "More room to sound up there, man. You can lay it all on me."

# Chapter 87

Loose took the stairs two at a time, admonishing me to "Hurry up, come *on* man!" The cat burst through the fire door and onto the roof like a bull in mind of makin' it with some fine brown-eyed jersey.

"Just hang on," I shouted. "I need to fall into my pad for a sec, grab a leak and a couple beers."

"Well make haste," the over-anxious alto man replied. "This is just too much, babe. I can't hold it in much longer!"

It looked like I was in for a long session. Maybe I should send out for a pizza or two, as this cat probably wouldn't turn my lobes loose until show time. I lost a pound of water into the big white telephone, then laid tracks to the fridge and loaded the plastic cooler with brews. Loose was pacing the ramparts when I scuffled outside.

"He called me, man, the cat called me *at home*. He has the Martin, say he's sorry we got our wires crossed before, but this time it is *mine!*"

"Whoa, Loose," I told him. "Cool it a minute, hold the weddin'. Sit down, slow it down and let's start over." I popped tops on a pair of cold ESBs, took a long pull on one brown bottle and offered the other to Lucian. Loose took his bottle in hand, but wasn't in any hurry to taste the juice.

"You say he called you at home? Had you, like, laid your number on this cat? Where did he get your number if you've only been doin' emails with the dude?"

"Probably copped it from Net Bid. Or maybe he just, like, let his fingers do the walkin'. Who cares, man?" Loose waved hands and bottle around as he spoke, spilling valuable ale and foam all over my patio. "He copped my number, he called and I'll get my horn, like, *Art Pepper's* horn. That's what matters! Wait'll I tell Sol, dude."

I had to cool this cats jets before he did a Peter Pan number off my roof and winged it into the vonce. "*Reet*, man, someone, *claimin'* to be the Net Bid seller rang your blower. You never dug his voice before so you can't be sure who your caller is, dig? Now if, just *if* this is the right cat, like, he's the wrong cat to swing with, you dig that? Bad news! Like, the stud they are puttin' their eyes out for is a stone cold-blooded killer, a *cop* killer. And this dude is one-and-the-same with your horn salesman, am I *root*?"

But Lucian was only facin' one lobe in my direction. His eyes were on a special prize in the long fallin' skies. He jumped up again and resumed his frantic footsteps along the ledge. It was a stone drag that I had to bust the kid's chops, but it was for his own good! He was steppin' into a rough riff, a bad scene, a hang-up that could put his lights out, like, *for all time!*

For at least a full sweep around the minute hand we danced around in a nutty little dance. I'd sit Loose down, try to hip him to the haps, and he'd pop up again and make with the freaky strut. My head was becomin' too twisted up in this bad scene. I left Loose guardin' the battlements and went inside to call Skoot for some back up. I was on my second ale. Loose was still wavin' a nearly full longneck. I hadn't seen him take a hit yet, the flask's only loss was what now dampened my deck.

Skoot was cool, put it straight that he'd be right over. I restocked my mini-cooler to wait for the bari-man's arrival.

Out on my patio, I could see Loose's constant motion. He had set his beer bottle down on the parapet by the fire escape ladder and was moving his feet in a circle around the corner of the rooftop, the top of the green and yellow Channel View sign showing behind him. I hung inside the sliding glass in my living room tryin' to get my head straight on how I was gonna tell Skoot that Loose had, like, totally flipped out, done his head.

Loose was talkin' to himself out there, arms flappin' and feet in constant motion. It was a groove scene when Skoot fell in. I painted him a quick picture before we split the pad to check Loose out. I laid it on Skoot how hung-up the cat was. "It's like he's on some freakish high, man," I told him. "He's jonesin' like a junky on speedballs. He's only got eyes for one thing, man, and it's gonna burn him down in solid four-four time."

"Wow, sorry dad," Skoot deadpanned, "Like, I forgot to bring the straight jacket."

I relayed all of what Loose had told me. Skoot was pinned to it, head noddin' and wheels turnin' in his beautiful wig. "Yeah," he said finally, "its wake--up to reality time for our little man out there. Let's go put him under the scope and dig where his head is headin'."

Catchin' our approach, Loose came runnin', arms aflutter, peeps wide and bright. "Hey, Skoot, man, good to see ya' pops. Did Lars clue you about my horn? I'm finally getting' my horn man, like tomorrow!"

"Yeah," Skoot replied, "I dug *somethin'* about that. Sounds a little shaky to me, though. You sure this cat called you is solid?"

Loose's face fell. "What do you mean, man. Why wouldn't the cat be playin' it straight with me? He's got the horn and he wants the bread."

"You ever heard of, like, scam artists?" Skoot asked him. "Maybe Jim picked up on your story some place like at the Dive, where he overheard your rap to one of us. Now this strung-out cat in need of a green fix is gonna hustle you for the bread, maybe bust your skull at the same time."

Loose shook his head, momentarily drug by the thought. "No, pops, can't be that. This cat knew too much about it. He was, like rattlin' off the Net Bid auction number and, like that. No, no, man, this cat has to be the real article and he's got the horn for me, I can feel it!"

"So then," I put in, "if he's genuine, he's very likely to be our murderous bad news cat, man You are quite likely gonna be facin' the freak who's killed at least three cops, includin' Salli who you knew, and God knows how many others both here and back East. Think about it, man. You're, like, just beggin' for this Capone-Clyde to punch your ticket!"

Tears came to the sax man's eyes. "No, man, no! I ain't pickin' up on that! I won that saxophone fair and square and the cat knows it and he wants me to have it."

Skoot and I calmed him down by soundin' Loose as though we were agreein' with him. Once he'd chilled, he lost his nervous thing, settled into a chair and took a pull or two from his now warm beer. Just to keep Loose chillin', Skoot asked him how and where he was suppose to score his prize, how he'd get the long daddy green to his mysterious caller.

"Not a *mystery* caller, man." Loose corrected. "He's the cat I won the auction on; cat who's got my horn for me!"

"Whatever," I threw out there.

"No, no," Skoot admonished. "Loose has gotta meet his connection to score his property, man. How you suppose to find him, pops?"

Now the story got really freakish frantic. Was Loose sayin' this? Did he dream it all in his up-tight state?

"Well," the sax man began, "I'm gonna meet with him tomorrow in the hills above Pasadena. I'll drive up there early, hike up a trail and make the exchange. Real simple stuff."

"Wait a minute," Skoot said. "This dude can't just come by the Dive or somethin' and lay it on you? What's this 'hike up a mountain' crap?"

"Loose, baby," I added. "Up a mountain, no one around? It's a perfect set up for you to find an early grave, no witnesses. Think about it. You're gonna walk up a mountain, single-o, with three large on your person. This is nuts, man."

"Hey, it's what he said, man." Loose was getting' agitated again. "You know how bad I want that horn? That horn is me! Like, I'm nowhere without it, just a burned-down shell of a cat!"

"Loose," I reminded him, "you're a fantastic player. You've copped a unique sound and style all your own. You got heavy ideas and all the technique to express'm. You blow a Mark VI Selmer that lots'a cats would kill for. You don't need the bad kicks of this horn, man, how do you even know it's really Art Pepper's horn? Sure, it's the same model Martin, but what does that mean? And that's if the horn really exists at all!"

"I've seen the photos of it, man." Loose protested. "I've dug the serial number, I've done the research, and I know what I'm buyin'. Just share some of my glow, man. Share my mellow stage. Wait'll you hear me blow through this baby, then you'll dig it all!"

"If you live long enough to put air into it," I corrected. "It's rough odds you got here, man. Like Lottery-City odds, against *you*. Get your head together for a minute and dig the *real* world. You're very likely dealin' with a freakish psycho killer, a cat that lives out where the trains don't run."

"Funny you should mention trains," Loose said, his face brightening with new information. "My man said I'm gonna be followin' an old train line to meet him. The old Pacific Electric line up Mount Lowe."

"Oh man." Skoot and I had groaned the line almost in unison. "Why up on the mountain, anyway, babe?" I asked.

"Cat's takin' a little heat right now, cause he got greedy and tried to hustle the axe to a few other customers, like double his score an' like that. He says he's got my sax buried up there by an abandoned trolley car that he's been campin' in. But it's cool, man. The hike will be good for me, fresh mountain air and all that."

"And the bullets?" Skoot inquired.

"Fuck your bullets, man!" Loose was losin' it again. "I know what I'm doin' and where I'm goin'. I went down to the Waterfront Red Car station by Utro's Café at Ports O'Call, they got a big map on the board there where you wait for the train and it shows all the old Red Car lines. The old Mount Lowe line winds around the mountain a bit. I even made myself a small map, just in case. I know right where I'm headin', man."

It was getting' close to suppertime by now. I hadn't ordered that pizza, and I was gonna have to think about grabbin' a bite before we started our five hour nightly gig.

So I caved. "Okay, Loose. If you're dead set on meetin' this guy, at least let me go up there with you, man. I can watch your back."

"I don't know," he pondered. "The man said to come alone, like not to alert *the man* or anything like that. It's s'pose to be just me'n him on this riff."

"Do I look threatening?" I asked him. "I'm just another musician, babe. Tell him I'm just there to check it out for you, like, swing to its authenticity."

"If you guys are goin' on this mad chase," Skoot added, "you better take some equalizers with you."

"Equalizers?" I asked.

"Yeah, equalizers, rods, weapons. I've got two old German side arms at home, I'm like, how would you say? A kind of collector. They're both old, one is from the 1930's, the other from World War II, but I keep'm oiled and cleaned, take them down to the police range every now and then, so I know they work well and fire a straight shot."

"Man, Skoot," I protested, "I ain't got eyes for guns, man, like I *hate* guns."

"For your own good, dude," the Skoot laid on me with a kind of superior look. "It increases your odds of comin' home, sax or no sax."

"You're a gun collector?" Loose asked.

"Like, I'm fascinated by war stuff," Skoot replied. "I got this weird hang-up, like I might have been a Nazi cat in a former life, you know, like the reincarnation bit? So I got eyes for old uniforms, guns, badges, crazy things like that.

"These pistols, like, they're both Carl Walther's. The old one is, like a police special, a Walther PP, and the other one's a German officer's side arm, a P-38, kinda like a Luger. The PP is, like, a 32 caliber. The P-38 fires 9-millimeter rounds, they're both very accurate and easy to fire. Just have to watch the kickback when they go off. And I got spare clips for both of them, so you'll have plenty of ammo."

# Chapter 88

Our crowd in the evening was swingin' better than the previous black right from the first bar of the chart. It was the "First Thursday" of the month once again, Santa Ana winds heatin' up the p.m., and the art crowd was millin' thick along the sidewalks. There were already a half-dozen or more Artwalk revelers drinkin' when we arrived at the Dive. When we started to blow, more cats and chicks poured themselves in the door as Ruthie poured the drinks.

The First Thursday crowd is mostly pretty hip folks and many were long time fans, so the black started off a stone ball for us all. We shared some Mingus, some Monk, and then we fell into Dave and Loose's Lennie Tristano bag, but with the full power of the sextet behind it, rockin' an' sockin' an' boppin'! Our first set flew by like a turbo-charged Super Chief diesel.

When we called time out, Skoot went into his bari case and came out with a small brown-paper-wrapped package. He invited Loose and I to Blondy's special booth in back, conveniently vacant, as Lady had left with Tom to check out the galleries on 7<sup>th</sup> Street. He unwrapped his package on the bench, against the shadowy back corner. Under the table he passed a brown leather case to me, and another to Loose.

I set my peeps on the leather holster in my lap. "Be cool now," Skoot warned. "Set these in your horn cases and keep'm outta sight. You don't wanna get popped with those things, they're loaded and that means, like, instant incarceration if the wrong cat sees'm."

I let loose with a plaintive, "Oh, man." Then I glanced sideways to see a nutty, wild look in Loose's bright lights. He already had his small gun out, his hand around the grips and his finger in the trigger guard. I was just hopin' he wasn't gonna turn into an even bigger problem for me now that he was armed.

"Just put the thing back in the holster till you get home, man," I hissed at him as *sotto-voce* as I could. "This shit isn't some kinda game, dude."

The man slipped his pistol back into the holster, and checked the spare magazine, which had its own little sleeve stitched onto the black leather of the gun's case. I decided I should study my own pistol a little closer. I glanced down in my lap. The holster Skoot had passed me was light brown cowhide, with two wide belt-loops on the surface and, just south of the loops was an embossed skull–and–crossbones with the words 'WAFFEN SS, Berlin 1943' in the middle of the surface. I felt an evil chill runnin' up my back. I turned the holster over. The other side featured a wide flap that buttoned over a silver knob. Liftin' the flap, I dug two chambers. The big one at the rear held the gun. I could see its beveled black grips. I slid the pistol out briefly, to check its size and weight and caught another surprise; on the black finish just above the trigger the weapon bore a small stamped eagle, wings spread wide and an encircled swastika in its talons. I shoved the evil thing back into its pouch, then tried the smaller compartment. In this spot was a long, flat metal shaft, set at an angle; the spare magazine. Through small vent holes, I caught a flash of bright brass. At the other end, I dug that the brass was a collection of bullets, loaded with a large spring that would feed them, one at a time, as the pistol discharged its uncool contents. I re-buttoned the flap, tucked the holster under my jacket, my arm holding it in my armpit while I made my way back to the stage and my gig-bag, where I could conceal this bad news.

Loose followed me, his holster palmed in full view. I was freaked, but no one in the room noticed. Loose set the gun in a large space designed to hold a clarinet besides his alto in the Selmer case. Back in the late fifties, when his axe was made, many sax players doubled on the liquorish stick and the Selmer cases of the day accommodated their extra horn.

No sooner had we stashed these old artifacts of evil when Tom and Blondy fell in, joinin' Skoot in the Lady's booth and callin' for martinis. Lady beckoned me with a toss of her locks and put a glass in my hand from the tray that had magically appeared on the tabletop. In my freakish, strung-out state, I inhaled two of the strong libations in as many minutes. Blondy winked and said, "Glad you're ready to swing, baby. Tonight is a gasser, isn't it?"

I was jittery the rest of the gig, couldn't complete a straight idea. I even lost my place in the changes a few times, which almost never happens. Loose was just flyin', feelin' no pain. I guess his conscious mind was hung on the horn he thought he would be coppin', and not the bad kicks he might be waltzin' into.

For the last set, Dave caught my discomfort and mostly called a lot of basic twelve-bar blues riffs. They were easier for me to follow, though my wig kept driftin' like bad news. When last call sounded, I was off like a shot, no pun intended, to try and cop some serious Zs before Loose might summon me in the morning.

# Part IV

## The View from the Mountain

# Chapter 89

It was still seriously dark outside my window when Loose appeared, tapping fingers on the glass like an Art Blakey solo. I got up and met him at the door in my night drapes. My alto man was shufflin' right foot to left foot and back again, like a child in dire need of a toilet. I invited him in, but he told me to just hurry up, he'd wait at the door.

I found jeans, a long-sleeved Swedish army pullover shirt and an old pair of war-surplus boots. I brushed my teeth, fed the boys and yelled to Loose, asking if he wanted a quick cup of coffee.

"We need coffee, we'll find a drive-through place on the way, man, come *on*, we gotta go!"

I never like goin' out without breakfast, especially without my caffeine boost, but I made reluctant tracks for the door. Loose's mother's Buick was around the corner, parked in front of the Dive. As we rounded the corner from Centre to 7th Street, Blondy shimmered out of nowhere, a large thermos in her hand.

I stared, incredulous that the Lady would be waiting, bustin' our supposedly secret mission. She seemed to read my mind.

"You can't keep secrets from Mother Wendy," she told me, then laughed. "Especially when the loose tongue of Loose is guarding the secret. I overheard you guys last night, dug you packin' heat in your instrument cases. I don't like the idea, and I had a long talk with Skoot about it last night. He said you're pretty solid behind the idea of meetin' up with this stud, so I figured I needed to at least warn you to be careful.

"I made some coffee for you. I know how you get, Loose, when you're jonesin' about something, and I figured you wouldn't spare a minute for Lars to eat his morning meal." Lady turned her deep green orbs my way. "Also, I'm not lettin' either of you go without some way of checkin' on you." The Blonde One jigged a hand in the pocket of her long coat and withdrew her cell phone, which she held out to me.

"I want you to stay in touch, Babe. You know I'm gonna worry about both of you." Then, with a nervous giggle she added, "I don't want to disappoint a heavy Friday crowd with just a quartet, so you guys better be back by show time, in one piece and ready to do your magic!" With that, she turned a military about-face and fell into her bar, kicking the door closed behind her, end of interview.

We folded ourselves into Loose's large motor, hung a sloppy U-turn, and booked out for Harbor Boulevard and the 110 Freeway. Loose drove hunched over, his knuckles white as they gripped the wheel, determination painted across his face in the light of passing street lamps. We were on our flight into the great mysterious unknown.

# Chapter 90

Loose followed the freeway to its end, where it narrowed to become Arroyo Seco Street in Pasadena. A Metro train was pacing us a block to our left, between Raymond and Arroyo Seco. Loose hung a *ralph* at California Street, motored another eight blocks to Lake, where he went left to point us toward a small, rounded mountain, faintly lit by the false dawn and dwarfed by the higher range behind it. More than half a century ago, someone had carved a huge letter "T" near the crest to commemorate the Thorp Institute, the forerunner to present day Cal-Tech. This was Echo Mountain, once topped by two grand hotels and a planetarium.

"Dude said he'd be up there watchin' us through some big eyes. Told me that from his perch up there he could watch our entire climb."

"Charming," I told Loose.

"It's cool," Loose smiled. He was becomin' more mellowed out as we were getting' closer to our destination. "I got the five-yards in the bag, it should be an easy exchange."

"Five?" I asked, *"five*? What happened to three? I thought you bid three grand?"

"Well yeah," he told me, lookin' sheepish. "It was three originally, but a lot has happened since the auction. Cat's taken some heat. Plus there's other bidders involved now, cats like Sol who are willin' to lay out much more long daddy green."

"Jeez, Loose, I think your wig is all twisted up, man." I was shaken my head at him. "Three bills was obsessive, now your layin' five on this dude for a horn you haven't even blown air through. Man, we gotta find you a serious wig doctor to shrink your conscious mind, dude!"

"Right," he said nonchalantly. "So anyway, is this Lake Street we're flyin' on? Cat told me we gotta leave our car by where Lake ends at Loma Alta Drive, walk up the hiking trail to the ruins of the old Echo Mountain Cable Railway cog house. From there, we're supposed to follow the original railway roadbed to its end by the concrete and stone foundation of the former Alpine Tavern. Dude told me we can't miss it. He said there's still steel rails set in the concrete up there. Like, no tavern, he said that burned down *donkey's ears* ago, but we'll know the spot.

"When he sees us arrive, he'll come down and lead us to the streetcar-cabin where the saxophone is waitin'." Loose turned his head to dig that I was pickin' up on all this. I felt like I should be takin' notes. Like, was all this gonna be on some final exam?

"Cat said, like, no police! Not a word to them,"

I thought about that little caveat. If Blondy was hip, like, Tom had to be in there with it as well. He might be already on our tail, hopin' we'd lead him to a multiple murder suspect.

"So where did you get another two yards a' cash?" I asked. His reply was a simple, "It's cool, man, don't get hung up on it. The bread is stashed in that Martin case we copped in the warehouse when all those crates came tumblin' down. The cat said to bring the ransom in the sax case so anyone saw us doin' the Jack and Jill bit wouldn't be suspicious eyeballin' us comin' back with the horn."

"Alright, Loose," I clued him. "You got the bread in the Martin sax case that you acquired on one of this dude's former attempts to cool your lights, like for eternity, and now you're good buddies and business partners? I can't get my head around this, man. I'm, like, total Clueless City, Wyoming!"

"When a treasure like this is involved, man, y' just do what y' gotta do. Like, strange bedfellows and that."

"Can't be much stranger then you, brother," I handed him with another negative head motion. "So, we're almost outta road here, what's the plan?"

Loose slotted the Buick into a space behind an older Chevy Blazer. I couldn't help but catch a white decal on the trucks rear window, 'Pedro Dad'.

I leapt from the *short* and quick-stepped up to check the machine out closer. It was black, with a New York tag and an IBLW longshore union bumper sticker plastered on the back gate. I took a stroll around this baby, pinnin' it closely. Gray primer covered the right rear quarter panel. The passenger side door didn't fit in it's frame quite right, like, maybe it was from a different model year. The front fender was creases and striped with dark gray paint, and the head light at the front was held in by wide strips of duct tape where the chrome frame and brackets had been knocked out of shape.

Without thinkin', I took out Blondy's small mobile horn and punched the Dive's number from the speed-dial. Lady grabbed it in the first notes of its phrase, her voice pourin' forth concern.

"We're at the trail head here in Altadena," I told her. She started askin' questions. I cut her off tellin' her we were fine, hadn't seen any *black hats* yet, but I had some straight dope she needed to relay to Tom as quick as she could grab him. The lieutenant's voice was there before I finished my sentence.

"Do we need to send a back-up team for you and Lucian?" he asked.

I told him, "No man, we're cool, but there is something here you need to fall in behind. I was lookin at a Chevy truck up here on the corner of Loma Alta Drive and Lake Street, right where we're set to pick up the trail. I think this may be your perp's *short*, man. It's got some serious scarrin' on the passenger side, like it could have run someone off the road, and its wearin' New York ID."

"Sounds like our friend Elwood's vehicle," he told me. "We'll check with the Sheriff's Station up in Altadena, have them put it under observation and I'll head that way with a couple investigators. We'll dress casual, so we don't scream 'cops' at the neighbors."

I said, "Cool!" and closed the phone.

"Who were you talkin' to?" Loose wanted to know.

"Just lettin' Blondy know were still mellow and breathin', bud," I lied. "You know the shortest road to the cop shop is to get Blondy shook. Long as she knows we're *stickin'* here, she won't give us away."

I walked back to the Buick. While Loose retrieved the sax case from the trunk, I threaded my belt through the loops of the ancient Nazi holster and checked its weight and placement, in case I needed to do a 'Gunsmoke' style quick draw. Loose caught my action and strapped his rod on as well. "We better un-tuck our shirts," I clued him. "Cover these guns so we don't freak out any hikers or tourist dudes."

# Chapter 91

The time was not quite 7:30 a.m. when we started along the trail just east of where Lake and Loma Alta Drive ended. At first it was all*reet*, just like headin' up 7$^{th}$ Street in Pedro, except surrounded by green brush turning brown, and some very mellow pine trees. But, like, me an' Loose, man, we're musicians. We're not mountain goats. I felt more like an *'old goat,'* out-of-shape and out-of-touch with nature. I've got the barroom tan to prove it! Like, stone night people.

We thought we were cookin' along, breezin' in the breeze until some *real* gray beards came sailin' by us; a Sierra Club Senior's group I later learned. Loose an' me were puffin' and getting' short winded. These grandpa and grandma folks marched easily up the grade, laughin' and talkin' without drawin' a deep breath.

"I wish I'd brought a back-pack full of beer instead of just two large bottles of Pedro Port City Water," I told Loose. Journalist Jack Baric had made a film called "Port Town," about San Pedro. As a promotion, he was giving out bottles of drinking water with the film's logo, the Angel's Gate Lighthouse, on the label. I'd copped a few that were left at the Dive on First Thursday, which I'd thought to put in my pack for the climb.

We wound around switchbacks and turns, the trail weaving up the hill in a looping climb until the newly risen sun was illuminating a toy town of tiny vehicles bookin' for day jobs and fightin' a fast movin' clock below us. I was on the comedown, feelin' the hours of sleep I'd missed.

At the top of the trail, as our path turned more level on final approach to the summit of Echo Mountain. I figured we were both ready to kick back for a hip little nap. "No dice," says Loose, "we gotta keep movin'."

I parked it on a *frantic* little set of concrete steps anyway. A voice behind us said, "That's where the incline cars used to discharge their passengers for the trip up Mount Lowe. Those steps used to serve as boarding platforms. You guys know Angles Flight in downtown LA? Well, similar cable cars used to bring folks up here from the bottom of Rubio Canyon 3000 feet below in Altadena."

I sensed that this white-wigged old bird was a talker, but then I says to myself, self, I says, "That's cool." Let the cat spew forth his wordage and I'll be able to catch my breath, at least until Loose cops to it.

But Loose was already up, he had the hilltop pinned, was diggin' on other bits of ruin and wild bougainvillea in red and yellow. I figured he was lookin' for the old trolley line where our climb was scheduled to drag on.

The senior cat held out a wrinkled paw and introduced himself. "Judson's the name, Judson Bailey. But just call me Jud. I love this place, so I lead these Sierra Club walks up here every month or so when the weather holds, which around here is most of the time." He sent forth a little chuckle.

"As you can see, this place used to be really something, course that was even before *my* time. I was two-years-old when this place caught fire and burned. Come on, Bud, let me show you around."

I was reet just sittin', but I stood and followed the cat's kicks. Jud led me around, pointed out stone foundations that had once supported grand, world-class hotels like the Echo Mountain House. The gardens were still there, though they had long ago gone native.

I told Jud I was a musician; a trumpet player and he said, "Son, back in them days, you could'a made a lot of money up here! The hot spots on this little hill had big dance orchestras, and they drew some crowds!"

Jud held forth on the extent of the one-time community on Echo Mountain; the Hotels, the Thorp Institute Astronomical Observatory and the Pacific Electric Railroad yards and shops. "We lost all'a this splendor and grandeur to the big fire of 1937," he said with a wistful look, almost like he was getting' ready to weep. "Fire started high up on Mt. Lowe, at the Alpine Tavern. Cook in the kitchen dropped somethin' and the place went up in a heartbeat, all ashes. The flames quickly swept down the mountain, destroying everything.

"Yeah," he breathed with a shake for his head. "These mountains are lovely, but they've al'ays been a big fire hazard. I think nature has programmed'm to burn every decade or so just to clear things up!"

His story dragged on; the rains that followed two years later and the floods that washed out the remaining rail lines. How WW II had sealed the resort's fate, no time or energy left to fix up or re-build. He could have gone on for the full bright, layin' down history and memories, but Loose had caught up with us.

"Hay, man, where you been, Lars. The road's over this way, the path where trolley's used to begin the climb up the grade, man, we gotta get movin'!"

Jud smiled, said "Nice talkin' to you Lars." With a questioning glance at Loose and has saxophone case, eyein' him up and down, he told me, "Enjoy your hike, son."

# Chapter 92

From Echo Mountain, the climb was uneventful. The old railway line was an easier hike, more like an ordinary walk. I remembered hearin' somewhere that street cars couldn't handle 'steep' any better than old horn players, so we made it skyward on a more copasetic grade. Every now and then we'd have to fall out from the old roadbed, head down a ravine or canyon where only the concrete piers stood in the thick foliage, reminders of the one-time bridges that crossed the more ragged contours of the scene. Other than that, I was gettin' into it, actually findin' my groove, getting' behind this hikin' thing. We had a spectacular view out over the land. Beyond the smog and roads and structures, the rise of Palos Verdes pointed us to where Pedro nestled against it, and the tip of Catalina Island capped the cloud bank beyond.

I was getting' hung up, thinkin' about how men, like, well over a hundred years ago, could have constructed all this wild paradise, like, on top of a *mountain*! These cats didn't have, like, helicopters, and if they had big cranes or grader things, how could they get them up these kinds of heights? Or back down again?

We legged it around a big sweep of curve and found ourselves on the backside of the mountain. Bridge supports were visible where trolleys full of cats and chicks must have swept out over the valley, lookin' straight down at empty air. Pasadena was no longer visible. Our peeps now kicked onto forested wilderness, like, everywhere. We'd dig the occasional telephone pole, uprights that in another world and another time held the catenary wires carryin' electric juice to power the big electric rail cars. I was trippin' on this scene. I'd have to find a book or somethin' when we got home to Pedro, hip myself to these weird earlier kicks. Man, I was getting' *boxed* on this riff. Nature was *ultra cool*! The wilderness was a *stone gas*! It was almost like I was strung out on some heavy weed or fungus shit. Heavy thoughts about why we were up here had flown from my conscious wig and I was just, at the risk of soundin' square, happy to be here.

# Chapter 93

My insane, lushed mood split my head when the trail turned into a tight, shaded glen with a mountain peak rising on one side and more *real* stone ruins along the other. Our path turned from packed dirt and stones to a wide concrete apron holding a set of steel tracks. We had arrived at the old Alpine Tavern. A Forestry Service plaque on a free-standing bulletin board marked the location.

Loose started running around in circles like a mad man, shouting, "Hello? Anybody home?" then turnin' to me, he began babblin' about how close we were and how he was gonna finally see his fine Martin axe.

His calls up the mountain were answered by a rifle shot from somewhere above us. The slug ricocheted off a set of stone steps behind our heads, but that wasn't enough to tighten up Loose's loose wig..

"Hey, we brought your money," The ecstatic sax man shouted in the general direction of where the shot had flown. "We're alone, man. What's the deal? Com'on man, its us, we got your *money* for you." He started to run up toward the incline.

I had to grab his shirt collar and pull Loose down onto the ground. I dragged the flailing cat back toward the stones.

"Hey, man," I whispered, "I think I just figured out that we've done a dumb thing here. Well, like, I mean I knew all along we were doin' a dumb thing, but this is turnin' real salty, real fast!. I think this cat plans to send us to the big sleep; keep the bread *and* the horn!"

I dragged Loose farther back. His peeps were showin' serious shook, pupils dilated to nothing. He copped to my words and we scrambled-up the stone stairs. At the top, we did a quick departure across what probably used to be the tavern's main room, toward a small stand of trees. At the far side of the old ground-works, I pulled Loose down and told him, "I think we better stay down, crawl behind this brickwork until we figure out where this cat is hiding."

We dropped flat with our bellies on the ground and scooted about seven feet toward the corner of the foundation that was our cover, Loose draggin' the alto case behind him. It was like bein' back in Navy Amphibs again. At the gone building's edge, I peered around toward the peak of Mount Lowe and found myself almost nose to nose with a resting serpent, catchin' himself some warm rays on the stone path. It was a Diamondback rattlesnake that looked like it could be as thick around as my upper arm. I eased myself backwards a few paces and hissed, "Crawl backwards! Fast! Snake!"

Loose, of course, panicked. He tried to jump up, probably getting' ready to run, charge right into the path of another rifle shot. I held onto the cuff of his jeans and pulled him back to earth.

"I don't think the snake's seen us yet, or smelled us or whatever they do. Just keep low and keep movin backwards until were in the cover of those trees."

We shuffled back on hands and knees, Loose scootin' awkwardly with the burden of the Martin case hampering his movement, towards the place we'd started. By the steps we sat up, leanin' our backs against the stonework. The snake had turned the corner now as well. He looked up in our direction, turned and slithered away into the thick brush. Loose was hyperventilating, sittin' rigid and lookin' almost catatonic.

"Snap out of it, dude." I shook him, slapped his face a couple times, like we occasionally had to do to guys in 'Nam that had just arrived and hadn't learned the drill yet. "That was too close, man. And he may have lots of family here, so I'm voting against crawling for now. Hey Loose, you with me?"

Loose nodded his head, glassy peeps still facing forward and unfocused. I pulled my alto man to his feet and led him on a few steps, scopin' out where our friend the snake might be headed. We must have blown our cover, as another shot rang out, drivin' into the ground ahead of us and much too close. The single shot was followed by a short burst of automatic weapon fire. It sounded like one of those Russian guns Charlie used to point at us all those years ago on another continent. A couple of the bullets struck the concrete of the steps behind where we stood, sending a shower of stone chips and sparks into the dry brush surrounding us. I tried to keep my wig straight, put my gray cells to work on this case. What had that Marine Captain told us about duckin' fire? Loose was headed for Panic City, New Mexico, sputtering nonsense, his eyeballs sweepin' the scene without takin' it in. Glancing around us, I saw a planted row of Cypress trees. If we took cover behind them, we might just make it to a faint overgrown trail beyond, leading away from the direction of the gunfire. "Wake up Loose," I said, "We gotta do a kinda Quasimoto run, ol' buddy. Keep hunched over, keep your knees bent and follow me. And it would be a lot easier if you dropped that silly sax case!" The cat clutched the box closer to his chest and shook his head 'no.' When I gave him a nudge, he moved the grip of the horn case back to his left hand and crouched as I'd showed him.

We'd covered only a short distance when I dug the faded red trolley farther along the path. We stepped up our pace, Loose had seen the old Red Car as well, but while I was bookin' it to shelter, my sax man was startin' to recite his mantra about Art Pepper's horn again.

We had nearly reached the rail car when we heard a loud whoosh behind us; felt a hot gust of strong wind. I turned to see a wall of flames dancing all around the stone foundation we had just split. Our gunman, Elwood or whoever he was had sent sparks into dry brush with his AK-47 rounds.

And as I thought of the shooter, his voice echoed out from somewhere above. "You're trapped, you stupid fucks. Now bring my money up the trail to your left, the one leadin' past that old Pacific Electric car. And you'd better hurry if you don't want to end up as Crispy Critters."

"You've got the sax to exchange? Tell us where the sax is. Is it safe?" Loose asked his questions in a high timbred voice, full of fear. Maniacal laughter echoed from the mountain in answer to his query.

"Where'd you get that horn," I shouted.

The laughter stop. The voice echoing back to us said, "I don't know why it should matter to you, you're dead men, but that stupid diStefani kid boosted it. Only he didn't know what he had. He was gonna pawn it, or sell it to some college student for a couple hunnerd bucks til I tol' him what he was holdin'. So if that answers your question, get up here with my money!"

Fortunately for Loose and I, the wind was blowing away from us, slowing the flames somewhat, but the roaring inferno was blocking our path of retreat down the trail. Loose wasn't registering the scene, out of his head hung up on his dream horn. He ran ahead luggin' that big brown case. He dove into the Red Car cabin, another shot chipping faded red paint just inches from his left shoulder. I was left no choice but to follow. I remembered the nasty Nazi pistol at my waist, unbuttoned the flap and drew the weapon out as I ducked behind the far side of the train. Steppin' into the ruined rail car, I found Loose on his knees. He knelt before an identical Martin saxophone case that rested in the corner of the space, just under a large black brake wheel.

# Chapter 94

I was feelin', like, real hincty listenin' to the roar of flames some 100 yards away, even if they seemed to be headin' the other direction from us. Loose, however, was solid gone, somewhere in a dream reality that fire, snakes and gunshots couldn't reach. But *I* had to *try*!

"Loose, baby, hey Loose." But he couldn't hear me. He grabbed the newfound Martin case, started to pick both boxes up, one in each hand.

"Wait a sec, Lars," came his plaintive wail." This is too light man, 'scuse me, but I just gotta check it out." Then he was back on his knees, poppin' the snap latches. When it opened to empty blue velvet lining, he ran his eyes over the inside of the car. "The saxophone must be here somewhere," he mumbled to himself, more than to me.

"Loose, man, I don't think there is a saxophone. Maybe there never was! Com'on, babe, we gotta get out of here!"

At that moment, a brief shift in the wind sent a shower of sparks over the streetcar. I could see the bright, glowing embers rain past the broken-out windows. I grabbed Loose, one of my hands on his belt and the other gripping his collar.

He was fightin' me, tryin' to break my grip so he could at least rescue the sax case with the cash in it. I planted my feet firmly against the bulkhead that had once separated the car's open-air section from the cabin and pulled with every fiber of muscle I could summon. We both fell backward, so I threw my weight into the fall with enough momentum to summersault us away from the streetcar and towards the trail

A paranoid glance over my shoulder registered that the tattered canvas coating on the car's roof was smoldering. I half-carried Loose through the thick brush away from the car *and* the trail.

Loose was screamin' and shoutin' loud enough for our attacker to hear us from a mile away. "Hey man, the snakes! And my money, my mom's money, man, we can't just let it burn!"

"Snakes or flames," I told him, "take your pick, man." Over a low rise I dropped Loose to the ground, pointed with my head and we ducked into the hollow of a stone wall that probably once formed the foundation of a small mountain cabin or storage shed set on the steep slope. I left my friend there, still dazed, as I made a thorough inspection of the area for reptiles or other livin' threats. I then re-drew the Walther from its holster, ready for another predator that I *knew* was out there somewhere. I raised my head just enough to peer over the wall. The flames appeared to be in retreat, moving in another direction, but that could be only temporary.

Up the hill, I could see a figure in camouflage fatigues with an assault rifle at port arms running full tilt behind the trees from the mountaintop. The fool was headed straight toward the burnin' Red Car screaming, "My money! Where'd you assholes put my money?" The man jumped through the wall of fire, into the trolley. A dull knock from down the pathway told us that either the man's rifle, his knees, or both had hit the floor of the streetcar. "He must be checking which case contains the money," I whispered to Loose. "They look so much alike."

Another loud whoosh. We instinctively pulled our heads down. When we poked our peeps over the stones again, the roof of the old car was a sheet of flame. As we watched, red tongues of energy quickly engulfed the entire structure. We could hear Elwood's screams from within the wall of heat and smoke.

Loose came back to life watching the trolley burn. "Shit, man, we better get out of here." He jumped the wall and started toward the flames, but I caught up with Loose, threw a full body tackle on him and brought him down hard, then I pulled him back to his feet and gave him a shove in the direction from which our attacker had come.

"Top of the mountain," I shouted over the roar of the nearby inferno. "I think that's, like, our best hope. Go up, man, go up." I pushed the confused saxophone player ahead of me and we climbed, stumbled and fell up the trail to the mountain's uppermost plateau. From our lofty perch, we looked down on the fast spreading fire, with the entire Los Angeles basin beyond winkin' at us through the smoke.

# Chapter 95

We sat for a moment, on the edge of the world, trying to catch our breath, and solid *shakin'*, I mean uptight vibratin' when we realized how close we had come; how close we were still hangin'. I looked down at the seemingly worthless Nazi sidearm I still clutched in my hand. What good could it possibly have done against a nut case with an assault rifle? Then I remembered Blondy's cell phone, another so far worthless attachment. I rummaged in my pockets till I found it. It was a long shot, but maybe the Blonde One would be there to save my biscuits one more time.

I punched Blondy's number on the speed dial. All I got was a lit-up green screen tellin' me I was outside the service area, no signal available. Totally freaked, I walked around the hilltop hittin' that button and shoutin', "Come on, baby, come on!" I stepped to the back edge, still no service. Finally, I leaned over the steep drop, my head and the lady's phone extended into space, six thousand feet above the city. When I hit the button, Blondy's number started ringing. She picked up almost instantaneously.

"Blondy, baby, we're on the top of Mt. Lowe and the whole world is, like, burning!" My voice was over excited; I couldn't help it. I was as full of fear and anxious vibes as I'd ever been, Viet Nam included.

"I know," came her calm reply. "We're diggin' you on the television over the bar. Tom's in a helicopter nearby, tryin' to keep tabs on you, babe."

It was then that I noticed the pulsing sound, looked up to see several choppers circling above.

"Can someone put this on hurry up time?" I asked. "It's getting a bit close to Bar-be-cue City up here."

But I was speakin' to dead air, the phone had died again. Like, no signal. Doornail City, Tennessee! I walked back to the other side of the peak where Loose is watching the blaze as it crept ever closer to our little island of safe and cool. The Red Car body was gone, vanished in smoke and ash as though it had never existed. Smoke was startin' to hamper our view in every direction. Loose sat on the edge of the world, chanting "Art's horn, man, Art Pepper's horn. Such a beautiful sound gone forever. Oh man, Art's horn."

I didn't mean to come on salty with the cat, he'd been through a lot in the past few hours, but it just came out. "If Art's horn was really ever here in the first place." My man turned hangdog at me; the saddest look I'd ever want to witness on anyone! I tried to explain myself.

"I don't think we could've trusted that dude, babe. He's probably sent the real horn to the collector in Japan and was just gonna fry us for the bucks. Like, I'm grievin' for you, man, grievin' *with* you, but I think this was just a bad scene from the first bar."

I got to my feet and decided to go back to the other side of the clearing, try Blondy's phone one more time. As I approached the drop off, a blue and gray helicopter rose in front of my eyes from the canyon below and up over the edge of the mountaintop.

# Chapter 96

Tom Cheatham stood in the open bay door at the side of the large whirly-bird, clad in an orange vest with some kind of safety line attached, the cable disappearing in the dimness behind him. His peeps locked on mine for a second and he raised his hands before him, thumbs up, as he rose past my eyes into the blinding mid-morning sun. My head followed the chopper's flight path while the pilot circled the mountaintop briefly.

The L.A. Police bird made three or four attempts to set down in the area between Loose and I, but aborted each time. The flames had found their way up to our perch. Loose had back-pedaled to the edge of the peak, where I stood waitin' for our rescuers to unfold their plan.

It seemed like each time the chopper tried to come down for us a wall of heat and smoke would rise up over the back edge of the summit. Each time I watched Lieutenant Cheatham at the open side door of the craft peering down expectantly, and each time I caught his disappointed face fallin' as he rose once more into the sky, the pilot shakin' his head as he lifted. Tom's wig turned often, instructing the pilot to maneuver towards us, then signaling for us to move ever closer to the drop off, away from the smoke.

But fire and thick smoke soon had us trapped on the edge of the world overlooking the San Gabriel Valley, no place left to run. Tom's pilot held the chopper at a hover some 40-feet above our heads.

Loose had totally lost it, cryin' like a baby, hands over his ears and head tight against his chest. At that moment, Tom left the bay door briefly and returned with a steel cable, something like a baby's canvas swing seat on the end. Turning his head once more, Tom shouted orders to another unseen player. The rope started payin' out, lowerin' towards us.

Diggin the steel line that swung before us, Loose came alive. He reached up to grab hold in a panic. "Get your butt in the sling," Tom shouted down to him. "We can't bring you up safely if you don't get into the sling"

Loose finally got the message after wasting seconds of valuable time. Tom called over his shoulder and Loose started his ascent into the helicopter, his body twirlin' back and forth in the smoky cloud over the valley while he rose in his canvas chair.

By the time the panicked puppy reached the safety of the helicopter, however flames had closed on three sides of me and I could feel the intense heat, like puttin' my head into an open oven. Occasional dark gusts sent gray smoke around me, fuzzin' my view of the rescue craft and leavin' me coughin' my lungs out.

With my sax man safe inside, the pilot started backin' the craft away, takin' it higher. He made a couple more passes, but he couldn't get close enough without exposing his rotors to the fire. The cops hovered over the valley, lookin' for a break. Behind them, I dug two smaller birds with television logos plastered on their bodies and cameras bristling from every opening. A red chopper passed above the others and over my head. Through the thick haze, I could see a pinkish load spill from the bird to the burning valley behind me.

A major gust of wind sent flames toward me. I dug a solid pain and looked down to see red and orange creepin' up the back of my left pant leg. I slapped it out as quick as I could.

The winds swirled around and shifted. Another heavy gust came up from the valley, cleared the lingering smoke and pushed the wall of fire into retreat for a few seconds. I saw Tom some fifty feet off wavin' hands around, shoutin' somethin' and the pilot revved his rotors, movin' towards me once more. Tom was leanin' out, rope and wench at the ready. He swung the heavy cable in my direction, but the wind shifted back. I felt my pant leg smolderin' again.

The bird had come closer to Mount Lowe in the short lull. I could make out Detective Carl Berger standing behind Tom. He was shouting encouragement at me with each forward movement of the line, "Come on, Lars Baby, jump, you can do it!"

Tom's added his voice to the chorus, "Come to papa! Com'on Lars!"

I didn't have a large book of choices. As the canvas sling came toward me, I bent my knees to push off and I sprung from the mountaintop, sailin' into the ethereal voutesphere without a net!

My left hand caught the slack bottom of the seat. I gripped it tightly, strainin' to get my right arm up and through the loop for a better purchase. My right leg was smoldering now, ready to burst into flame. I could feel heat on my back, what felt like intense heat on the rear of my head, as the winch drew me towards Tom, Carl, and an airborne safe haven. I felt strong hands take hold of my arms, pullin' me the final inches to safety. I cast my peepers downward to dig Eaton Canyon and Hastings Ranch beneath us, a 6,000-foot free-fall that I had almost copped.

I fell face down into the steel bird. The last thing I remembered was Carl throwing a gray blanket over my roasting back and legs. I came around in time to dig that the pilot had set us down outside my pad, on the roof of the Channel View.

A police medic was leanin' over me and something very frosty was pasted over my backside.

Two of my plastic chairs had become toast beneath the big bird's skids and I probably would have two very salty felines to deal with when I found their hidin' place inside, but I was home and safe. Some extra tuna might make amends to the boys when I located them.

# Chapter 97.

Saturday found me an' Loose back in Blondy's Waterfront Dive. My alto man had joined the blonde one and Tom Cheatham in Lady's favorite booth. I was happier standin'. I had a nutty collection of ointments and bandages covering the rear half of me, and wildly singed patches up my back to the rear of my skull. I was also tanked up on the bean, wiggin' out behind some serious opiates the medics had scored for me on my overnight hospital stay. The police medic may have landed me on my own patch, but Tom and Blondy had dragged me up to San Pedro Peninsula Hospital for 24-hours of observation.

Blondy assured me that Yard and Art had swung out of hiding, copped a large helping of Trader Joe tuna and were *voot* with life once the police bird had winged it off their patch.

Lieutenant Tom had been in meetings late into the previous black. Lady's cop friend had filed his reports for his own captain, and then been 'de-briefed' by the FBI, who'd had a pair of agents waitin' when my rescuers touched down on my roof. Los Angeles Port Police had been standin' by for a piece of Tom as well.

The feebs had, in fact, been watching Billy Adrian/Elwood de Gier for some time. He was their prime suspect in the longshore thefts, to be charged with multiple crimes, including murdering three police officers and six others, as well as racketeering: collecting protection money from the shipping companies and heading a ring that stole cargo and sold it to the highest bidder. The feds had been collecting vast amounts of evidence to back that suspicion. They said they were only hours from making the arrest when the suspect seemed to drop off the face of the earth.

The sunlight outside Blondy's was a strange orange hue, filtered through the smoke as the San Gabriel Mountains continued to burn. Santa Ana winds were makin' life difficult for a few hundred fire fighters locked in combat with the quick movin' blaze. On the *idiot box* above the bar, the camera eye was sweepin' my charred perch of twenty-four-hours earlier. Mount Lowe was bleak, black, bald, and unconcerned that it had seriously burned-down one young musician's dream.

Astrid had phoned me three times in the past twelve hours. Her last call was to let me know she had requested another five-weeks of emergency family leave from streetcar duty and was flying back to America to play nurse to me and care for my burns. Her plane would touch down six hours from now at LAX.

No one has, as yet, found Art Pepper's Martin saxophone, but it could have been shipped anywhere or sold to anyone with no way to trace it unless that person or another with the knowledge was willing to come forward. Possibly the coveted horn would turn up when more arrests were made and more suspects interviewed. On the bright side, the government agents had mentioned a reward that had been put out on de Gier. I told Loose he could have it if, indeed, such a reward was paid. If he copped it, Loose would easily be able to buy the horn of his choice and still return the considerable sum he owed his family.

I was late for work that night. After remarking, "I thought you would have burned faster up on that mountain with all the alcohol you usually have in your system," Blondy had said she really didn't expect me to get behind the gig, but I told her it was probably the most positive therapy I could have aside from Astrid's presence. Carl Berger had taken me to the airport in a slick back panda car, so it was no problem parkin' in the loadin' zone in front of the Bradley Terminal to wait for my girl. Airport police would ask no questions.

Astrid laid a silly smirk on me when she dug that we would be ridin' home in the back of a cop car, but official vehicle or not, she was all over me in the back seat. Behind the wire mesh cage I felt lushed all over with Astrid's careful hugs takin' note of my sensitive' legs and back.

As soon as we had stowed Astrid's bags at my pad, we headed down the stairs. I picked up my silver flugelhorn and limped to the bandstand.

"A few little burns is all," I told the large assemblage of friends and fans, "but they hurt like hell!"

Loose cast his peeps down at the floor. "Sorry man, I panicked," he whispered at my side. "I'm really drug about it, man. Like I wasn't trying to ace you out or nothin'."

"I know that, man. And it's cool," I answered, puttin' a brotherly arm around the man's shoulders. "We're cool, babe. We got real hot there for a while, but now we are both here bein' cool an' that's what matters. Solid chill!"

# More Excerpts from Lars' Dictionary of Hip Words and Phrases

**Action:** What is happening. "What's shakin' baby, where's the action?"

**Axe:** Musical instrument or any tool with which you make your living.

**Baby:** A friendly form of address, used for persons of either sex.

**Bad:** Good. "Lars blows some bad riffs!"

**Bad News:** A dreary, unpleasant or dangerous person.

**Bag:** Very general term for a set of circumstances, a complex of behavior patterns, etc.

**Ball:** A pleasurable experience.

**Ball All Night:** To party until after dawn.

**Ball, to:** To have sex.

**Behind:** Under the influence of.

**Black:** Nighttime, the dark hours.

**Blow:** To play any musical instrument.  Also to make or assemble, as in "Blondy blows a  mean Martini," or to lose, as in "If I'm late one more time I'm gonna blow this gig!"

**Boss:** Very good, "The saxophone  is one boss axe!"

**Box:** A phonograph, jukebox.  Sometimes a piano.

**Boxed:** High or stoned.

**Bread:** Money

**Bright:** Daytime, daylight hours.

**Bug:** To annoy or irritate

**Bug Out:** To split or leave the scene.

**Burned, to be:** Cheated or swindled.

**Burn Down:** To create a scene where no good action is possible, to blow it.

**Bring Down:** A depressing person or thing.

**Busted:** Arrested by the man, or caught at something uncool.

**Cat:** A with-it person or musician, usually of male gender.

**Changes:** Originally musical chord changes, but can also refer to emotional or psychological swings.

**Changes, to put through:** To do purposeful violence to a cat's state of mind or mental health.

**Changes, tough:** Hard times.

**Chick:** A with-it female, or a girl in general.

**Chops:** A musician's embouchure or lips, extended to mean any part of the body used to play an instrument.

**City:** A suffix used for emphasis, usually in a negative bag.

**Clock:** a face.

**Clyde:** An offensive square, a hick.

**Come down:** To return to normal from a high, or to be thrown into depression by a person or event.

**Connection:** The man from whom you buy what you shouldn't be buying because it's illegal or harmful to your person.

**Cook:** To play really fine, or do to whatever you do well.

**Cool:** Safe, good, all right, appropriate, a positive attitude.

**Cool it:** Stop it, cease, desist, mend your ways.

**Cool out:** Straighten your head, stop what you're doing for a while to give your system a break.

**Cop:** To obtain or score, either by purchase or by theft.

**Cop out:** An excuse or cover story. To fail to own up to your actions.

**Cornfeds:** Hicks, yokels, innocent squares

**Crazy:** Excellent, swinging, generally good.

**Crib:** Home, apartment. A place to crash.

**Cut, cut out:** To leave, split the scene.

**Dig:** To understand or appreciate, also to look at or listen to, to pay attention.

**Digs those mellow kicks:** Knows how to live well.

**Do up:** To use up or destroy.

**Drag:** A person or thing that is depressing or boring.

**Drapes:** Fine clothes, a Zoot Suit or other outrageous attire.

**Drug:** To be or become depressed. A heavy sad state of mind.

**Dues:** The disadvantages you will put up with in order to obtain the things you really want. Punishment you take for uncool behavior.

**Eye, the:** Television set (see Tube).

**Eyes:** Desire or lust. "I got eyes for a pizza!"

**Face:** A person or character.

**Fall by:** Visit or come around.

**Fall in:** Enter

**Fall in on it:** Really play it for all its worth.

**Fall out:** Suddenly go to sleep or nod off. To become out of favor.

**Far Out:** Weird, Strangely motivated, beyond the norm in a cool manner.

**Fine Brown Frame:** A lady of African heritage with a voluptuous body.

**Flip, Flip out:** To go crazy, or to like something very much.

**Forget it:** An expression of contempt.

**Frantic:** Happening, exciting, excellent.

**Freak:** A cat that likes something very much or exclusively.

**Freakish High:** High as a kite!

**Freak scene:** A swinging party, or a bi-sexual happening.

**Freaky:** Weird or odd.

**Gas:** A superlative expression. To really wow someone.

**Gaters:** Swingin' friends or fellow musicians. Cats that can really swing.

**Gates:** Cats that really swing. From "Swings like an open gate."

**Gen:** Information. The genuine article or facts.

**Geets:** Small change, or homemade slugs to cheat vending machines.

**Get in the wind:** Split, leave, cut out.

**Get straight:** Make a deal, work it out. Also to come down from a bad high.

**Gig:** Job, or to work.

**Good people:** Solid cats or chicks, people you can trust.

**Grease: Money.** To pay the tab or pay the man.

**Groove:** A good feeling or scene.

**Groove behind:** To like or enjoy, to really dig.

**Groovy:** A complimentary adjective.

**Hangup:** A fascinating object or concept. Also a psychological block or personality quirk.

**Hat:** A chick or a female companion.

**Head:** A cat freaked over or hooked on a thing. "That cat is a stone jazz head."

**High:** Intoxicated by drugs, music, a fine chick or a great scene.

**Hincty:** Paranoid, overly nervous about a scene or event.

**Hip:** To know or be aware.

**Hipster:** A fully dues-paid member of hip society.

**Hippie-dip:** A hipster want-to-be. A square trying to act hip.

**His story is great:** A successful man about town.

**Hold back the dawn:** Go on forever, keep up the groove.

**Hook:** A mania or uncontrollable desire.

**Hooked:** Addicted or locked into something.

**Horn:** The telephone.

**Hubcap:** A low paying gig. Less than a wheel (see Wheel to turn).

**Hung up:** Neurotic. Also fascinated by something, or in a position where you're robbed of choice, frustrated.

**Hustle:** To work in a field other than your own. A musician's day job.

**Insane:** Really cool or exciting. "Man, that chick is insane!"

**Into something:** A high compliment. A cat putting forth good creative ideas would be said to be "into something."

**Jim:** An uncomplimentary form of address. A put down.

**Jive:** A fearsome insult, originally coupled with a term regarding sex with a person's female parent.

**Joint is jumping:** The club is full of customers and in full swing.

**Juice, juices:** Liquor, intoxicants.

**Juiced:** Drunk.

**Juicehead:** A lush or habitual drunk.

**Kick, a:** An extended obsession. A hang-up on a mental riff, a style or a fashion. "The cat was on a Dixieland kick."

**Kicks:** thrills, ideas or happenings that bringing satisfaction.

**Knock me:** Give me or send my way. "Knock me your lobes, a got a word to lay on you."

**Laid it down and left it there:** Made the ultimate sacrifice. Paid with their lives.

**Later:** Goodbye. Also a derogatory term meaning "don't bother" or "forget it."

**Layin' it on straight:** Telling the truth.

**Lay on:** To give.

**Like:** A form of verbal punctuation. The extensive use of this word would seem to indicate that the hipster is unconsciously aware of the fact that he can never communicate exactly what he wants to say, and that what he is saying is at best an approximation of what he intends to communicate.

**Lobes:** Ears, hearing.

**Long Daddy Green:** Bread, cash, spondoolicks, spendable folding stuff.

**Loose Wig:** To be free to create or to be creative in general is to have a loose wig. Feeling creative.

**Lushed to all ends:** Extremely drunk, close to passing out.

**Main Day Charge:** wife, Significant other or serious partner.

**Make it with:** To have an affair with someone. Or to have an almost sexual experience with a instrument, a piece of music or other thing.

**Man:** A neutral form of address for either sex. Originally a term of respect, as opposed to Clydes calling hip cats of ethnic origin "boy."

**Man, The:** The police.

**Mellow:** Copasetic or agreeable.

**Motha:** A very *unfriendly* form of address, reserved for bad and uncool faces.

**Mother:** A friendly form of address when said in a cool manner and fully pronounced.

**Motor:** Car or other transportation. To move by personal vehicle.

**Nod:** A brief hip nap. Also to sleep in some circumstances.

**Nutty:** Nice, good, attractive. Also a phrase of agreement or ascent.

**Out:** Similar to, but more complimentary than "far out."

**Out-of-this-world mellow stage:** Ecstatically drunk.

**Pad:** A hip home or apartment. Also can mean a mattress or place to sleep.

**Peepers or Peeps:** Eyes.

**Penny kick:** An low paying or unsure gig.

**Pick up on:** Pay attention to, listen to, or discover.

**Pin:** to put your full attention into examining.

**Pitch a ball:** Have a good time.

**Popped:** Busted, arrested.

**Put down:** To reject or denigrate. Also an insult.

**Put on:**  A favorite sport of hipsters, occasionally vicious.  A form of practical joke in which the victim is unaware that he is being had.

**Really in there:**  Knows all the answers.

**Riff:**  Originally an improvised jazz solo, but can also be a conversational solo or a hip idea.

**Salty:**  Angry.

**Salty, to jump:**  To "come on" in an angry manner.

**Same beat groove:**  Bored or boring

**Satori:**  A sudden flash of "enlightenment, " or a profound realization.

**Scarf or Scoff:**  To eat or consume.

**Scene:**  Where the happenings happen!

**Score:**  To make a successful deal with a connection.  To get lucky with a chick.

**Scuffle:**  To hustle.

**Shakin':**  Happening.

**Shape in a Drape:**  Well dressed, looks good in fine clothes.

**She Cat:**  A female musician or a chick carrying a lot of wiggage.

**Short:**  Car or vehicle.

**Short line:**  Very little money.

**Sides:** Recordings. Records or compact discs.

**Slam:** Jail or prison.

**Somethin' else:** A very good person, happening or object. "That cat is somethin' else!"

**Sound:** To ask or inquire.

**Sounds:** Music or recordings (see sides).

**Split:** To leave, get in the wind.

**Square:** Conventional, unimaginative. A Babbitt.

**Straight:** High, or stoned. Also can mean not high, not stoned. To "get straight" can mean to get what you need to do you gig.

**Straighten, to:** To give a cat what he needs, or to lay the correct information on him.

**Stone:** Complete, or in the extreme. "Blondy is a stone beauty!"

**Stoned:** Very high.

**Stash:** A secret hiding place for illicit goods, often elaborate or imaginative. A place to put the stuff that you scored, but *The Man* says you shouldn't have, so *The Man* won't find your kicks and throw you in the slam.

**Stickin':** Doing well financially.

**Strung out:** Far gone, physically or mentally.

**Stud:** A male. A solid stud would be a man with connections or influence.

**Swing, to:** To be happy, successful, or both. To enjoy one's self. To groove.

**Take it slow:** Be careful, cautious.

**Taste:** A sample. An alcoholic beverage.

**There you go!:** A friendly greeting. A hip "hello."

**Tight:** On close, friendly terms.

**Tossed:** Searched by the man.

**Tough:** Very good.

**Tough changes:** Hard times.

**Tube:** The television. Also known as "the idiot box."

**Turn on:** To get high. Also to become interested in a person or object.

**Twisted:** High, very straight.

**Uncool:** Dangerously un-cautious. Menacing.

**Up tight:** In a difficult position. Under psychological pressure.

**Urban Assault Lorry or UAL:** A large truck-like "sport" vehicle driven by squares and cops.

**Ville:** A suffix used for emphasis, usually in a positive bag.

**Vonce:** Heaven, the heavens, or a very far-out state to be in.

**Vouty or Voot:** Cool to the extreme!

**Vout-O-Reeny or Vout-O-Rooney:** A very vouty scene.

**Voutesphere:** The heavens, or a very far out state of mind.

**Wasted:** Very high. Also, to inflect damage on someone is to "waste" him.

**What's shakin':** What is happening?

**Wheels:** Car, vehicle, transportation.

**Wheel to turn, a:** A decent gig. "Skoot couldn't find a wheel to turn."

**Wig:** Brain or head

**Wig Out:** To crack or fry your brains, to lose your cool, or to cook very creatively.

CPSIA information can be obtained
at www.ICGtesting.com
Printed in the USA
FFOW02n1907160514
5469FF